Why everyone is raving about
Johanna Edward's debut novel

# The Next Big Thing

"In this saucy sendup, a feisty young Memphis publicist . . . drops the pounds, but learns that fame has a cost . . . and that being skinny isn't always pretty."            —*US Weekly*

"Edwards addresses image issues with wit and candor. . . . Fans of Jennifer Weiner's realistic female protagonists will find a new favorite here."            —*Booklist*

"Reality TV meets actual REALITY! Take a bunch of women struggling with weight, body image, and relationship problems and lock them in a house with a gym, a trainer, a pantry full of treats and nothing but time, and what you get is a perfect combination of catfights and self discovery. In *The Next Big Thing*, Johanna Edwards asks us to wonder what life on such a reality show would be like, and through the eyes of her feisty herioine Kat Larson, we get a pretty good idea of the ups and downs. But more importantly, we get a very clear picture of the diversity and humanity of women who are dealing with their own feelings about their weight issues, as well as society's hang-ups. Kat is as flawed as any of us, and on her journey discovers that her flaws actually have little to do with her size and more to do with her attitude. Funny, but also honest with some real power, *The Next Big Thing* is a very entertaining read that makes you think. Great fun!"
            —Stacey Ballis, author of *Inappropriate Men*

*continued on next page . . .*

AUG 0 3 2008

"A deliciously dishy tale of life behind the scenes of reality television. Peeking into the lives of contestants on *From Fat to Fabulous*, Johanna Edwards has created a cast of characters who keep you rooting for them from start to finish (as well as a few you'd like to strangle!). Protagonist Larson is a sympathetic and complex plus-size gal who gives readers a real feel for what it's like to be an overweight woman in America. While poignant and touching, Kat's plight keeps readers laughing throughout this delightful tale."   —Jennifer Coburn, author of *The Wife of Reilly*

"Loved it!"
        —Melissa Senate, author of *Whose Wedding Is It Anyway?*

"With tell-all honesty, pitch-perfect sass, and a generous and tender heart, Johanna Edwards brings to life the public burdens of being overweight . . . Like reality TV, *The Next Big Thing* is highly addictive." —Jennifer Paddock, author of *A Secret World*

"More addicting than any reality show, *The Next Big Thing* is a terrific read that kept me laughing and cheering until the last page."        —Sara Mlynowski, author of *As Seen on TV*

"From the first page to the last, Johanna Edwards' debut novel is fabulous fun. I couldn't help cheering for Kat as she comes face-to-face with the reality behind TV."
                —Jennifer O'Connell, author of *Bachelorette #1*
                and *Dress Rehearsal*

# Your Big Break

*Also by Johanna Edwards*

THE NEXT BIG THING

Withdrawn/ABCL

3 9075 03466408 3

# Your Big Break

## Johanna Edwards

BERKLEY BOOKS, NEW YORK

THE BERKLEY PUBLISHING GROUP
Published by the Penguin Group
Penguin Group (USA) Inc.
375 Hudson Street, New York, New York 10014, USA
Penguin Group (Canada), 90 Eglinton Avenue East, Suite 700, Toronto, Ontario M4P 2Y3,
Canada (a division of Pearson Penguin Canada Inc.)
Penguin Books Ltd., 80 Strand, London WC2R 0RL, England
Penguin Group Ireland, 25 St. Stephen's Green, Dublin 2, Ireland
(a division of Penguin Books Ltd.)
Penguin Group (Australia), 250 Camberwell Road, Camberwell, Victoria 3124, Australia
(a division of Pearson Australia Group Pty. Ltd.)
Penguin Books India Pvt. Ltd., 11 Community Centre, Panchsheel Park, New Delhi—110 017,
India
Penguin Group (NZ), cnr. Airborne and Rosedale Roads, Albany, Auckland 1310, New Zealand
(a division of Pearson New Zealand Ltd.)
Penguin Books (South Africa) (Pty.) Ltd., 24 Sturdee Avenue, Rosebank, Johannesburg 2196,
South Africa
Penguin Books Ltd., Registered Offices: 80 Strand, London WC2R 0RL, England

Copyright © 2006 by Johanna Edwards
Cover design by Honi Werner
Text design by Tiffany Estreicher

All rights reserved. No part of this book may be reproduced, scanned, or distributed in any
printed or electronic form without permission. Please do not participate in or encourage piracy of
copyrighted materials in violation of the author's rights. Purchase only authorized editions.

This is a work of fiction. Names, characters, places, and incidents either are the product of the
author's imagination or are used fictitiously, and any resemblance to actual persons, living or
dead, business establishments, events, or locales is entirely coincidental.

PRINTING HISTORY
Berkley trade paperback edition / March 2006

ISBN: 0-425-20784-6

Berkley is a registered trademark of Penguin Group (USA) Inc.
The "B" design is a trademark belonging to Penguin Group (USA) Inc.

This book has been cataloged by the Library of Congress

PRINTED IN THE UNITED STATES OF AMERICA

10  9  8  7  6  5  4  3  2  1

To James Abbott

# Acknowledgments

I am extremely grateful to all the readers who took a chance on a new author and picked up a copy of *The Next Big Thing*. You guys made my lifelong dream come true and put me on the best-seller lists for nearly three months! Thanks also to everyone who took the time to e-mail or come to one of my readings. Your kind words and encouragement have meant the world to me.

Many thanks to my savvy agent, the awesome Jenny Bent. Without her, I'd still be sitting around waiting for *my* big break. My undying gratitude to the phenomenal team at Berkley: Leslie Gelbman, Kara Cesare, and Tess Tabor. A big thank you to the Penguin marketing and sales force for working so hard to get my books out there. And, of course, many thanks to Allison McCabe, who got the ball rolling in the first place.

Publication is a crazy time. I owe a lot to my family and friends who put up with me during the most neurotic year of my life (and that's saying a lot!) and who offered much love and support. Thanks especially to my parents, Paula and Les, and my sister, Selena, as well as all my aunts, uncles, and grandparents, and cousins.

Two people were very instrumental in helping this book see the light of day. I am grateful to James Abbott, who read and critiqued both *Your Big Break* and *The Next Big Thing* on incredibly short notice. Thanks to my Boston buddy, Susanne Enos, for giving me the scoop on Beantown.

I am also grateful to: Candy Justice, Chris Allen, Christy Paganoni, Virginia Miller, Chris Carwile, Karin Gillespie, Stephen Usery, Dr. Cynthia Hopson, and Dr. David Arant. Thanks to everyone in Memphis for rallying around a hometown girl and showing your support.

Last, and definitely least, to all the boys who ever dumped me, rejected me, or otherwise broke my heart—thanks for the inspiration.

# 1

**YBB INC. EMPLOYEE RULE #1**
Always meet in a public place.
Coffee shops are ideal.
Never go anywhere that serves alcohol.

I am a liar. My job forces me to be one.

Every day I spin falsehoods, tell people what they want to hear.

"Of course he still finds you sexually attractive!" *He just finds you sexually attractive in that "we're better off as friends" way.*

"It's not you. Yes, I know everyone says that, but it's so *not* you."

"No, he doesn't hate you." *He just never wants to see you again as long as he lives.*

"Your receding hairline and beer belly have nothing to do with why she left."

I say these things because that's my job, to sugarcoat the bad stuff.

I even lie to my family.

My parents have no idea what I do for a living. They think I write promotional copy for websites. It's not that I'm embarrassed by my job, but, well, my folks are kind of old-fashioned. Especially my mother. She's kissed three men in her entire life and was a virgin until she married, a fact she reminds me of on a semi-regular basis. If she knew I made my living busting up relationships, she'd be crushed, mortified. I made up the whole Web thing to buy time, so I could slowly introduce my parents to the idea of Your Big Break Inc. But the trouble with lying is you can't tell just one fib and be done with it. You have to make up more lies to cover your original lie.

Long story short, I still haven't gotten around to telling my parents the truth.

Maybe I *am* embarrassed.

But as crazy as it seems, I took this job because I wanted to help people. Breakups are horrific and devastating—Your Big Break Inc. makes them civilized. I do whatever I can to help people transitioning from couplehood to single life. But good intentions or not, the fact remains: I *am* a liar.

"Are you Jason Dutwiler?" I ask, entering the downtown Boston Starbucks and locating a forlorn-looking man nursing a cappuccino.

"I was expecting a guy," he says, eyeing me up and down.

I clear my throat. "Jason Dutwiler?" I ask again, and he nods.

"My assistant said I had a meeting with someone named Danny," he explains. "I thought it'd be a man."

"Dani," I tell him, extending my hand. "It's short for Danielle."

Jason is clean-cut with light brown hair and eyes. He works as a CPA at FleetBoston. According to my notes, he's thirty-six years old, but I find that hard to believe. He looks much younger.

"I never thought Lucy would leave me for a *girl*," he says, amazed.

I smile and slide into the seat across from him. I'm carrying a small, black duffel bag, which I place beside my feet. "She's not leaving you for anyone, Jason. It's not about that." I pause. "Lucy's at a crossroads in her life," I begin.

"Crossroads? Give me a fucking break." He groans. "Did Lucy tell you to say that?" Before I can answer, he rushes on. "Forget it. I've been putting up with her BS for months now."

He takes a sip of his cappuccino and we stare at each other.

"She used to be fun, the kind of girl you take to a Red Sox game and then down a few beers with, you know?" he finally says to me.

A CPA enjoying beer and baseball? The way Lucy described Jason, I'd expected a hardcore number-cruncher whose idea of a good time was analyzing cash-flow statements.

"Now she's gone all Gwyneth on me," Jason continues.

"Gwyneth?"

"As in Paltrow. Lucy's obsessed with wheatgrass shooters and yoga and not eating meat. She wants to find herself." He rolls his eyes. "She wants to be 'at one with the universe.' "

I don't have the heart to tell him that what Lucy *really* wants to be at one with is her new acupuncturist, Nate. "Jason doesn't do it for me anymore," Lucy had confided during our initial consultation. "He's too clingy. And, physically speaking, he's not what I want. Nate, on the other hand . . . Nate's amazing. He practices tantric sex." And, besides, I'm not sure how much I buy Lucy's hippie vegan routine. Last time I talked to the girl, she was preparing to become an actress.

I shake the image out of my mind. I'm supposed to be giving Jason the cold, hard facts. "Okay, I'll be blunt," I say, locking my eyes on his. "Lucy's fallen out of love with you."

He looks like he's about to vomit.

I place a reassuring hand on his arm. "I know this is hard to hear, but, unfortunately, it's the truth."

"When?" he asks in a voice barely above a whisper. "When did it happen?"

"She's felt this way for several months now."

"My God," Jason breathes, his body visibly tense. "And she doesn't even have the nerve to tell me? She sends some friend to do her dirty work?" He swats my hand off his arm.

"She couldn't find the words," I say. "She can't bear to hurt you."

The truth is, Lucy's reached the point in the relationship where all she wants is a clean break. And she doesn't have the guts to tell him to his face. Most of our clients are cowards.

"What are you, her spokesperson or something?"

"In a way, yes." This is always the worst part. There's no easy way to explain what I do, so I usually come right out with it. "Here," I say, handing Jason my business card.

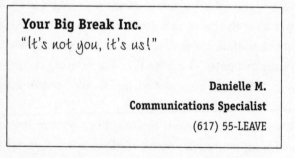

**Your Big Break Inc.**
*"It's not you, it's us!"*

**Danielle M.**
**Communications Specialist**
(617) 55-LEAVE

"I work for a breakup service. Lucy was afraid things might get complicated, so she hired me to help sort through the details," I explain as Jason stares blankly at the card.

"She *hired* you to dump me?"

I nod. His jaw drops.

"I didn't even know you could do that!"

"Your Big Break Inc. is one of the first companies of its kind. There was a huge article on us in *The Boston Globe* last month. Did you see it?"

"No, I did not," Jason snaps. He runs his hands through his hair, the shock on his face palpable. "Let me get this straight— you make your living dumping people?"

"Yes." And ending friendships. We'll even quit your job for you if the price is right. Your Big Break Inc. offers all sorts of services: Breakup Recovery Kits, personally crafted Dear John letters, counseling phone calls, property and pet retrieval, and guilt gifting (the dumper placates the dumpee by sending him or her specially arranged packages of baked goods, balloons, and massage certificates). Our fees range from $25 to $350—a real bargain, if you think about it.

"This is fucking unbelievable!" Jason exclaims loudly. A few people turn to stare.

"My job is to help you two transition to single life while remaining on good terms." He seems too stunned to speak, so I continue. "Lucy had some things she wanted to tell you, and she felt it best to put them in a letter."

I give Jason the envelope and he sets it down on the table. "I'll read it later," he mumbles.

In actuality, every word of the letter was written by me. I interviewed Lucy extensively about why she wanted to end things, and then reworded her answers into what I hope is a concise, heartfelt good-bye note. It's a tough balance. You have to be straightforward and honest, while letting them down easy. I pick up my duffel bag. "Lucy also wanted me to give you these," I say, holding it out to him.

Jason glances at the bag suspiciously.

"Go on, take it," I prod. "It won't bite." *But it may sting a bit.*

He unzips it and peers inside, pulling out Your Big Break Inc.'s official Breakup Recovery Kit, which I prepared for him this morning. There are a few standard items that go into every box: a list of the fifty best breakup songs, a guide to Boston's least date-friendly restaurants (the goal is to keep the dumpee away from as many happy couples as possible), a selection of counseling resources, and a mix of humorous and serious articles about getting over a broken heart.

Each Breakup Recovery Kit is tailor-made to fit the individual who's receiving it. We add as many little extras—aka *guilt gifts*—as the budget allows. In Jason's case, Lucy sprung for a pair of tickets to a Red Sox game and a DVD of *Die Hard*.

Jason digs through the duffel bag, locating a copy of *Under the Table & Dreaming*. "My Dave Matthews CD!" he exclaims. "I've been looking for this forever." He retrieves a boxed set of *The Sopranos* DVDs, a framed photo of the once-happy couple, and a dog-eared guidebook about northern California. "This was our first big trip together," he says, looking pained. "I took Lucy to San Francisco for her thirtieth birthday. I told her I loved her in front of the Golden Gate Bridge." His voice is quavering.

"Jason," I begin, "do you need me to—"

He holds up a hand to silence me. "No, I can do this." He continues digging through the bag, taking stock of everything. "I see she's kept all the jewelry I've given her."

*They always do.*

Jason narrows his eyes. "You must get some sick pleasure out of dumping me. For her," he clarifies.

I've heard this one before. "Believe me, nothing could be further from the truth."

"That's crap. Isn't this what you do? Profit off of other people's misery?"

"I'm a communications specialist," I say. "I help facilitate a smooth ending to a troubled relationship."

"And how many 'smooth endings' have you facilitated this month, Dani? Do tell."

If you include all the kiss-off phone calls, e-mails, and in-person meetings, I believe the total comes to thirty-three. But who's counting? "Jason, my intentions are to help you. Lucy still cares about you, but she thinks you're better off as friends."

"That's pathetic. *She's* pathetic for hiring someone to dump me."

"Believe me, there are worse ways to break up with people."

"Yeah, right." He snorts. "What do you know?"

"A lot, actually. This is my area of expertise," I remind him. "I've seen people pull all kinds of breakup moves: leaving their lover on Valentine's Day, a birthday, at Christmas."

There are dozens of crappy ways to dump someone: via e-mail, cell phone text message, AOL Instant Messenger, postcard, or Post-It; on an answering machine; through a friend; over dinner. But by far the most popular method seems to be the duck-and-run.

"Most people pull the old 'drop off the face of the earth' routine," I tell Jason. "They decide to dump someone, and, rather than tell the person, they just avoid them and hope they'll take the hint. At least Lucy's being straightforward." I smile sympathetically. "I wish *my* last boyfriend had hired someone to break things off."

Jason looks skeptical.

"The way he did it was publicly humiliating."

For the first time since we've met, Jason relaxes a bit. "Why, what'd he do? Take out a billboard?"

"You're not far off. He dumped me on the radio."

I'm leading into The Story—my own personal breakup horror tale that is sure to put Jason at ease. All of the employees of Your Big Break Inc. have one, and we pull them out when things get sticky. The only difference is mine's one hundred percent true. My two coworkers embellished theirs.

"Did your boyfriend call up and dedicate 'N Sync's *Bye Bye Bye* to you? No, wait, let me guess! It was *Fuck Off* by Kid Rock."

I give him a tight smile; that *is* kind of funny. "It was Ben Folds Five's *Song for the Dumped*. My ex-boyfriend was a DJ at WBCN," I say, citing Boston's biggest rock station. "He broke up with me on-air during the drive-time show."

In the eleven months since it happened, I must have told The Story a hundred times. Now it almost seems as though it happened to someone else. "I hadn't heard from Garrett for over two weeks." I lean across the table and lower my voice conspiratorially. "I'd been leaving messages at his house, calling him at work, the whole nine yards. Then I turn on my radio one day after work and—boom! There he is, talking about how he'd gotten laid the night before by some Hooters waitress."

"He *obviously* wasn't referring to you!"

My hands instinctively fly up to cover my less-than-ample breasts, and Jason's cheeks turn pink.

"Oh, God, I didn't mean it like *that*. Nothing I say ever comes out right." He smashes his face against his hands. "It's like my foot is surgically implanted in my mouth. That's probably why I can't keep a girlfriend." He gets really quiet, and I'm afraid he might start crying.

"Everybody has failed relationships," I say. "Think of them as practice runs. They prepare you for the real deal. Not that your relationship with Lucy wasn't genuine," I throw in, before I get myself into trouble.

Jason laughs. "That'd fix her, wouldn't it? Lucy always likes to think of herself as a star player in everybody's lives. She's such a drama queen. She'd hate it if I considered her a 'practice girl-friend.'"

I can see he's starting to head off down the bitterness track, so I quickly shift the topic back to The Story. I find it calms people and distracts them. "So, anyway, about Garrett and the Hooters waitress . . ."

"Ah, yes," Jason says, brightening. "You were getting to the good part."

*Why do we get so much comfort out of other people's misfor-tunes?* I push the thought aside and continue. "After he made the announcement about his Hooters hookup, one of the other DJs said, 'Dude, I thought you had a serious girlfriend.' Garrett laughed and replied, 'Not anymore. I dumped her weeks ago.' Which, of course, was news to me. Then he cued up the Ben Folds Five song."

"Ouch! What did you do?"

I shrug. "What *could* I do? At first I thought it was a joke, but when I talked to him off the air, I learned he was serious. I cried and screamed and shredded pictures of him. I left ram-bling messages on his answering machine. I even threw a drink in his face when he came over to drop off my stuff. I was totally nuts for a little while."

"Sounds like a normal response to me."

I could tell him about the five stages of getting dumped, but I want to wrap up this job. "Getting back to the matter at hand, Lucy gave me a list of things she left at your place." I pull it out of my purse and hand it to him. "I'll need to arrange a time to pick these up."

His face falls. "She's actually doing this, isn't she?"

"I'm so sorry, Jason. I really am."

"Please," he begs. "I don't want to do this."

"Lucy's mind is made up—"

"Talk to her for me!" he interrupts. "Tell her I'll do anything! I'll give up cigarettes. I'll meditate! I'll take up Tan Chi!"

"Tai Chi," I correct.

"Whatever! I just want her back. I'll completely overhaul my life if that's what it takes!"

"You shouldn't change yourself for someone," I caution. "It never works."

"Dani," he says, glancing around to make sure no one's listening. "You don't understand how much I love this girl. All I want is a second chance to prove myself to her. I don't think that's too much to ask."

"I'm afraid Lucy's mind is made up."

He places his hand gently on mine. "Then help her *un*make it."

"I can't."

Jason draws in a deep breath. "Will you at least do one favor for me then?"

"That depends."

"My brother's getting married in a few months down the Cape, and Lucy is supposed to be my date. If I show up alone, my parents will go ballistic. They'll give me the third degree about why we broke up. I come from a large Catholic family—they're already upset that I haven't gotten married and given them grandchildren yet."

For a brief moment, I'm worried he's going to ask me to go with him. Not that he's grossly unappealing, but that would be a serious violation of protocol.

"Convince Lucy to come to the wedding and pretend we're

still together," Jason says, and I breathe a sigh of relief. "One last date to really say good-bye."

"I don't know. . . ."

Craig McAllister, my boss and the founder of Your Big Break Inc., is always citing one of our cardinal rules to me: Do *not* get personally involved with a client. I can hear his voice in my head now, warning me. But how do you break someone's heart—even a stranger's—without getting personally involved?

I sigh. "Give me a couple of days. I'll see what I can do."


People always talk about the five stages of grief: denial, anger, bargaining, depression, and acceptance. But what's just as common are the Five Stages of Breakup Hell: nervous breakdown, sour grapes, rebounding, backsliding, and letting go.

It's not just a cliché: Breaking up *is* hard to do. And forget about the recovery rule—that the relationship mourning period lasts one month for every year you were together. That's totally untrue. More often than not, people get it backward, taking one *year* to recover from a one-month fling. There's no reliable way to measure when a broken heart will mend. Even at stage five, when the dumpee sadly accepts the inevitable, they never *completely* get over it. Some part of them will always be connected to the person who broke their heart.

Since Garrett dumped me, I've become a real pro at ending love affairs.

# 2

# We Need to Talk

It's eight o'clock Thursday, and I'm standing in my parents' large, stucco kitchen, drinking red wine and watching Mom make Cajun food. My family doesn't have a lot of traditions, but this is one of the few: We get together every other Thursday for a sit-down dinner of spicy food. My brother is usually missing in action until the very last second—he opts to hang out upstairs and watch TV instead of socializing. He rushes down just in time to eat, stuffs his face, and then bolts.

"We need to talk," Mom says.

I cringe because, really, has anything good ever followed that statement?

"Wait, let me guess. You burned the jambalaya, and we're having pizza for dinner," I joke.

"I'm concerned about you, Dani."

"Concerned?" I repeat, running my fingers through my shoulder-length blond hair. I study her face as she stirs the rice. It amazes me sometimes how much my mother and I look alike. We're both short and slim, with good skin, green eyes, and wheat-colored hair. If it's true what they say—that your mother is a mirror image of what you'll look like when you're older—then I'm pretty lucky. My mom has held up very well over the years.

She stops stirring the rice. "You're twenty-eight years old, Dani. In two years, you'll be thirty. Thirty!"

"Gee, Mom, thanks for reminding me."

"When I was thirty, I was married with two children, a house, and a successful career. You're still living in that tiny apartment in Cambridge, fumbling around, trying to get your life in order."

"My life's in order," I grumble, gulping down my glass of wine and pouring myself a fresh one. The truth is, in a lot of ways I'm lucky. Your Big Break Inc. may not be the most serene place to work, but the pay is really good. And I desperately need the salary—not only did Garrett leave me with a broken heart, he left me with a drained bank account as well. I'm still paying off the debt I incurred while mourning our breakup.

"No, it isn't. Dani, you try to pretend like you're happy, but I can tell you're not. These are the best years of your life. You're in your prime!" Mom says. "You're supposed to be out having a good time, meeting people, living it up. In a few years, you'll be too old to have fun."

*Too old to have fun? Where is this coming from?*

"You have the social life of a senior citizen," Mom says, smiling wryly.

I gasp. "Do you want me to be immature?"

"I just want you to live it up a little."

"What about Sean?" I ask, trying to change the subject. "At

least I have my own apartment; Sean's twenty-five and he still lives at home. And he only works part-time at Blockbuster."

"Your brother is about to start medical school," she counters. "He's saving his money."

My brother has been "about to start medical school" ever since he graduated from Northeastern two years ago. As far as I can tell, all he does is loaf around the house, playing video games and watching TiVo.

Fortunately, my dad wanders into the room before things get hairy. "Hey, hon," he says, pecking me on the cheek. Seeing my pained expression, he adds, "You driving her nuts again, Beth?"

"Just showing a little motherly concern."

"Yeah, I know how overbearing your 'concern' can be."

"Just doing my job," Mom says, looking tense.

"Mind if I borrow Dani for a minute?" Dad winks at me. "I've got a couple of boxes in the car. I could use some help bringing them in."

Mom waves us away. "Sure, Paul, that's perfectly fine." I can tell she's irritated that Dad interrupted her rant, but I'm relieved to make it out of there alive.

"You doing okay?" Dad asks as I follow him outside.

"Yeah, I'm doing pretty well. Aside from the Spanish Inquisition."

"Oh, your mom?" He shrugs. "She's been kind of stressed lately."

I nod. "I know. Plus, she's turning fifty-five."

Dad opens the trunk of his Audi and begins pulling out large filing boxes.

Six months ago, my mother retired from her position as a corporate trainer and strategic analyst. I say "retired" as though she had a choice in the matter. She didn't. The board of directors wanted to bring in "new blood." In the process, several people, my mom included, were let go via early retirement. Mom hasn't quite been the same since it happened.

Dad hands me a box. "Thanks for helping out."

"What is all this?" I ask, hoisting the box in my arms.

"Clients' files." Dad grunts, slamming the car trunk shut. "I've really fallen behind—it's going to take me all night to go through these." Even before my family moved to Boston ten years ago, my dad was a total workaholic. He puts in long days as a financial analyst at Merriwether Payne Investments, and frequently stays at the office till all hours of the night.

We trudge up the front steps and into the house, carrying the boxes to Dad's small workspace off the living room.

"I could help you sort through these if you'd like," I offer.

"Oh, no." He shakes his head. "I'm not putting you to work." He slings an arm across my shoulders and smiles. "What do you say you and I go catch a few minutes of the Bruins game before dinner?"

It's not often that Dad makes time for me. He's usually too busy working to hang out. Lately, this seems to be changing. "Sounds like a plan."

We're halfway to the den when Mom yells, "Paul! Get in here a sec. This jambalaya's a little . . . crispy."

"Oh, brother. Duty calls," Dad quips, jogging off into the kitchen.

"Looks like we'll be having pizza after all," I quip.


Fridays are generally slow at Your Big Break Inc. People like to get their relationship-ending done and over with early in the week, or else they go for one last weekend of sex before calling it quits.

"Dani, are you familiar with the term 'binding arbitration'?" my boss Craig asks, planting himself in front of my desk. "Did you guys have that down in Louisiana?"

Craig thinks everything south of Washington, D.C., is made up of swamps, dude ranches, and farmland. Never mind the fact that I've been living in Boston for more than a decade, or that New Orleans—where I was born and bred—is a bustling metropolis. I toy with him. "Is that one of them fancy legal shindigs you have here in the big city?"

"Dani!" He sounds ready to explode.

I laugh and gesture to the chair opposite my desk. "Have a seat." He thinks it over for a minute, his brow furrowing rapidly, then plops down. "All right, Craig, yes, I know what binding arbitration is. Why?"

"You know Evan Hirschbaum?"

It's a rhetorical question, but I nod. Evan Hirschbaum is our biggest client. He practically single-handedly keeps us in business.

"Well, Mr. Hirschbaum was in the middle of binding arbitration this morning when Sophie Kennison—the girl he hired you to dump last week—barged in and started screaming obscenities at him. It threw him off so badly, he nearly blew the case." Craig smirks. "Though, of course, he didn't."

"Of course."

Craig looks at me. "Be straight with me, Dani. Did you or did you not inform Sophie Kennison that Mr. Hirschbaum no longer wants to see her?"

"Yes, I did the deed last Monday." I sigh. "She was pretty devastated."

*Devastated* doesn't even begin to describe it. Sophie didn't stop crying for two hours. I wound up pigging out on Häagen-Dazs with her in an attempt to smooth things over. I don't know how much more client heartache my waistline can handle.

"Well, apparently, the breakup didn't take."

"Apparently," I agree.

"At any rate, Evan's deeply upset about what happened, Dani."

*Oh, brother.* I suppress a laugh. Try as I might, I can't imagine Evan Hirschbaum shedding a tear over anything, much less one of his disposable girlfriends. The guy's rock-solid, through and through. "I'm sorry to hear that." Sometimes it seems like all I ever do is say I'm sorry. I say it to my boss, to our clients, and, especially, to the people I break up with. Maybe that's what my business card should read: *Danielle M., Professional Apologizer.*

"You'd better get down there," Craig instructs.

"Get down where?"

"Sophie's apartment. The address is in your file, right?"

"You mean Sophie's not still at the law offices?"

"No, of course not." Craig shakes his head. "Evan kicked her to da curb."

Craig has a habit of picking up slang that sounds ridiculous coming from a middle-aged Irish-American guy. At our office Christmas party, he kept slapping his hands together and exclaiming "True dat!" every time someone made a statement he agreed with. I often feel embarrassed for him. The poor guy means well. He founded Your Big Break Inc. four years ago after his wife left him for a fledgling musician. Craig used to be a traveling salesman, but he returned home one day to find a "Dear Craig" letter taped to the refrigerator. His ex-wife drained his bank account and broke his heart. Craig hasn't been the same since.

"Let me get this straight," I say. "Sophie Kennison burst into a closed proceeding today and shouted out a string of cusswords. Yet the arbitrator let her go? She's not in any legal trouble or anything?" I don't know much about legal matters, but that doesn't sound right.

Craig throws up his hands. "Who knows? I'm not clued in to how the legal system works. Mr. Hirschbaum can explain it better. Speaking of which"—he rises from his chair and points to my phone—"you'd better square things away with him before you go see Sophie."

"I'll make it my top priority."

"That's the spirit! You're going to have to do your damn best here, Dani," he says, turning to go. "When I talked to Mr. Hirschbaum this morning, he was furious. It's going to take a real—"

"Don't worry, Craig," I say, cutting him off. "I'll kiss his ass."

He smiles. It's exactly what he wants to hear.

# 3

# It's Not You, It's Me

Evan Hirschbaum is quite possibly the world's most prolific dater.

As I sit in the reception area of Hirschbaum, Davis, and Klein: Attorneys at Law in the John Hancock Tower downtown, I mull over his never-ending list of exes.

There is, of course, Sophie Kennison, who I'm here to discuss. Last month, it was Holly O'Henry. Before her, Shiri Friedman. And let's not forget Annie Shields, Heather Canatella, and Tina Graber. Beyond that, my memory gets fuzzy. After a while, Evan's gal pals start to blend together. They all have similar professions (wannabe actress/model/singer), similar appearances (drop-dead gorgeous) and similar shelf lives (six weeks, max). Evan keeps Your Big Break Inc. on retainer, which basically means we—usually me—remain at his beck and call.

I've been waiting in the reception area for nearly forty-five minutes. I pass the time flipping through outdated issues of *The*

*New Yorker* and sending text messages to my best friend, Krista Bruce, on my cell phone. Krista is the business manager for a small catering company in downtown Boston. We make plans to grab dinner at The Cheesecake Factory tonight after work, and then I put my cell phone away. I glance down at my watch again. I'm giving Evan fifteen more minutes, and then I'm bailing. I'd hoped to schmooze him via phone, but Evan's secretary instructed me to come to the office. "This isn't the sort of thing Mr. Hirschbaum is comfortable discussing over the phone," she snapped.

Which was news to me.

Evan and I conducted most of our business via phone. We'd met in person only once before.

I flip open my briefcase and pull out my Franklin Covey day planner and make a quick note: *Call Lucy about Cape Cod wedding w/ Jason.* I grimace. That's going to be a tough one. Lucy is going to be pretty peeved when I ask her to see Jason one last time. I should have given him a flat no, but something in his face—*desperation?*—really stung me. I just couldn't bear to see him so upset. My stomach growls. It's almost 2 p.m., and I haven't had lunch. I'll have to grab a quick sandwich at Au Bon Pain on my way to Sophie Kennison's apartment. I stand up and approach the receptionist's desk to tell her I'm leaving.

She clicks off from a call. "You can go on back now."

I head down the hall past a seemingly endless array of conference rooms and tiny cubicles. I don't see one person who looks genuinely happy. I make my way to Evan's gigantic office and rap lightly on the door. His head's buried in a file.

"Come in," he says, not bothering to look up.

I stroll inside and come to a stop in front of his enormous mahogany desk, which is covered with hundreds of manila folders, piled in stacks. I stand there for a minute before he further acknowledges me. "Dani, great to see you!" he says brightly, standing to greet me. We shake hands, and he holds my grip for a second too long.

Evan's tall with inky black hair and large dark eyes. He's in his early forties and is strikingly handsome in a polished, intimidating way. When I first met him, I thought he looked like a soap-opera stud, not a Boston attorney.

"Would you care for some water?" he asks, sitting down.

I perch on the chair opposite him. "That'd be great."

He buzzes his secretary. "Martha, bring me two bottles of Trump Ice."

Evan Hirschbaum, I realize, is the only person I know who would actually drink bottled water with Donald Trump's face on the side.

A pretty young woman comes bustling in a second later with two waters. As soon as she's gone, I begin sucking up.

"Mr. Hirschbaum, I can't tell you how sorry I am, sir—"

"None of this 'sir' business. It makes me sound ninety. How long have we known each other, Dani? Four, five months?"

"About a year."

There's a long pause, and I'm afraid he's going to argue with me. "So call me Evan." He smiles. "We're on a first-name basis now."

*We are?* This is news to me. Even Craig doesn't call him Evan.

"Dani, the reason I asked you here is simple. I've been paying for your services for a year, and I think that entitles me to a certain level of commitment."

I hate the way he says "services." It makes me sound like a prostitute. "You can rest assured, s-Evan"—*I just called him Seven!*—"you're our top priority."

"I'm glad to hear it." He nods. "However, I didn't feel like a top priority this morning. Can I assume Craig brought you up to speed with what happened?"

"Yes, Craig filled me in on all the details. I understand Sophie Kennison caused some trouble for you during a binding arbitration."

"Trouble," he scoffs. "She completely intruded on my workspace!"

I grimace in sympathy. "I can't imagine how horrible that must have been."

He takes a swig of Trump Ice. "Would you like to hear my life philosophy, Dani?"

*Not really, but what choice do I have?* "I'd love to."

He stares straight at me. "Everything's business. *Everything*. Treat your life that way, and the world's your oyster."

"That's interesting." I take a quick sip of Trump Ice.

"The problem with people is they let their feelings dictate how they live their lives. They become slaves to emotion. Me, on the other hand—I take nothing personally."

I'm not sure what to say to this. "That's one way of looking at the world," I finally offer.

Evan shakes his head. "It's not *one* way. It's the *only* way. Do you see what I'm getting at? How this applies to Sophie?"

He's lost me, but I try to hide it. "I think I do, yeah."

He leans back in his chair and props his hands behind his head. "I trust you to keep my romantic relationships in order. Ideally, I prefer clean partings. But when messes occur, I trust you to clean them up promptly."

"I'll handle Sophie."

He shakes his head. "She got to me today, and I don't appreciate that."

"What exactly did she say when she barged in? I understand she was cursing?"

Evan laughs. "Cursing isn't exactly the right word, though it was bordering on profane. See for yourself." He reaches into his Cole Haan trouser pocket and pulls out a Motorola cell phone. "It's the first text on the screen."

I take the phone from his hands and open the message.

*Evan,*
*I miss the way you kiss me, I miss scratching my nails down your back. I miss your eyes, your hands, your tongue, your two-hour hard-ons . . .*

I snap the phone shut. "I don't really think I need to read the whole thing."

"But you get the picture."

*Loud and clear.* "So tell me about the part where Sophie burst into the room. How did the arbitrator react?" I ask, steering things onto less embarrassing ground.

"She never came into contact with the arbitrator."

*Huh?* "But I thought she intruded on your case?"

"It wasn't a physical intrusion, per se."

*I wish he'd just get to the point.* "What do you mean, exactly?"

"Sophie sent this"—he grabs for the phone—"semi-erotic text to me in the *middle* of the arbitration! I made the mistake of reading the damn thing right at a crucial moment."

"You had your cell phone on during a legal proceeding?" I ask. Surely that's violating some law? At the very least, it's incredibly rude.

"I'm only human."

*Could have fooled me.*

"And when I read Sophie's text, I was utterly distracted."

*This from the man who takes nothing personally?* "Craig said Sophie barged into the proceedings—"

"She wasn't *there*, but I felt her presence quite strongly"—he glances down at his lap—"if you follow."

*Oh, Christ.* I'm thoroughly grossed-out. I can't believe this is what my life has come to. I have a master's degree in communications from Tulane University, for crying out loud. "Look, sir . . . Evan," I begin. "Sophie's having trouble adjusting. She cared about you a great deal. I'll talk to her, make sure she's coping okay. And I'll see that she doesn't bother you again."

"Music to my ears."

I get up to leave. "I've got to run, but I'll take care of this first thing."

Evan rises from his chair. "Why the rush?" He cocks his head to the side. "How about grabbing a late lunch with me? It would give us a chance to get to know each other better. I'd like to find out what makes you tick, Dani."

*What makes me tick? Has he lost his mind?*

Evan strides around the desk and touches my shoulder. "It's really a shame we aren't better friends."

"Friends?" I repeat.

"Yes, you seem like someone I'd enjoy getting to know."

*Oh, fuck, is Evan Hirschbaum hitting on me?* I feel my face flame up. I'm not Evan's type! As Jason Dutwiler so bluntly pointed out, I'm not exactly stacked. And for Evan Hirschbaum, that's an important quality. His taste runs more Carmen Electra than girl-next-door.

"I'd love to have lunch, but, unfortunately, I've already eaten. And I could eat again, except I had such a big, big meal." My stomach, naturally, picks this moment to growl. "I ate pasta. At Bertucci's," I babble.

"Do you always ramble when you're nervous?" he teases.

*Oh, fuck, Evan Hirschbaum is* definitely *hitting on me!* "I'm not nervous, I'm just . . . full."

"Another time, then." He releases his grip on my shoulder.

"Yes, another time." *Not if I can help it!* "But now I'd better get over to Sophie's place."

He shakes his head. "Sophie's visiting her parents in Connecticut for two weeks. Which you would have known, had you read the *entire* text message."

"I'll talk to her as soon as she gets back, then." I begin inching toward the door.

"Sophie's a loose cannon, Dani. I don't know what I ever saw in her in the first place."

"Beauty. Same thing you see in all your women," I say before I can stop myself.

Evan winks. "You make me sound shallow. As though I chew people up and spit them out."

"You do break a lot of hearts," I tell him, and he beams, like he's proud of it.

"It may appear that way, but I've merely had a string of bad luck," Evan says as he shows me out of his office. "Some women are too annoying, too fat, too clingy to merit a lasting relationship. I seem to know them all."

I can't get out of there fast enough.


I meet Krista for dinner at The Cheesecake Factory after work. I never did stop for lunch, and I'm absolutely starving. I'm about to crack a joke about how hungry I am when my cell phone starts ringing. I quickly pull it out of my purse and answer. "Hello?"

"Hi, honey." It's my dad.

"Hey, what's up?"

"Not a lot. I was calling to see if you're free to go shopping this weekend. I'd like to pick out something really nice for your mother's birthday next week, and I could use your help."

"Sure, my schedule's wide open."

He chuckles. "I find that hard to believe. I bet you've got a wild time planned with your friends."

Actually, I don't. And it's really more like *friend*. Singular, no "s." Other than Krista, I don't have a lot of close pals. I let a lot of my friends slip away when I was dating Garrett. It's a mistake I've deeply regretted, and one I vow never to repeat.

"I'm sure I can squeeze you in," I tease Dad.

"Great! How does Sunday sound?"

We make plans to meet at two o'clock.

"Sorry about that," I apologize to Krista as I hang up the phone. "Looks like I'm hitting the mall with Dad this weekend."

Krista raises an eyebrow. "That's weird. Since when is your dad the shopping type?"

"Since he needs a gift for Mom's birthday."

"He's such a workaholic, I'm surprised he even remembered."

"Tell me about it," I begin, then think better of it. "You know, Dad's been a lot better lately. He's been making a real effort to spend time with the family. It's actually kind of cool. I've never gotten to know my father very well. Other than watching the occasional Bruins game, he keeps to himself. But he seems to be opening up a lot more these days."

"That's great! I wish my parents would do the same. I barely see either one of them," Krista says. "So, how was your day? Did you have to go see that Ethan guy again?"

"Evan." I grimace.

"Sorry, I can never remember," she apologizes as she thumbs through her menu.

"I wish I could forget," I say, thinking back to our bizarre conversation.

# 4

*"Your suspicions are correct: I slept with your boyfriend. The sex was mind-blowing. I came five times. . . ."*

"I can't go through with this," I say, dropping my pen mid-sentence.

Your Big Break Inc.'s newest hiree, Amanda Portney, looks up at me and grins. "You're only giving the client what she wanted."

"I know, but it seems so . . . cruel."

"Read me the rest," Amanda prompts, kicking her feet up on my desk.

It's Monday morning and we're sitting in my office, conspiring to end a six-year friendship. Amanda just started at Your Big Break Inc. last week, and we're still training her on the finer details of terminating relationships. She's going to be working for us on a part-time basis while she finishes her psychology degree at Boston University. Amanda's primary duty is to maintain our website, but she still needs to know what we do and how we do it, so I've included her in this drafting session. Her official title is Assistant Support Specialist.

Which, as my colleague Trey so eloquently pointed out, spells ASS.

With the addition of Amanda, Your Big Break Inc. is now a five-man operation. There's Craig McAllister; Trey Shaunessy, my fellow Communications Specialist; me; Amanda; and Beverly, our administrative assistant. We work on commission, so the hiring of more personnel is both a blessing and a curse.

"Okay, so the next paragraph starts, 'We were like two rabbits, constantly humping—' "

"Take out the rabbit part," Amanda weighs in. "Too gross."

"That's a direct quote. The client specifically instructed me to use that line."

Amanda makes a face. "It's a disgusting image. Is that what you're aiming for?"

"Not exactly." I flip through my notes. "I'm aiming for drama, bitchiness, and major shock value. She wants the letter to sound like it was written by a soap-opera vixen."

"A soap-opera vixen who's into bestiality," Amanda cracks.

I ignore this and continue reading aloud, " 'Your fiancé and I have been carrying on a torrid love affair for two months.' "

" 'Torrid love affair'?"

"I'm going for high drama, remember?"

Craig pokes his head into my office. "What are you two chicas meeting about?"

"I'm teaching Amanda how to break up a friendship."

He raises an eyebrow. "I thought platonic relationships were my man Trey's department."

"Usually. But Trey's in Milwaukee this week," I remind him.

"Milwaukee? When did I agree to let him take a vacation?"

"His mother's having knee replacement surgery, remember? He went there to help out."

"Oh, right," Craig mumbles, looking embarrassed. "Gimmie the four-one-one on this case you two are working."

"Two twentysomething girls from Brookline—friends for six years, roommates for two—had a bitter disagreement over a guy."

"What other kind of bitter disagreement is there?" Amanda asks.

"Our client, Jamie, discovered that her best friend, Lyndsey, was sleeping with her fiancé. So Jamie bedded down Lyndsey's boyfriend, and now she is kicking Lyndsey out of her apartment and her life."

"A revenge affair," Craig muses. "I like it!"

"Shows style, huh?" Amanda chimes in. "What I wouldn't give to see the look on Lyndsey's face when you deliver that letter."

Oh, yeah, it's going to be a real treat. *Maybe Lyndsey will slap me across the face out of anger.* A few months ago, one jilted woman spit on my shoe after I informed her of her new single status. And a mortified ex once commanded her dog to attack me. But it was Pekingese, so the only casualty was the left corner of my Dooney & Bourke tote.

"Good work, ladies," Craig calls, ducking out of my office.

"So, do you wear a Kevlar vest when you go out on a job?" Amanda jokes.

"Funny." I roll my eyes. "No, I don't. But that being said, make sure you always follow rule number two."

"Rule number two?" she asks, giving away the fact that she hasn't read the company handbook very carefully.

"Rule number two is: Never reveal your last name. It's not that you're in any danger, but you don't want to open yourself up to potentially harassing situations—angry exes phoning your house or leaving a flaming pile of dog poop on your front door. That kind of thing."

Amanda shrugs and wrinkles her nose. "I'm glad I won't be working in the field."

Steering us back to where we were before Craig interrupted, I resume my instructions.

"Breaking up friendships is the same as breaking up lovers: The most important thing is to adhere to the client's requests," I explain. "We're here to make the parting as easy for them as possible, yet we have to keep their preferences in mind."

"Obviously," Amanda agrees. "But can you be really vicious? Can you tell a guy his girlfriend left because his dick's too small?"

Technically, yes, but I don't tell Amanda this. "I always try to let them down easy."

"But what if the client asks you to be rude? Like with Jamie?"

"Then I'll be a teeny bit rude. But never outright hurtful. Any other questions?"

"Yeah, what are some good, standard lines you use to dump people?"

"We try to avoid using run-of-the-mill excuses," I say.

It's true. If people want clichés, they could come with them on their own. There's a whole secret language to dumping somebody. I've cracked the code. I flip to the back page of my legal pad, where I've scrawled out:

### The Ten Biggest Breakup Excuses, Redefined

**Excuse:** It's not you, it's me.
**Translation:** It is definitely, without a doubt, one hundred percent you.

**Excuse:** We're better off as friends.
**Translation:** The thought of having sex with you turns my stomach.

**Excuse:** I think we should date other people.
**Translation:** I'm already dating other people.

**Excuse:** I don't deserve you.
**Translation:** I actually deserve someone much better than you.

**Excuse:** In another time or place, this could've worked out.
**Translation:** If you were hotter/richer/less boring, this could've worked out.

**Excuse:** I'm still getting to know myself, finding out who I am as a person.
**Translation:** I'm gay.

**Excuse:** I used to you think you were The One; now I'm not so sure.
**Translation:** You weren't this fat when we started dating.

**Excuse:** I want my space.
**Translation:** I want to sleep around.

**Excuse:** This hurts me as much as it hurts you.
**Translation:** My pain ends after this conversation; your pain lives on forever.

**Excuse:** I'm getting back together with my ex.
**Translation:** I no longer even speak to my ex, but I'd rather die alone than spend another second with you.

"That takes all of the fun out of it," Amanda says, interrupting my thoughts.

"What does?" I ask, startled. I quickly flip my legal pad shut before she can read it. The last thing I want to do is give Amanda any clichés she can use.

"Being nice. It's so easy and dull."

*Easy? Dull? Is she clueless?* "I hate to tell you, but dumping people isn't exactly a walk in the park."

"But breaking up *in* parks is good, huh?"

By the way she says it, I can tell she's embarrassed about being caught out on rule #2. "That's right—rule number one, any public place will do." I quickly outline Your Big Break Inc.'s five basic rules.

**Rule #1:** Always meet in a public place. Coffee shops are ideal. Never go anywhere that serves alcohol.

**Rule #2:** Never reveal your last name.

**Rule #3:** Avoid cheesy euphemisms.

**Rule #4:** You are an impartial observer.

**Rule #5:** Do *not* get personally involved. This is the cardinal rule and must be followed above all others!

Then I get back to the friendship-ending letter.

*According to Newton's Laws, for every action, there is an equal and opposite reaction. Your action was to have sex with my fiancé. My reaction was to bed down your boyfriend. Turnabout is fair play, my dear Lyndsey. I hope you're up for the game of a lifetime.*

"Too dramatic?" I wonder. I don't know why I'm asking Amanda. She hasn't even worked here a full week.

"Nope, not too dramatic, not too plain," she says, grinning. And in a voice that reminds me of Goldilocks, she adds, "That sounds *juuuust* right!"

I have this ritual when I get home from work. It starts with a piping hot bath (bubble, if I'm so inclined), followed by some of my favorite music (U2, No Doubt, and Tori Amos—all the must-haves), topped off with a scrumptious meal from whatever take-out place comes next in the rotation, which goes: Chinese, pizza, deli sandwiches, Indian.

Then I plop down on the couch to write breakup letters, pick out "guilt" gifts for the dearly deserted, and match-make. Okay, so maybe that last one doesn't have much to do with Your Big Break Inc. In fact, it's in direct conflict with the business. But I really enjoy fixing people up and, like an addict, I can't seem to stop myself.

Can you blame me? I have an endless pool to choose from.

Every day I meet newly single people, all of them ready to jump back into the dating world. It's fun to try to pair them up. Evan Hirschbaum's ex-girlfriends are always good. Over the last year, I've found dates for five—count em, five!—of Evan's former flames. Granted, only one of these fix-ups actually turned into something lasting, but it was fun nonetheless.

Tonight, I'm planning to tackle the Jason/Lucy fiasco. Maybe Jason was onto something when he suggested taking Tai Chi to impress Lucy. I'm going to recommend that he try a few introductory classes.

It certainly couldn't hurt.

Even if he doesn't win Lucy back.

# 5

## YBB INC. EMPLOYEE RULE #3
Avoid cheesy euphemisms.

A full-figured, voluptuous red-haired woman is standing in my doorway. It's early Tuesday afternoon and I'm chewing on a pencil, reading a case file. "Can I help you?" I ask.

"A man named Craig sent me back here for a free consultation," she begins. "He said you could help me. I'm having a problem with my"—she pauses—"*in*significant other."

"You want to tell me about it?" I ask, inviting her to sit down.

"I don't even know where to begin!" she cries, flopping on the chair opposite my desk. She brushes back a lock of her curly, red hair. "I'm sorry, I don't mean to fall apart. I'm usually much more composed than this. I'm just so upset over what's happened!"

"Can I get you something to drink?" I offer, smiling encouragingly. "Coffee? Water?"

She shakes her head. "No thanks, I just want to get this over with."

I study her face. She seems embarrassed, nervous. "Get what over with?"

She squeezes her eyes shut and blurts, "Dumping the bastard! That's what you do, right?"

*That's one way of putting it.* "I help people sort out messy relationships," I clarify, putting down my file and devoting my full attention to her.

"Then you're exactly the person I need to see." She snorts. "Because if things don't change soon, I'm going to throw myself off a bridge!"

"Ah, come on. It can't be that bad."

"Worse."

I raise an eyebrow. "Well, then, we'd better get started right away. I'm Dani, by the way." I lean across the desk and pass her one of my business cards.

"I'm Gretchen Monaghan." She pauses, then stuffs the card into her Kate Spade tote.

I smile reassuringly and pull out a legal pad and flip to a clean sheet. "I'm going to take a few notes as we go along," I explain, to prepare her. Sometimes it makes people nervous when I start writing down their responses. I think they feel as though they're lying back on a couch, confessing all to a shrink. I can understand the feeling. There are definitely some similarities.

Gretchen settles back in her chair. "Where to begin," she says. "I know, I'll tell you about Lester. Stockbroker bastard."

I lean forward and write *Lester* on my legal pad. Underneath it, I jot down *stockbroker*. "How long have you two been involved?" I ask.

"We got engaged last Christmas," she says, and I quickly hold up a hand to stop her.

"We actually don't handle marriages or engagements," I explain.

Gretchen laughs. "Oh, Lester and I aren't engaged *anymore*. We broke up when he checked himself into McLean."

I gulp. "McLean—as in the mental institution?" McLean Hospital is legendary in Massachusetts. It's known for having once housed Sylvia Plath and Ray Charles, among others.

"Mmm-hmm. Don't worry, he's not dangerous or anything. In fact," she bemoans sadly, "Lester was perfect in every way—until he turned out to have borderline personality disorder."

I let out a low whistle. "Borderline what?"

"Take your pick. Borderline jerk. Borderline asshole." She sighs. "It's a bunch of psychobabble. What it basically means is that he's incapable of having a meaningful personal relationship, that he's chronically unsatisfied. Once he gets something, he no longer wants it. No woman will ever be good enough for him . . . blah, blah, blah."

"That sounds like pretty much every guy I've ever dated," I joke.

For the first time since I met her, Gretchen smiles. "You, too? And I thought I was the only one with a penchant for jerks."

I laugh. "Nope, it's a common problem. Many women today suffer from it."

"Well, anyway, after the whole Lester debacle, I'd sworn off men forever. That is, until I met The Big Jackass six months ago. He drew me in right away; I couldn't resist him."

"The Big Jackass?" I repeat.

She groans. "At first he was a dream come true. Totally devoted, handsome, great personality, great in bed. The total package. Of course, his 'package' wasn't fully operational without Viagra," she recalls, flexing her fingers. "But considering he's in his late fifties, I'd say it's par for the course."

"Late fifties!" I exclaim. I don't know how old Gretchen is, but I'm guessing early thirties.

As if reading my thoughts, she says, "I'm thirty-five; it didn't seem like that big a stretch. Besides, I've had such bad luck with men my age."

"But now I take it things with this older guy aren't working out too well?"

"That's the understatement of the year."

"How did you two meet?" I ask.

"I answered his online personal ad."

I nod and jot that down.

"I don't know what I was thinking," she continues. "I'm a fiery Leo and he's a hardheaded Capricorn, so we were doomed from the start. But he seemed so sweet, and I really do like older men. . . ."

We're getting off track, so I change the subject. "Before we go any further, I need to ask you a few questions."

"All right, fire away."

I have to make sure that Gretchen understands how Your Big Break Inc. does business, and that she's willing to abide by our rules. Likewise, I have to find out if I'll even be able to take on her case. Certain things we just don't do: marriages, engagements, or anything that feels "unsafe." A lot of it is guesswork. I have to watch out for volatile personalities, potentially violent situations, and anything that generally seems too risky.

"Does this guy—"

"The Big Jackass," she supplies.

"Right. Does he have a history of violent behavior?"

"No."

"What about mental instability?"

She shakes her head.

"Does he abuse drugs or alcohol?"

"No."

I write down her answers. "Any obsessive tendencies?"

Gretchen gives me a pointed look. "Are you asking me if he's a stalker?"

"I have to be on the lookout for potentially dangerous situations," I explain.

"Believe me, The Big Jackass isn't dangerous. He's a moron, but he's harmless."

"So you've never felt threatened by him in any way?" I prod.

"Oh, God, no! He's one of the sweetest, most lovable people I've ever known. He was so considerate of my needs; he treated me so well." Her lower lip trembles. "He always bought me thoughtful presents, took me to romantic movies."

I drop my pen and lean forward. "Gretchen, can I be frank?"

"Please."

"Are you *certain* you want to break up with this guy?"

She nods vigorously. "One hundred percent."

"Because, from the looks of it, you're still in love with him."

"Oh, I love him all right. But I'm done with him."

I lean back, setting down my legal pad. "What did he do?"

"He deceived me."

"Deceived you?"

"He's a liar," she says. "All this time I thought he loved me, and he was full of shit."

"And you came to this conclusion when?" I ask.

"When I found out that the jerk has a wife."

"So he's a two-timer." *Now we're getting somewhere.*

She swallows hard. "I can't believe I ever trusted him. I mean, I found out he had a wife a few months ago. But he said they were separated; he said he was in the process of divorcing her so he could be with me. And now I find out that they're still living together as man and wife!"

"Married men always say they'll leave their wife. Most never do."

"I know, Dani, I know," Gretchen says, dissolving into tears. "This just feels so . . . it just hurts so much!" she sobs.

I open my desk drawer and retrieve a small box of Kleenex. "It's going hurt for a while." I get up from behind my desk and walk over to her. "But you'll get over this; you'll get over *him*."

"I want him out of my life, but I don't know if I can handle being alone."

I place a reassuring hand on her back. "You'll be fine. You're a strong, independent woman."

"You barely know me!"

I offer her a tissue. "Hey, you got over that borderline personality creep—that's no small feat."

She smiles and blows her nose in a Kleenex. "Thanks, Dani."

"Anytime," I tell her.

"So, how will you do it?" Gretchen asks. "How will you dump him?"

"I'll call him, preferably at work," I explain. "Set up a meeting on neutral ground. Break the news to him over coffee."

She nods, reaching into her purse for a pack of gum. "How soon?"

"With any luck, by the end of this week. We try to do things as quickly as possible. Like pulling off a Band-Aid." I pick up my pad and prepare to write. "Where does he work? Oh, and what's his name, by the way? I can't just call and ask for The Big Jackass."

"No, I suppose not." Gretchen laughs. "Though it would serve him right, the asshole." She pops a piece of gum into her mouth and starts chewing. "His name's Paul Myers."

I sit there for a second, staring at her dumbly.

"Paul Myers?" I repeat, struggling to keep my voice steady. *Maybe I didn't hear her right. Maybe the gum distorted it.*

"Yes, he works in the financial district. He's an analyst at Merriwether Payne Investments," Gretchen says, but I barely hear her because suddenly, my ears, my eyes—my whole body, really—seem to have stopped working properly. I'm slipping, fading fast.

*Paul Myers?* Her boyfriend's name is Paul Myers? And he's an analyst at Merriwether Payne Investments? She's got to be kidding. It's got to be a coincidence. Paul Myers is a fairly common name. There must be forty—fifty?—of them in Boston alone. *Right?*

"I'll give you Paul's direct line," she says, reciting the digits, and I don't write them down, partly because I'm in shock and partly because I don't have to.

I already know the number by heart.

# 6

**STAGE ONE OF BREAKUP HELL:**
*The Nervous Breakdown*

The jilted man/woman stumbles around blindly, desperately trying to figure out how his or her picture-perfect love affair suddenly turned into a nightmare. Tears are shed. Work is missed. Numerous vices are indulged, including (but not limited to) alcohol, drugs, shopping, and food binges.

*My father is having an affair.*

This is the man who taught me to ride a bicycle, who took me trick-or-treating, who held my head when I was sick. And now he's diddling a thirty-five-year-old.

My life has officially become a cliché.

I just don't get it. My dad is not the kind of man who runs around on his wife. That category is reserved for cads like Evan Hirschbaum: players, adulterers, cheaters. The kind of guys who make women collectively roll their eyes and declare, "Men are scum." My dad isn't slick or conniving. He has bi-focals, a thinning hairline, and a quiet disposition. He likes playing solitaire, cheering on the Bruins, and reading all the latest sports news online.

*Or does he?*

The more I look back, the more I review, the stranger it seems. There were signs. Dad spends an awful lot of time on the computer—he always claims to be on ESPN.com, but God knows what he's really up to. After all, he met Gretchen through an Internet personal ad. *What if there were others before her? What if he has a whole secret online life, where he visits lurid chat rooms, answers Match.com personal ads, and . . .*

*Oh, God.*

I'm queasy. I wonder what his ad said? *Middle-Aged Man in Search of Redhead.* Or *Married Bastard Looking to Cheat on Wife.* Yeah, that was probably it. Gretchen's right. He is a big jackass!

Poor Mom. She hits her mid-fifties, and her husband, being The Big Jackass that he is, trades her in for a younger model. No wonder she's been acting so stressed-out lately. Deep down, she must realize something's not right in her marriage.

I can't believe I ever loved my father, can't believe I ever trusted him, thought he was someone good and pure and true when he so obviously was not.

And now his mistress has hired me to dump him.

I told her I couldn't do it, of course. I said I had too many cases, that it sounded complicated, muddled. Not the sort of thing Your Big Break Inc. could get mixed up in. I don't know if she believed my story or not—she looked completely baffled by my sudden shift in personality. I didn't stick around to find out her full reaction. I got the hell out of there, told Craig I had a "family emergency" (it was the truth), and took off running down the street. Trouble is, I didn't have anywhere to run.

Now here I am, standing on the corner of Massachusetts Avenue and Inman Street, fighting back waves of nausea and struggling to keep myself from crying.

This changes everything, absolutely everything. No more family vacations down the Cape. No more warm and happy Christmases, sitting around the fireplace, sipping hot chocolate, watching *It's a Wonderful Life* and listening to Sean play Madden NFL 2005 on his computer. And my wedding—the one I'm going to have as soon as I meet a smart, gorgeous, successful man who loves me for me—is totally ruined. How can I have my father walk me down the aisle when he clearly doesn't respect the sanctity of marriage? I can't believe it. I'm not even engaged yet—I don't even have a boyfriend—and already my father has ruined my wedding.

*I'm gonna kill him.*

But before I kill him, I'm gonna to talk to him, find out why he did this. *But how? How can I make myself broach the subject? "So, Dad, I met your mistress today . . ." How can I say those words?*

I think I'm going to throw up.

I blow off work for the rest of the day and take solace at The Thirsty Scholar in Davis Square. It's a quaint, traditional Irish pub that attracts a crowd of wannabe poets, writers, and drifters. I slump down at a corner table and order a Glenlivet on the rocks. Then I call for reinforcements. She answers on the second ring.

"Fintane Catering; this is Krista."

I mumble something that sounds like hello.

"Dani?"

"Mmm." I pull the cell phone closer to my mouth, banging it against my lips.

"You okay?" she asks, sounding concerned.

"I'm drinking Scotch in the middle of the day, if that tells you anything."

Krista pauses. "Scotch?"

"Yeah. Glenlivet, to be exact."

"Dani, you don't even like hard liquor! I've never seen you drink anything stronger than a wine cooler."

She's right. But this day is so horrific, I feel obligated to have something potent. "I'm guessing you're not at work," Krista says.

"Good guess."

"Where are you?"

"The Thirsty Scholar in Davis Square."

"In Somerville?" She sounds baffled.

"Yeah. I left work and hopped on the Red Line and rode around for a while. Somehow, I wound up here." There's a long silence, and I can tell Krista's trying to figure out what to say. I decide to just come right out and tell her. "My father's having an affair." He is no longer "Dad." From this day forward, I will always refer to him as "Father."

Krista gasps. There's a long silence on the line. Finally, she says, "You're kidding, right?"

"No, I'm not kidding. He's got a girlfriend. I met her this afternoon."

"Oh, fuck!"

"Literally," I deadpan.

"Wow . . . that's just . . . how? Did you catch him red-handed?"

"No, but I caught him red-*headed*, so to speak." I quickly fill her in on what went down. When I finish, Krista lets out a low whistle.

"Jesus, Dani," she says, and I hear her fumbling around in the background. "Sit tight; I'll be there in twenty minutes. We'll have lunch or something."

I take a huge swig of Scotch. It goes down like fire, scorching the inside of my throat. "It's three o'clock in the afternoon. Haven't you already taken a lunch break?"

"Nobody will care. Besides, you shouldn't be alone right now."

She makes it sound like someone's died, but I appreciate her concern. "Thanks, Krista."

"This is so weird," she says. "The way you found out. It's so . . ."

"Comical?" I supply.

"I was going for ironic. Or shocking. Or fucked up."

I snort. "How about all of the above?"


True to her word, Krista makes it to The Thirsty Scholar in less than twenty minutes. I'm just starting my third drink. I downed the first two in record time, and my head feels light and fuzzy. I'm not used to Scotch, but I'm finding it suits me. Krista comes bustling in through the door and rushes over to my table.

"Hey," she says, throwing her arms around me in a hug.

This makes me burst into tears. I remember the last time we hung out, at The Cheesecake Factory. Everything's so different now.

"Shhh, Dani, don't worry," Krista says, stroking my hair. "Everything will be okay. Just give it some time."

I wipe the tears from my eyes and pull away. "This isn't one of those 'time heals all wounds' kind of situations. My father's a liar and a cheat. My family is over." I start sobbing harder.

"Maybe there's another explanation," Krista suggests, sitting down beside me.

"And to think, I just went shopping with that jerk two days ago," I say, ignoring her. "I helped him pick out an Anne Klein shirt for my mother—my *mother*! The woman he's cheating on!"

Krista motions for me to keep my voice down. "It's going to be all right, Dani."

A thought occurs to me. "Maybe this is some kind of karmic payback?"

"Meaning?"

"I make my living ruining relationships; it's only fair that mine get ruined, too."

"You can't be serious. By the time people come to Your Big Break Inc., they're ready to jump ship. It's not like you tear them apart; if anything, you make the breakup easier on both parties."

"That's just it," I say. "I ought to be bringing couples together, not pulling them apart."

Krista shrugs. "You can't force people to do anything. If they want to break up, they're going to break up. It doesn't matter whether you help them or not."

My cell phone starts ringing. It's work calling. "Oh, shit!"

Krista looks alarmed. "Your dad?"

"No, it's Craig." I quickly answer the call. "Hello."

"So you *are* alive."

"Barely," I mumble.

"You left me in a real bind, Dani."

"I know, and I'm sorry."

"The phone's been ringing off the hook since you left!"

"It has?" I ask nervously. This can't be a good thing. What if Gretchen somehow figured out that Paul Myers is my father? What if she tracked my mom down and told her about the affair? What if my parents—

"A Jason Dutwiler has called *four* times, looking for you. He says it's urgent."

*Oh, crap.* That's right. I'm supposed to convince Jason's ex-girlfriend Lucy to consider reconciliation. Between the Evan Hirschbaum creep-out and Gretchen's big bombshell, I've completely forgotten.

"He said you promised to get back to him in a few days but never did. That doesn't reflect well on our organization."

"I'm sorry, Craig, I totally dropped the ball."

Craig sighs. "Actually, that's not my concern. I looked through your computer files and, well, I'm just gonna come right out and ask. Dani, did you promise Jason Dutwiler you'd find him a date for his sister's wedding?"

I take a swig of Scotch, trying to stall. "Kind of. I promised I'd try to convince his ex-girlfriend to go with him."

He draws in a deep breath. "I was afraid of that. Dani, have you forgotten about rule number five?" He pauses and then recites it: "Do *not* get personally involved. This is the cardinal rule and must be followed above all others!"

"I know better than to get personally involved," I mumble.

"And yet that is exactly what you've done with Jason Dutwiler!"

"It's no big deal. I can handle it."

"There shouldn't be anything *to* handle! You dumped the guy;

that ought to be the end of it. We're not running a matchmaking service, for God's sake!"

"I'm not matchmaking," I assure him. "I'm just helping out with the healing process."

"The healing process!" Craig explodes. "You're not a guru, Dani."

"I know that," I say, defensively.

"Apparently, you do not. First, you tried to reunite that couple from Jamaica Plain—"

"And that worked," I jump in. "Last I heard, they were engaged."

He ignores this. "Then you gave that computer science student from Tufts a makeover—on company time, I might add."

"Craig, the guy had a ten-inch ponytail! That wasn't a makeover; it was an intervention. If you'd seen him, you'd understand why I took him for a haircut—"

"And to Banana Republic for clothes. Don't forget that part."

"He'd just been dumped by his Internet girlfriend! He needed a confidence booster. There's nothing in the rules about taking a client out for a haircut and makeover."

Craig continues, "And last month, you went to end one of Mr. Hirschbaum's relationships, and five hours later, you came back raving about the latest Keanu Reeves film!"

"Okay, well, see, that . . ." I struggle to think of a way to explain it. My head is starting to spin from the alcohol. Krista slowly scoots my half-finished Scotch across the table, replacing it with a water. I yank it back.

"Dani, if you keep this up," Craig is saying, "I'm going to have no choice but to—"

"But to what?" I demand. "Fire me?" I'm usually not this bold; it's the Scotch talking.

"No." His tone softens. "Nothing that drastic. But suffice it to say, I'm going to be keeping a close eye on you. And you're going to have to learn to abide by my rules. They're not here to torture you; they're here to make the business run smoothly. Understand?"

"Yeah, I get it." I roll my eyes at Krista. I know I have no right to get snippy with Craig, but I can't help myself.

I think I'm about to get off easy, but then he adds, "Now, you wanna tell me the real reason why you left in the middle of a client consultation?"

My mood crashes as thoughts of my father come flooding back. My lower lip starts quivering, and I feel as though I'm on the verge of tears again. "Craig, my life is so messed up right now. You have no idea."

"*Give* me an idea, then."

"It's my father."

Craig gasps. "Is he sick? Dying?"

*Well,* I think wryly, *he's dead to me.* "No, he's alive and well. But the situation's personal."

"Are you coming back to the office today or not?"

I glance at my watch. It's almost 4 p.m., and I'm in no state to work.

"Can I take a half day or something?" I beg. "I'll stay late tomorrow, I promise."

He pauses for a moment. "Oh, all right," he says, giving in.

"Thanks, Craig."

"If that Dutwiler dude calls again, I'll tell him you had to leave early," he says briskly. "But I want you to straighten out this mess first thing tomorrow."

"Sure, Craig. No problem."

We quickly say our good-byes and hang up.

"You get away with murder at that place," Krista says. She reaches across the table and squeezes my hand. "So, do you . . . do you want to talk about what happened?"

"I just keep going over it in my mind, trying to understand. No matter how hard I think about it, it doesn't seem real."

"It's pretty shocking," she agrees.

"How could my father *do* this?" I ask in disbelief. "Yesterday, we were great friends; now I feel like I don't even know him anymore."

"Are you going to confront him?"

"I have to." Hands shaking, I pick up my cell phone and start punching in his work number.

"You're going to do it *now*?" Krista exclaims, stopping me mid-dial.

"It's now or never!" I say, a little louder than I intended.

"Maybe you should take a few days to, uh, sober up. You know, figure out what you want to say. And besides, don't you want to do this in person?"

"I don't *want* to do this at all."

Krista smiles sympathetically. "I know you don't, sweetie. And I'm here for you, whatever you need."

"Thanks." I swallow hard, struggling to keep my composure. As long as I can keep it together, everything will be fine.

"Maybe you shouldn't deal with this yourself," Krista suggests. "It might be better if your mom confronts him." She stops, thinking it over. "Yeah, you should probably go to your family first."

*My family.* I think of my mother and brother and how devastated they're going to be and the bottom drops out from under me. The nervous breakdown I've fought off suddenly hits and I can't move or speak. I feel paralyzed, rooted to my chair.

"Dani?" Krista says, and her voice sounds very far off.

I cradle the cell phone in my hands and burst into tears.

# 7

# Girls' Night In

I wake up the next morning feeling a thousand times better.

I've realized something: Gretchen is a liar.

It's so glaring, so obvious that I can't believe I didn't see it immediately. So what if she *claims* to be sleeping with a financial analyst named Paul Myers? That doesn't make it a *fact*. What proof do I have, other than her word? So she knows my father's name and where he works. *Big deal*. His bio is in the Merriwether Payne information booklet that the company gives out to potential investors. It's also posted on their website. She's obviously a stalker or something.

I'm in such a good mood, I go into the office early. The first order of business is Jason Dutwiler. I try his house and don't find him there, so I leave a message. I'm about to phone his ex-girlfriend, Lucy, when Craig comes bustling in.

"Word up, Dani!" he calls out, sailing into my office.

"I think you mean 'what's up?' "

"Close enough. It's good to see you're up and running."

"Good to see you, too," I say brightly. Even my throbbing headache—the result of yesterday's Glenlivet indulgence—can't drag me down.

"I booked you an appointment for tomorrow afternoon," he informs me. "Erin Foster-somebody-or-other." He digs into his briefcase and pulls out a memo. "Meant to leave this on your desk," he says, passing it to me.

I look down at his scratchy handwriting.

*Erin Foster-Ellis*
*27*
*from Beacon Hill*
*Wants to cut ties with long-term bf*
*Initial consultation w/ Dani, <u>Thurs., May 12, at 2:30 p.m.</u>*

"Beacon Hill. Impressive."

"My thoughts exactly." Craig gives me a sly smile. "Hit her up for our most expensive package. Make sure she feels nice and guilty so she'll send this poor dude some expensive 'parting gifts.'"

"I'll do my best," I promise. Sometimes I wonder how I make it in this business. As soon as Craig leaves, I get back to work. I'm in the middle of checking my e-mail when the phone rings. I don't recognize the number. "Hello?"

"Hi Dani, Evan Hirschbaum here."

"Hi, Evan," I say. "You got another job for us?"

"No, I'm calling about Sophie Kennison—the job you've yet to finish."

"As soon as she comes back from Connecticut, I'll pay her a visit," I say. "She won't bother you again."

"She's been bothering me for the last week," he gripes.

"I thought she was out of town," I say nervously. I hope I haven't gotten the dates screwed up.

"She is. But she's been e-mailing me every hour on the hour since she left!"

*Uh-oh.*

" 'Dear Evan, Why don't you love me anymore?' " he begins reading in a singsong voice. " 'Tell me what I've done to drive you away. Am I too fat? I'll lose weight. Bad in bed? I can be kinky, try anything you want . . . ' "

*Oh, no. Not the sex talk again.*

" 'Am I boring? Not smart enough? I can read the same books you do. I'll learn to cook your favorite foods, cheer on your favorite sports teams . . . ' " He reverts to his normal voice. "It goes on for two pages. And I've got another twenty just like this one!"

"Forward them to me," I instruct him. "I want a copy for our records."

"Screw your records!" he shouts down the phone. "Just get her to stop."

"I'll speak with Sophie ASAP. Do you have her parents' phone number in Connecticut?" I ask, picking up a pen and preparing to write. "If not, I'll call her cell."

"No, I don't have the number," he barks. "Why would I?"

"Right, I understand." I'm starting to get worried. Evan is our most important client, and I am screwing everything up.

"This Sophie situation is out of control," he continues. "Up to this point, I've been ignoring her. But if she writes me again, I'm going to tell her to fuck off. Now, I'm going to Chicago for a few days, but by the time I get back, I hope you'll have this mess sorted out."

"Absolutely, sir. And don't worry about Sophie. I'll straighten her out. Count on it."

Evan chuckles. "Again with the 'sir' business. You're making me feel old."

He clicks off the line before I have time to respond. I'm flustered, but I feel relieved that he didn't fire me—or ask me out to lunch again.

I pull up Blackbaud on my computer and locate Sophie's cell number. I dial it, hoping she'll answer, but instead I get voicemail. I leave a brief message: "Hi, Sophie! This is Danielle from Your Big Break Inc. I understand you've been e-mailing Evan Hirschbaum, and I'm going to have to ask you to stop. I realize you're feeling upset and a bit lonely, but, unfortunately, you're going to have to let Evan go. He isn't interested in pursuing a relationship with you. I hope you're doing well. Let's meet for coffee when you get back in Boston."

For the life of me, I hope that tides her over.


The Gretchen-as-stalker theory takes me through the first part of the morning, but by mid-afternoon, I'm starting to get worried again. What if I dismissed the whole thing too easily? What if— *what if*—Gretchen is actually telling the truth? I'm ninety-nine percent sure she's a pathological liar, but there's that little one percent of me that's still questioning it.

Actually, it's more like five percent.

*Maybe I should investigate, do some checking. Just to be sure.*

I start by calling Dad's office. His assistant, Lorne, picks up.

"Hey, Lorne, this is Dani. Is my dad around?"

"Hang on, let me check."

He puts me on hold. I listen to elevator music and contemplate what I'll say when Dad picks up. Maybe I should just come clean about why I'm calling. Of course, I'll have to confess that I don't really work on websites for a living. Knowing Dad, he won't be too upset, just bewildered. And when I inform him about psycho-stalker Gretchen, he'll be worried, or quite possibly confused. But he'll get to the bottom of the situation and he'll fix it, the way he always fixed things when I was young. Whenever I had a problem—whether it was a loose tooth or a rickety bike wheel or a sadistic algebra teacher—Dad always knew how to solve it. All I had to do was talk to him, tell him what was bothering me. Then he'd work his magic and everything would be normal and happy and safe.

"Nope, he's not back yet," Lorne says.

"Back from where?" I ask, twirling the phone cord around my fingers.

"He had a breakfast meeting today."

"*Breakfast* meeting!" I burst out. "*It's one o'clock in the afternoon!*"

"I guess it ran long."

"What time did he leave?"

"Hmm . . . let me check." I'm back on hold again. "The meeting started at 10 a.m."

"Do breakfast meetings typically last three hours, Lorne?"

"Not typically. It might have turned into lunch."

*Or sex at a seedy motel in South Boston.*

The part of me that doubts Dad has jumped from five percent to fifty in one fell swoop. "Do you have a number where I can reach him?"

"Just his cell. He didn't leave the name of the restaurant."

"Thanks, Lorne."

"You want me to have him call you?"

"No, don't worry about it." I hang up and quickly dial Dad's cell phone. It goes straight through to voicemail. "Hi, you've reached Paul Myers with Merriwether Payne Investments. I'm not able to take your call at the moment, but please leave a message . . ."

I hang up before the beep.

My doubt is now up to seventy-five percent.

I go to see my mother after work on Wednesday. As I walk through the front door, the house feels strange, alien. *I shouldn't be here. I'm not ready to face her yet, knowing what I know.* The guilt is overpowering. My mother doesn't deserve to be cheated on, to be lied to. I find her camped out on the sofa, TiVo remote in hand. Ever since she lost her job, my mother has become the queen of Lifetime, Television for Women—if Lifetime shows it, my mom watches it. TV addiction is the one thing she and Sean have in common.

"Hey, Mom, what's going on?" I ask.

"Dani!" She's surprised. "What are you doing here?"

"I had the evening free. I thought I'd come see you."

She scoots over on the couch, making room for me. "Have a seat."

"Thanks." I sit down next to her.

"Something to eat?" she asks, not taking her eyes off the television set. "I think we've got some leftover zucchini cake."

*Zucchini cake?* "Leftover from what?" I ask.

"My yoga class had a potluck the other night."

"You're in a yoga class?" *How is it that I know so little about my parents?*

"I am," Mom says. She hits pause on the TiVo remote and

turns toward me. "It's so great to see you, Dani. I'm so glad you stopped by."

"Thanks."

"When you were younger, we used to hang out together all the time. Go to movies, go shopping. Now you're all grown up and I barely see you, except at family dinners." She grins. "We need to change that, starting now." When I don't respond, her eyes search my face. "What's wrong?"

I take a deep breath. I have to tell her.

"Life moves so fast," Mom says, looking pensive. "It seems like only yesterday your father and I were getting married."

*Oh my God! Why is she talking about this?*

"And then before I knew it, I was pregnant with you, and then Sean . . . and then both of you grew up so quickly. Sometimes it feels like my life got out from under me. Before I knew it, I was old and gray and all of these opportunities had passed me by."

"You're not old and gray," I jump in.

She grins. "You're sweet, Dani, but I have to face facts. I'm past my prime. I've got to make the most of what I have left."

She sounds so fatalistic, so depressed that I want to cry.

"Ever since I quit my job," Mom continues, and I grimace. I hate the way she's in denial about this. "I've really reexamined my life. That's why I said what I did the other night."

"The other night?"

She leans over and tousles my hair. "About you getting out and experiencing life. I want you to be happy, Dani, to live it up while you're young. God knows I didn't."

I'm not sure what to say. All of my professional heartbreaking skills are leaving me. I sit there, dumbfounded. "You shouldn't be so sad, Mom," I finally manage.

"I'm not sad. I'm just nostalgic. I used to have girlfriends.

I used to go out and have fun. I haven't done that in thirty years. I got married and I let them all get away from me."

*The same way I let all my friends go when I hooked up with Garrett.* My mind is swirling. I've lost control of the situation. I can't do this now. I bail. "We're going to hang out!" I say enthusiastically. "We'll have a girls' night out, just the two of us."

Mom looks so pleased, I'm afraid I might crumble.

I'm going to have to regroup.

There's only one way left to play this: I'll go to my brother.

# 8

# I Don't Deserve You. I Actually Deserve Someone Much Better Than You

"Are you Danielle? I'm Erin Foster-Ellis."

My 2:30 appointment breezes into my office, all long legs; thick, chestnut hair; and huge boobs. She's decked out in a sharp Prada pencil skirt, and carries a Christian Dior saddlebag purse. I'm wearing a gray DKNY dress—one of the nicest, most expensive outfits I own—and I feel totally outclassed.

"The one and only."

She doesn't look amused.

"I'm here about my boyfriend—"

"What's his name?" I ask immediately, to avoid another Gretchen nightmare.

Erin sits down in the chair opposite my desk and crosses one slim leg over the other. "Brady Simms."

*Okay, that's good.* I've never heard of the guy. I nod.

"I'd like to get Brady out of my life, and I'd like to do it as quickly as possible."

"Have you ever used a breakup service before?" I don't usually ask this question, but Erin strikes me as the type who might have some experience in this area.

"God, no." She makes a face. "To be perfectly honest, I'm not even sure if I want to hire you. It seems a little *tacky*."

I go into salesgirl mode. "What about Your Big Break Inc. makes you uncomfortable?"

"Oh, I'm not uncomfortable. I just find the concept obnoxious."

"I can walk you through how we work, if that helps."

"Not necessary." She waves a hand dismissively. "I read the article in the *Globe* last month." Erin pauses. "Let me be blunt: What can I get for twenty-five bucks?"

So much for Craig's instructions—Erin Foster-Ellis isn't going to be a big spender. "That's our entry-level package. It means I'll craft a Dear John letter and, after you approve it, I'll deliver it via e-mail or snail mail. Your choice."

"No, no, no." Erin shakes her head. "I have some expensive things at his apartment. I'll need you to go get those back. Can you do that for fifty?"

"We don't do in-person for less than a hundred. It also depends on what kind of stuff you've left at his place. If it requires a moving truck, for example, it's going to be more expensive."

"Small things. Earrings. A watch. Some clothes and shoes." Erin fishes into her Christian Dior purse. "I made a list."

She hands it to me and I quickly look it over. "These shouldn't be a problem." Surprisingly, Erin opts for a few additional services, including a Breakup Recovery Kit. I do some quick calculations and give her a price quote of $110.

"I suppose that's fair." She smiles, showing off a mouthful of perfectly veneered teeth. "Can you terminate the relationship when you get my things back? I'd rather this go down in person."

"Sure. I'll need to arrange a time to meet with Brady in a public place. We usually do these things over coffee."

She claps her hands together. "Perfect! You can see Brady tonight. He's got a poetry workshop at Barnes and Noble every Thursday at eight. There's a café right in the bookstore, if I'm not mistaken."

"He's a writer?" I ask.

"Hardly. His stuff's not worth the trees it's printed on. Here's a picture of him," Erin says, passing me a wallet-sized photo. She laughs. "He always stands up and reads a poem." She shakes her head, as if the mental image of Brady Simms reading a poem is beyond ridiculous. Then she stands to leave.

"Hang on a sec," I stop her. "We still need to go over a few details."

"I don't know what else we could possibly discuss," she says as she sits back down.

I pull out my legal pad. "I need to ask you a few questions." I begin quickly running through our standard fare: relationship history, mental stability, and so on. Everything is clean and normal until I ask, "Can you tell me why you're leaving him?"

"Do I have to answer that?"

"No. But it would be helpful."

"Because I'm not sure if I want to."

I put down my notepad. "There's no need to be embarrassed. Trust me, whatever you have to say, I'm sure I've heard worse."

"I bet you haven't," she counters, narrowing her eyes at me. I get the sense she's challenging me.

I think it over, trying to come up with the most humiliating situation I've dealt with in the recent past. "Did he fall in love with a man?" I ask.

"God, no!"

"Are you leaving him for his brother?"

"No." She folds her arms across her chest and gives me a smug smile. "I want to dump him because last week he quit his job to become . . ." She pauses dramatically.

"A garbage collector?" I can't resist. "A male stripper?"

Erin rolls her eyes. "When we started dating two years ago, Brady was a successful corporate attorney. Now he's a high-school English teacher! Apparently, being an *English teacher* is his life's dream."

"So he quit being an attorney to follow his dream?" I ask.

"Yes."

"And this bothers you because . . . ?"

"I do not date high-school teachers," she says matter-of-factly. "I date physicians, lawyers, investment bankers."

"I see."

She leans forward and lowers her voice. "I'm not going to waste a pair of tits like these"—she points to her chest for emphasis—"on some goddamned civil servant who makes less than forty grand a year!"

I stare at her, dumbfounded. How do you follow up a statement like that? "It's certainly your prerogative," I finally say.

"Yes, it is. Now, are you going to Brady's poetry workshop tonight?" Erin asks.

I check my schedule and confirm that I'm free—kind of sad, considering it's such short notice. *Maybe my mom is right. Maybe I don't get out enough.* "I'll pop in, see if I can catch him," I promise her.

"Lightning efficiency." She smiles. "I like that!"

I turn his photo over in my hands. "He's a good-looking guy," I tell her. With his dark brown hair and piercing blue eyes, Brady is definitely attractive. I'm surprised she's letting him go. "How old is he?" I ask.

"Thirty-one. I spent two years training the idiot, and look what he does."

"Training?"

"Men are like blank slates," Erin continues. "Or dogs. However you prefer it."

"Let's go with blank slates."

"I taught Brady everything he knows about pleasing a woman. I practically drew him a map of the female body, taught him what I like and how I like it."

This is more information than I need. "Do you want me to give him a kiss-off letter tonight, too?" I ask, changing the subject. "It's short notice, but we should be able to bang something out."

"Does that cost extra?"

"No, it's included in the price."

"Fantastic!" Erin rises from her chair. "Let me know how it goes."

"You don't want to çollaborate with me on what goes in the letter?"

"No. You can tell Brady whatever you like. I honestly don't care."

With that, she leaves. Then my phone rings—it's Beverly, our receptionist. My 3 p.m. appointment is waiting.

* * *

*Dear Brady,*
  *I'm rich, you're poor. Here's the door. Any questions?*

I have to stop goofing around and be serious. But how can I
come up with a heartfelt breakup note when Erin's given me
nothing to work with? I mull the situation over and try to reach
a decision. I know it's against everything Your Big Break Inc.
stands for, but I'm going with fluff. I take out a clean piece of paper and write.

*Dear Brady,*
  *This is a difficult letter to write. I want you to know that
I'll always love you.*
  *But people change, and because they don't change to-
gether, they drift. . . .*

I've just finished sealing the letter in an envelope when the
phone rings. I check the caller ID. It's my brother's cell phone.
Sean never calls me at work. I can't imagine what he wants.

I pick up the receiver. "Hello?"

"Hey, Dani, are you busy?" he asks.

"Not really. What's up?" I tuck the Dear Brady letter into my
purse.

"I just got off the phone with Dad."

"You did?" My heartbeat quickens.

"Yeah, he called me from work and—"

"Are you sure he was calling from work?" I interrupt.

"I guess so, why?"

"What number showed up on the caller ID?"

"I don't know. I think it was his cell phone."

*Aha! His cell phone. Jesus.* It's four o'clock in the afternoon. Dad—excuse me, *Father*—probably ducks out of the office every day for a mid-afternoon romp with his mistress.

"He wanted me to let you know dinner's canceled next Thursday."

"Canceled? Oh my God!" I exclaim, my voice catching in my throat. "Did he say why it's canceled?"

"Yeah. He has to work really late every night for the next couple of weeks. Apparently, he's super-swamped at work."

*Well, that's that. He's definitely having an affair.* I'm one hundred percent sure of it now. "This is a nightmare," I whisper, blinking back tears.

Sean laughs. "Hey, chill out. We're free and clear, no family obligations. Why are you being so melodramatic?"

"Sean, there's something I want to talk to you about," I begin, then stop. *Should I tell him? Can he handle it?* I decide the answer to both questions is yes. "It's personal."

"Fire away."

"Not over the phone. Can you meet me for a late lunch?"

He's quiet for a minute. "Not today. My shift starts at Blockbuster in twenty minutes."

"Tomorrow?"

"I guess." He sounds annoyed. "What's this about, Dani?"

I let out a sigh. "It's a long, complicated story."

"Great," he says sarcastically. "My favorite kind."

We make plans to meet at Chili's at Copley Place at one o'clock.

Sean and I don't always see eye to eye on things, but he's my brother and I love him. And I know he'll want to do whatever he can to keep our family together. Telling him about Gretchen is going to be tough, but we'll talk it over, we'll cry, and then we'll figure out what to do. Together.

Now I just have to make it through tonight.

The Barnes & Noble poetry workshop is packed—who knew there were so many wayward poets in Boston? I pull out the wallet-sized photo that Erin gave me and scan the crowd for Brady Simms. I feel like a hitman, zeroing in on my target. Or should I say hit*woman*? Either way, Brady's a marked man. Breaking up with strangers is a cumbersome task. We've never met, yet I know this giant secret about Brady's life—and all the ways it's about to crumble. And he has no idea. I search the sea of faces but don't spot anyone who resembles Brady. *Oh, well.* I hope I'll be able to locate him once the workshop starts. I slip into a seat near the back as the crowd continues to swell.

At eight o'clock on the dot, a short, stocky woman walks up to the front of the room and introduces herself. "I'm Sal, and I'll be your moderator for tonight." She scans the room and smiles. "Welcome back, returning poets and poetesses! And a big hello to all our fresh-faced pen-pushers."

*Fresh-faced pen-pushers?*

"As usual, we'll begin with a few short readings, then we'll open up the floor for comments," Sal says. "I'd like to encourage those of you who haven't joined us before to read your work first. Any volunteers?"

No one responds, and I'm scared that she's going to start drafting people. I'm not about to get up there and wing it. I glance around the room, but there's still no sign of Brady Simms. He had better show.

"No newcomers? All right, then, let's start with the old stand-bys. . . ."

I sit through a rambling piece on unicorns and a haiku about the Irish potato famine. Then a burly, bearded man ambles up to the front of the room. "I'm Walter," he says, as though it's spelled *Walt-ah*. "I'm gonna read ya a poem called *Colors You Can't See*. It's about my mother, who is colorblind."

> *Red bird, blue flame,*
> *to you they look the same.*
> *Green light, Rainbow Brite*
> *doll I had when I was young.*
> *Orange sun, yellow moon,*
> *pink roses in bloom—*
> *all these colors you can't see.*
> *But, Ma, can you see me?*

Walter ends the poem with a flourish, dropping down to one knee and thrusting his arms skyward. I look around the room to see if I'm the only one who finds this amusing. Apparently, I am. A guy in the back claps and says, "Good job, Walter. That took a lot of courage." I turn around to see who spoke and my eyes lock on an attractive, dark-haired man in a pair of black slacks and a gray button-down shirt.

*Brady Simms.*

I glance down at the picture in my hand for confirmation. Yep, it's him. He must have snuck in late.

"Would you like to go next?" Sal asks Brady.

"Sure." Brady makes his way to the front of the room. "Hi, everyone. I'm Brady." He smiles brightly.

My heart starts to race. I feel as though he's looking

directly at me, as though he knows what's about to happen.

"I appreciate your listening. Ever since my father died two weeks ago," Brady begins, blinking rapidly to hold off tears, "I've had a really hard time dealing with things."

I jerk upright in my chair. *What? His father died two weeks ago? Did I hear that right?*

Obviously, this is some sort of mistake! Erin can't possibly want me to ditch Brady. She must be confused. Maybe she thinks I'm some sort of a relationship counselor, hired to patch things up? Deep down, I know that's bullshit, but I can't think of a better explanation.

I start to panic. *What should I do? Should I talk to Brady? Should I bolt?*

I decide to confront the situation head-on. As soon as the readings are over, I jump up and make my way to the back of the room. Brady's sitting by himself, leafing through a notebook.

"Hi, Brady, my name's Dani!" I say brightly. My face turns red. I'm talking too loudly, being too enthusiastic. I'm thrown off my game. I can't seem to focus. "I'm a friend of Erin's," I finally manage.

He looks up, surprised. "Erin Foster-Ellis?"

"The very same."

"Nice to meet you, Dani." Brady shakes my hand. "Any friend of Erin's is a friend of mine."

Now that I'm face-to-face with Brady, I can't think of what to do. I realize that I'm staring at him, and my mind races desperately for something to say.

He eyes me quizzically. "Is everything okay?"

*Not even close!* "Of course! I was just hoping you and I could catch up on a few things tonight."

"Catch up on what? We've never met before," Brady points out.

"True." I'm really digging myself a hole here. "But now's a great time to get to know each other!" I sound like an idiot. "Like you said, any friend of Erin's—"

Brady opens his mouth, and I think he's about to question me when Walter yells, "Hurry up, Simms! Time's a-wasting."

"I've gotta go," he apologizes. "We have to do critiques."

"No sweat. So I'll catch you after the critique?"

"Okay, see you then," he says, walking off to join his group. He throws a confused glance over his shoulder as he goes.

I kill time browsing through Barnes & Noble's magazine aisle. I cast periodic glances at the meeting-room door, waiting to catch Brady the minute he emerges. I made such a fool of myself, I want to remedy it. More important, I need to find out if what Brady said is true—if his father really *did* die two weeks ago. Maybe he meant to say two *years* ago. Or maybe he was using poetic license? The poem he read wasn't that good, but the fact that it was about his dad *who had just died* gave it added effect. . . .

I need confirmation of the facts to figure out how to proceed.

I'm halfway through a magazine article when someone taps me on the shoulder. "Penny for your thoughts."

"Yaaaa!" I shriek, dropping the magazine. I didn't hear him come up behind me.

"You seem flustered," he says.

"I'm fine," I chirp, red-faced. I can't believe I've lost sight of my own target. "Is your critique finished already?" I ask. It's only been about ten minutes.

"I ducked out early."

"You did?"

"I wanted to talk to you. Did Erin send you here to look for me?" he asks.

*Oh my God, he's onto me! He knows I'm here to dump him!* "Why do you ask?" My voice comes out in a squeak.

"It seems odd that we'd both end up at the same poetry workshop, and that you'd approach me the way you did. I don't recall ever meeting you before tonight."

"Well, we haven't met before—"

"Then how did you recognize me?"

"Well . . ." He's staring at me. I think furiously, and then I say, "Erin told me her boyfriend took this great poetry workshop and suggested I check it out, because she knows I'm interested in poetry. I knew what you looked like because she showed me your picture." I feel a warm glow of professional pride. My lies are coming out smoothly. "If I'd known it would freak you out so much, I wouldn't have come," I throw in, with what I hope is an inviting smile.

Brady smiles back, relaxing. "Sorry about the third degree. It's the lawyer in me talking."

"I thought you gave up law." I say before I can stop myself.

"I did," he admits. "But legalese has a nasty habit of sticking with you. I overanalyze everything."

"Was it weird changing careers? High-priced attorney to high-school teacher seems like a pretty big leap."

"Erin told you?"

"She did. Why the drastic move?"

Brady stuffs his hands in his pockets. "Do you know much about the legal profession, Dani?"

"Only what I've seen on *Law & Order.*"

He laughs. "Trust me, it's far less glamorous in real life. Extraordinarily long hours. Endless piles of paperwork."

I picture Evan Hirschbaum's desk, with its mile-high stack of manila folders.

"It's a brutal, brutal profession," he continues. "Lawyers square off in court, play every dirty, backstabbing trick in the book on each other. Then they walk out, shake hands, and make a date to play golf." Brady sighs. "I left work every night feeling like I'd been beaten up. It got to the point where it just didn't make sense to put myself through that anymore."

"Then why did you go into it in the first place?" I ask.

"The short version of the story is I did it to make my parents happy. My teaching career"—his eyes light up—"I'm doing that to make *myself* happy."

"That sounds fascinating; I'd love to hear more about your new job sometime."

He flashes me a grin. "How about we grab a cappuccino? My treat."

*Cappuccino*. At the mention of coffee, my mind flashes back to Your Big Break Inc. I have to find out the facts about his father before I drop Erin's bomb on him. "I'd better not," I say. "I've already had nine cups of coffee today." This is actually true. Given my job and rule #1, I drink enough caffeine for a small army.

"You want to help me find a book, then?" he offers. "Since I started coming to this workshop, I buy at least one new novel every week, always on someone's recommendation. Tonight, you can pick something out for me."

"Sure, sounds fun." We stroll over to the fiction section. "What are you in the mood for?" I ask him.

"Anything," he says, and it makes my heart flutter a little to meet his eyes. "I'm at the mercy of your decision."

"Are you, now?" I say coyly.

"Yep. Whatever you tell me to buy, that's what I'm getting."

"Hmm . . . what if I purposely choose something really

strange? You know, like *Smart Women Finish Rich*. Would you read it?"

"It's not a novel." Brady chuckles. "But, yeah, I'd read it. Trust me, you can't top Walter. I let him pick one week and he chose a kids' picture book. *Baby Duck Goes to the Circus,* I think it was called."

I laugh.

"Oh, it may seem funny now. But I accidentally left the thing in my briefcase and it fell out in the middle of a pretrial meeting. The guys at the office never let me live it down."

"All right, no baby ducks," I promise, patting him lightly on the arm.

He winks. "I knew I could trust you." He pauses and then asks, "What's your favorite novel?" His light blue eyes are still studying my face.

*"High Fidelity,"* I say.

He brightens. "I loved the movie; never got around to reading the book."

"The book's better," I chide.

*"High Fidelity,"* Brady repeats. "So that's your favorite novel?"

"I don't know if it's my *all-time* favorite, but it's really good."

"I'll buy it tonight, and I'll let you know what I think." We find a copy, then walk over toward the register. "Did you enjoy the poetry reading?" Brady asks as we get in line.

"It was an interesting experience," I say honestly.

"I'll let you in on a secret." He leans close. "I love reading poetry. I detest writing it."

"You do?" I ask incredulously.

"Erin's the one who encouraged me to join the workshop. When I first started coming, I hated it. But I fell in love with the people and the atmosphere here. Now I really enjoy myself."

I'm speechless. "It was *Erin's* idea that you take this workshop?" I finally ask.

He nods. "Her last boyfriend used to write her love poems. She wanted me to do the same." Brady groans. "Everything I write sounds stiff and unnatural."

"I thought your poem was sweet," I tell him, semi-honestly. We move forward in the line.

"How did you and Erin meet?" Brady asks.

This is it, the moment of truth. This is where I'm supposed to tell him. I hesitate. *How can I do this? How can I break his heart?* It's never bothered me so much before. But I think about his father—about *my* father—and all the pain that comes from being betrayed.

"We met at Starbucks," I lie. *That's a safe bet, isn't it? Everybody goes to Starbucks, right?*

"How long have you known each other? I don't remember her mentioning you."

"Oh, we've known each other for a while now. We weren't that close at first. But we're starting to become better friends, practically best friends." Even to my own ears, this sounds made up. Fortunately, Brady doesn't seem to notice.

"So I guess she told you about my father, that he passed away two weeks ago."

*So it is true.* "No, I only found out tonight when you said something. I'm so sorry, Brady. That's awful."

"Erin's been acting kind of weird since it happened." His face clouds over. "She's been distant, for lack of a better word. To be perfectly honest, I've been sort of worried."

"There's no need to be," I quickly reassure him. "Everything's fine! Erin loves you very, very much." *Now, if only it were true!*

"You really think so?" he asks.

"Absolutely."

Brady steps up to the cash register and places *High Fidelity* on the counter. A salesgirl rings up his purchase and drops it into a bag.

"Thanks, Dani, you've really helped me out," he says.

Then, holding up the Barnes & Noble sack, he adds, "In more ways than one."

# 9

# Starbucks Redux

I dial Erin Foster-Ellis's cell phone the second I get out of Barnes & Noble. It rings four times and voicemail picks up. I leave a brief message: "This is Dani from Your Big Break Inc. Call me as soon as you get this!" A few minutes later, I dial again. And again.

After seven tries, she finally answers.

"Hello?" She sounds annoyed.

"Erin, this is Dani from Your Big Break Inc.—"

"Who?"

"Dani, from Your Big Break Inc.!"

"Oh!" I hear the recognition in her voice. "Danielle. Right, now I get it. Did you just call me?"

"About ten times." I sit down on small ledge outside the building.

"That's a tad rude," she says. "Sometimes when a person doesn't answer her phone, it means she's busy."

*And sometimes a person might be a heartless shrew*. I don't say this, of course. Instead, I say, "I've got to talk to you immediately." Come hell or high water, I'm going to convince her not to dump Brady Simms.

"So talk."

"Not over the phone." Am I becoming like Evan Hirschbaum, demanding in-person meetings? First my brother, and now Erin. "Can you meet me somewhere tonight?"

"It's awfully late."

"It's only nine o'clock," I argue.

"I guess I could spare a few minutes."

"I'll be quick, I promise." I feel desperate to fix her relationship with Brady. As if patching things up between them will somehow patch things up in my life. "I'll come out to your house."

"No," she says. "That's not necessary. I'm spending the night in Back Bay."

"Back Bay?" I repeat. Back Bay is a trendy little area of downtown Boston.

"There's a Starbucks on Newbury Street," she says. "It's next to—"

"I know it," I say, interrupting her. I know every single Starbucks within a 100-mile radius. I often joke that my real office is a coffee house. If they made frequent-drinker cards, I'd have earned enough points to open my own store. "I'll be there in fifteen minutes," I promise, snapping my phone shut. It's funny. Earlier tonight, I told Brady that I'd first met Erin at Starbucks. Now here I am, going there to meet her. *Does that make my lie the truth?*


Newbury Street is just a short walk from Barnes & Noble. I hoof it down Mass Avenue for a few blocks, then cut over to

Newbury Street. Even though I make it in less than ten minutes, I arrive to find Erin already waiting, a tall latte in hand. I spy her through the window as I walk inside. She's decked out in another Prada outfit, different from the one I saw her in earlier today. It's been only a few hours. I can't believe she's already changed clothes.

I'm about to walk over to Erin's table when a Starbucks staffer flags me down. "Tall iced nonfat mocha!" she shouts, waving the drink in the air.

Erin stares at me as I make my way to the counter.

"Haven't seen you in a while, Dani," the barista says as I pay for my drink on my Starbucks credit card. "What's it been? Four or five days?"

I hear Erin laughing in the background. "Sounds like somebody has a little coffee addiction," she quips as I walk over to the table. "Good for you for ordering nonfat," she says approvingly. "You definitely don't need the full."

I ignore her snide comment. We've got important business to attend to. "You can't break up with Brady," I announce, sitting down across from her. "I think—"

"I can do whatever I want," she cuts me off. "Thanks for your concern."

I fold my arms across my chest and stare at her. "I saw Brady at Barnes and Noble."

Erin takes a few sips of coffee before answering. "How'd he take it?"

"He didn't. I couldn't."

Erin wrinkles her brow. "You didn't tell him I want to end things?" She squints at me. "I thought you said you would take care of it."

*Here we go*. I take a deep breath and look her straight in the eyes, defiantly. "I couldn't go through with it. As soon as I heard about his father's death—"

"Oh. That." She wads her napkin into a ball and shrugs her slim little shoulders. "He passed away a few weeks ago. He was in his early sixties, I believe."

"And you left out this information because . . . ?"

She crosses her long legs. "I didn't think it was relevant."

"You didn't think it was relevant?" I ask incredulously.

Erin narrows her eyes. "Honestly, Danielle. I don't owe you an explanation. So Brady's father died of colon cancer a couple of weeks ago. It's tragic, but it doesn't really have anything to do with our relationship. The two are completely unrelated. That's his family life. I'm not involved in that."

"What do you mean you're not involved in that?" I ask. "You've been dating the guy for two years! How can you not care about what happens to his family?"

"Family's overrated," Erin says, waving her had dismissively. "Only saps care about that kind of thing." She pauses. "You act as though losing your father is a big deal."

I want to punch her. *How can she say a thing like that?* Losing your father is a *huge* deal. *My God, I ought to know. . . .*

I don't say anything, and Erin continues: "Brady's a grown man; he'll be fine."

She's unbelievable. Why any man would want a shallow girl-friend like Erin is beyond me, but Brady obviously sees something in her that I don't.

"Don't you kind of think dumping Brady right now would be"—I pause, choosing my words carefully—"insensitive?" I feel so bad for him. I don't want to do this. I don't want to ruin his world.

"The timing's not great, I'll give you that." Erin takes another sip of coffee. "Did you get to hear any of Brady's writing?" she asks, shifting topics.

"As a matter of fact, I did. Brady read a showstopping poem about his father. His *late* father." *Showstopping* might be stretching it a bit, but I've got to work all the angles. "Brady said you were the one who encouraged him to take that poetry workshop," I say.

"You and Brady-boy did an awful lot of talking tonight," Erin notes, raising her eyebrows. "A shame you didn't talk about what I paid you to talk about." She smiles in a patronizing way and looks around the coffee shop. "I suggested he take that poetry class because I wanted to have Thursday nights free."

I wince. "Erin, can I ask you a personal question?"

"You can ask. I don't know if I'll answer."

"Is there anything I could do to convince you to give Brady another chance? He seems like a nice guy. I mean, he only started this whole teaching thing a few weeks ago. Maybe he'll find out he doesn't like it."

Erin smirks. "It doesn't matter. I'm not interested."

"Even if Brady went back to being an attorney?" I ask.

"Even then. Look, Danielle, I'll be honest with you—it's over between me and Brady. There's someone else. There has been for a while."

"Someone else?"

"A TV producer for PBS. I met him a few weeks ago. In fact, I'm going back to his place as soon as we finish up here." She eyes her watch.

*Back* to his place. "You just came from there?" Now I know why she was in Back Bay tonight, instead of Beacon Hill.

"Not that it's your business, but I stay over at his place most nights."

So that's what's going on. She's cheating on Brady. During our consultation this afternoon, I'd asked her, point-blank, if there was another man. "Why did you lie when I questioned you earlier if there was someone else?"

"My God, you're nosy!" she snaps. "What other details do you want to know? If I'm sleeping with him? Because I am. And I haven't had sex with Brady in three months. Happy now?"

Looks like getting Erin and Brady back together is out of the question. There's nothing I can do to help him, no way to make things right, and I feel horrible. Lower than pond scum. I'm about to get up and leave when something occurs to me.

"Here's what I'm thinking," I begin. "Brady's going through an extraordinarily bad time right now—maybe you could hold off on breaking up with him."

"Hold off?"

"Yeah, wait until things settle down." I hang my head. "He's going to be crushed if you do this to him right now."

"And he won't be crushed tomorrow? Next week? Next month?" she demands.

"Obviously, he's going to be crushed no matter when you do it. But dumping him right now is like kicking him when he's down."

She yawns. "Honesty's the best policy."

"No, it's not. Not always. There are times when you have to do things—dishonest things—to spare someone's feelings."

I can tell by her facial expression that she doesn't agree. "Look, I'm going to end things with Brady. I've already decided that. What difference does it make if I do it sooner or later?"

"You've got to wait this out, give him some time to heal. He's just gone through a major loss. The last thing he needs is to face losing you."

"I don't know."

I swallow hard, gathering up my courage. "Please, Erin. You mean so much to Brady. It would destroy him—literally destroy him—if you left right now." I'm pleading, begging even. But I can't let her go through with this. For once in my life, I want to do something nice for somebody. "Can't you stick it out one month?"

"One *week*. I'll give this one week."

I make a counteroffer. "Two weeks."

She shakes her head. "Nothing doing. One is already pushing it."

I square my shoulders. "You give two weeks' notice when you leave a job. Why not give two weeks' notice to leave a boyfriend?"

"I've never had a job," she informs me, looking bored.

"Then think of it as giving him one week for every year you've been together," I say. "It's the least you could do."

"No, the least I could do would be to give him *no* notice." She chuckles. "But I'm not a monster." She thinks it over. "What the hell. I can wait two weeks. I can't promise I'll be a faithful and devoted girlfriend, but I'll hold off on shoving him out the door, so to speak."

That's not great, but it's better than nothing. I feel better. One less broken heart on my conscience. "Thanks, Erin."

"I've got two conditions."

"Okay." *This should be good.*

"I want you to handle everything—*all* the details. After I dump him, I don't ever want to see or speak to Brady again."

"Of course. I can't guarantee that he won't try to contact you at some point down the road, but I'll do my best to stop him."

"Good." She sounds pleased. "Now, for my other condition. And this is non-negotiable."

*Uh-oh*. I get the feeling she's about to play hardball.

"You have to knock seventy-five bucks off the price."

"Seventy-five bucks!" I exclaim. "That's like a sixty percent discount!"

"Sixty-five percent," she corrects. "And that's my offer, take it or leave it."

"How about twenty-five dollars?" I suggest.

"Nope."

I'm going to have a tough enough time convincing Craig to discount this at all, and I know there's no way he'll go for seventy-five dollars off. But, frankly, I'm too tired to put up a fight.

"All right." I sigh. "Seventy-five it is. That brings the price down to thirty-five bucks."

"Pleasure doing business with you."

We shake, and I'm about to respond when Erin throws her head back and laughs. "You're not much of a negotiator, Danielle."

I shrug it off. "You drive a hard bargain."

"Yes, I do." She smiles. "But I'll let you in on a little secret." She lowers her voice to a mock whisper. "I'd have done it for fifty."

# 10

# Gretchen Guy-Getter

"You wanna tell me what this is about?" Sean asks as we sit down in a booth at Chili's the following day.

I pick up my menu and thumb through it. "After we order."

My brother rolls his eyes but agrees. A few minutes later, after a waiter has brought us soft drinks and taken our food orders, I begin. "Okay, the reason I've asked you here today is, well, it's complicated."

"Dani, you're going to have to speed this up," he says, tapping his watch. "I can't afford to listen to some two-hour story. I've got a lot of stuff to do today, you know."

I lean back against the booth, settling in. "I thought this was your day off."

"It is," he says, slurping his Coke.

"Then what's so pressing? Is your favorite TV show on right now or something?"

"No, *General Hospital* doesn't start until three."

"You're joking, right?"

He blushes. *Oh my God, he's not joking.*

"You watch *General Hospital*?"

"I might," Sean huffs, averting his gaze.

I can't help giggling. "Since when?"

"Since I discovered how many fine chicks are on the show."

"Fine chicks?" I repeat, leaning back in the booth.

"Hell, yeah." He rubs his hands together in anticipation. "The girls on *GH* are so freaking hot. And they're always running around half-naked."

"Isn't it set in a hospital? Shouldn't they be wearing scrubs?"

"You'd be amazed how often they end up in bikinis and lingerie. You should check it out, Dani. You'd love it."

*Oh, yes. Fine chicks in bikinis. That sounds right up my alley.*
"Are the men cute?" I ask, being conversational.

Sean slurps his drink. "How should I know?"

"You watch it."

Sean runs his hands through his shaggy, light brown hair. "Yeah, but I don't watch it for the men. Besides, I can't tell if a dude looks good or not."

"Oh, come on." I give him a look. "You honestly can't tell if another man is attractive?"

He shakes his head.

"So you couldn't say who was hotter: Tom Cruise or Tom Arnold?" I insist.

He drinks his Coke. "Nope. All men look the same to me."

*Why do guys always claim this?* "Then, how do you know whether or not *you're* attractive?"

He ponders this. "I guess I don't."

"But you spend time primping in front of the mirror," I point out. "Why bother, if you can't tell the difference between when you start and when you finish?"

"Dani, what the hell does this have to do with anything?" he says, setting down his soft drink. I've irritated him.

It doesn't. But it was a fun distraction. Now it's time to get down to business. "Okay, okay . . . back to the story."

"Finally."

I clear my throat. "You know how I work for a breakup service?"

"No!" Sean clasps his hand over his mouth in mock-horror. "And all this time I thought you were a Web mistress."

Here's my opening. "Funny you should mention the word *mistress*," I say, taking a quick sip of my Sprite. "That's sort of why we're here."

"What, does Dad have some little number on the side?" he cracks.

"Yes," I say flatly.

"Puh-*lease*." Sean laughs. "Look who's into soap operas now."

"It's no soap opera." My voice drops. "I met her a few days ago. She's thirty-five. Her name's Gretchen Monaghan."

"Yeah, right. You're off in la-la land, Dani." He sits upright and peers around the restaurant. "Where's that waiter? I'm starving."

"I'm serious, Sean! A woman named Gretchen Monaghan came in to Your Big Break Inc. on Tuesday and asked me to"—I pause, choking up at the memory—"to break up with *our father* for her."

He stares hard at me, trying to decipher whether or not I've lost my mind.

"What the fuck," he mumbles, raising an eyebrow.

I reach forward and put my hand on his arm. He jerks it away. "Sean, I—"

In a classic case of bad timing, our lunch arrives at precisely this moment. Neither of us speaks while the waiter sets down our dishes. I stare at my plate, which is piled high with food. Why did I order chicken tacos with a side of fries? I'm not the least bit hungry.

Sean's appetite doesn't seem to be affected. He pours ketchup all over his fries and digs right into his burger with gusto. "You're so dramatic, Dani," he says between bites. "Always letting your imagination run wild."

I stare him straight in the eyes. "I'm telling you the truth. Our father's having an affair."

"Dad couldn't pull something like that off. He's way too mild-mannered. Plus, he works all the time."

I nod. "Exactly. Perfect cover." I poke at my chicken tacos with a fork, scooting them around on my plate. "He pretends to be working long hours when he's actually out running around on Mom."

"Did you ever stop to think Dad just might be a workaholic?" Sean asks. He wipes some ketchup off his cheek.

"Well, then how do you explain Gretchen?" I take a tentative bite of a french fry.

Sean considers this. "You're *positive* this woman was talking about Dad?"

I nod my head yes.

He pops some fries into his mouth and quickly downs them. "All right, tell me how this went down."

I start at the beginning, and work my way through the entire story. I close by recounting the conversation I had with Father's assistant, Lorne, yesterday. "So, as you can plainly see, there's only one explanation," I finish.

Sean, who has been munching quietly on his food the entire time, finally speaks. "There's an explanation, all right."

I take a small bite of my chicken taco. "Dad and this Gretchen woman are obviously . . ." I pause, searching for the right word. *Dating? Too high-schoolish. Lovers? Too nauseating.* I settle on *involved*.

"Oh, I don't doubt they're involved," Sean says. "You wanna know what I think?"

"Fire away."

"It's payback." He sets down his hamburger. "Dad's paying you back. Hell, Mom's probably in on it, too."

"What are you talking about?"

"For the past year, you've been lying to them about where you work."

I cringe and start to defend my actions, but he holds up a hand to silence me. "Somehow Mom and Dad found out the truth. So they decided to get even, to teach you a lesson you'd never forget," he announces. "This whole thing's staged. Gretchen's probably an actress, hired for the occasion."

"An actress?" I nearly choke on a fry.

"Sure. We played that same trick on my buddy M.J. a few years ago."

I stare at Sean blankly. "You've lost me."

"It was M.J.'s twenty-first birthday, and he had this big party at Callaghan's downtown. A couple of us hired this singing-telegram chick named Pregnant Patty to embarrass him. Man, it was great!" He smiles at the memory. "She came storming into the restaurant, decked out like a knocked-up hooker—thigh-high leather boots, fishnets, a pillow stuffed under her lacy dress."

Sean chuckles. "Pregnant Patty totally berated M.J. for leaving her alone with their unborn child. M.J. got all flustered and claimed he'd 'never seen this woman before' in his life. Which, of course, he hadn't. Then she threw a drink in his face, flipped on a karaoke tape, and launched into a rendition of *These Boots Were Made for Walking*. Don't you see? That's what Gretchen is—a hired singing telegram!"

My brother is insane. "You can't be serious."

"As a heart attack." The waiter brings Sean a refill and he heartily gulps it.

"You think our parents hired some novelty act . . . named, I don't know, Gretchen Guy-Getter . . ."

"Hey! That's pretty good," Sean says admiringly.

I ignore him. "And sent her out to play a practical joke on me?"

"If the shoe fits."

*The shoe so does* not *fit.* "I met her. Trust me, she wasn't an actress!"

"Be logical!" Sean exclaims.

He's *telling* me *to be logical?*

"Of all the breakup services in Boston, what are the odds of Gretchen picking yours?" Sean asks.

"Pretty high, considering Your Big Break is the only breakup service in the entire state of Massachusetts!"

"Whatever." Sean rolls his eyes. "My point is, it's too coincidental that Gretchen came to see *you*. It's got to be a setup."

Maybe he's onto something. I hadn't really considered that option. "I suppose it's possible. . . ."

"It's not just possible, it's probable," he insists. "I still live with the 'rents, remember? If Dad were having an affair, I'd know about it. There'd be signs."

"But how do you explain his weird behavior? The breakfast meetings that last all day? The family dinner cancellations?"

"Dad's a busy man. Remember all those boxes he brought home the other night? He's right in the middle of some huge project, and he's working long hours to catch up."

I'd forgotten about the boxes. That's a good point. No, make that a *great* point! "So you don't think we should tell Mom?"

"No way," Sean says, chowing down on the last of his burger. "Let me investigate it, get to the bottom of what, if anything, is going on. Then, *if* I come across any definitive proof, we'll go to Mom."

The more Sean talks, the better I feel. Maybe, just maybe, the situation isn't as bad as I initially imagined? Maybe it *was* payback. Maybe my family is going to be okay after all. By the time our waiter deposits the bill, I'm feeling refreshed, relieved.

"We'll get to the bottom of this," Sean promises, "figure out what's going on."

"You really think it's one giant misunderstanding?"

"Definitely. But just to be on the safe side, I'll check into it, do a little poking around," he says, waving his fork at me. "If Dad's up to anything—anything at all—I'll find out."

"Thanks," I say, and I genuinely mean it. I vow to put it out of my mind until Sean finishes his investigation.


When I get back to the office after lunch, there's a message from Sophie Kennison on my machine. I hit the playback button.

*Hello, Dani. This is in response to your voicemail. While I'll be happy to meet up with you when I get back to Boston, I will not—I repeat, I will not—leave Evan Hirschbaum alone.*

*I just called his office and discovered he's gone out of town for a few days. Since you're Evan's little go-between, please tell him that I'll be phoning him as soon as he gets back. Good-bye, Dani.*

"Great," I mutter, sinking down in my desk chair. If I can't figure out a way to get Sophie off Evan's back, I'm going to be screwed. Evan will be furious, and he'll undoubtedly call Craig to complain. Craig will come down hard on me for messing things up—again!—with our biggest client. He's already pissed off enough about the Jason Dutwiler situation. And what if Craig discovers what a slipshod job I've been doing since discovering my father's affair?

I've got to act swiftly, get all my ducks in a row.

It's time to devote myself fully to Your Big Break Inc.

# 11

# The Dearly Deserted

I spend the next few days figuring out how to break Brady Simms's heart.

*Poor guy.* He has no idea what's about to hit him. I need a well-fleshed-out plan. I'm going to cushion the blow as best I can. What will Brady need to help him pull through? I jot down a short list.

1. *Support*
2. *A fun night out with friends*
3. *A stellar Breakup Recovery Kit*
4. *A rebound girl*

I look over my list. What concerns me most is that Brady may need some kind of professional counseling. I'll put a list of local grief counselors in his Breakup Recovery Kit.

The second one's pretty tricky. Right after the breakup

happens, Brady will need a night out on the town to cut loose and forget his troubles. I jot down a few options: *Sports. Beer. Junk food. Strip clubs.* The tricky part is, I don't know any of his friends, and I don't think it would help him if he completed these on his own.

Number three's also going to be tough. Making Breakup Recovery Kits for guys is always hard. If it's a girl, you can give her chocolates, chocolates, and more chocolates. Guys . . . not so much.

Plus, Erin's thirty-five dollars won't allow me to put together a stellar Breakup Recovery Kit. In fact, for thirty-five dollars I could barely put together a lame Breakup Recovery Kit. I could spend a little of my own money, maybe throw in a mix CD, some humorous magazine clippings. I brainstorm for a few minutes and come up with a few other cheap options: a journal for his poetry, a handmade sympathy card, some Blockbuster gift certificates that Sean can get me at a discount, a giant-sized bottle of hand sanitizer to "wash away the germs of your old relationship." I laugh at that last one. Is it too tacky? Nah, I decide to go for it. I'll pick up the items for Brady's Breakup Recovery Kit this weekend. I want to make it extra special. Brady's been through a lot lately. I want to do whatever I can to help him heal.

By far, the hardest thing to accomplish will be finding Brady a rebound girl.

I'll have to give it some serious thought. He needs someone sensitive, someone understanding, someone who's been through a terrible breakup herself, like my breakup with Garrett. For a brief moment, I debate taking him out myself, but I quickly push the thought out of my head. It's not like I could go do it. That's totally against company policy.

In the meantime, I might as well work on my other project:

reuniting Jason Dutwiler with his ex-girlfriend, Lucy Dooley. Talk about a pair of bad last names. I scrawl *Lucy Dooley-Dutwiler* on a piece of scrap paper. *Yikes*. No wonder she wants out.

I've been putting this off long enough. I look up Lucy's phone number on my computer and then pick up the phone and give her a call.

"Dooley residence," a voice says.

"Hi, is Lucy available?"

"May I ask who's calling?"

"This is Danielle from Your Big Break."

"Oh. My. God! Hold please." I hear the phone drop, followed by shouts of, "A lady wants to give you your big break!"

"Hello?" Lucy answers, breathless. "Who is this?"

"Danielle from Your Big Break," I say, wishing whoever answered the phone would have just given her a straight message.

"Oh. I thought you were a talent scout," she explains. "I sent out a batch of headshots yesterday. Mom thinks the offers are going to start pouring in."

"That was your mom who answered?"

"Uh-huh."

"You live with your parents?"

"I do."

I glance down at Lucy's file, which says she's thirty-one. Thirty-one years old and she still lives at home? Maybe I ought to fix her up with Sean? No, she's probably still seeing the acupuncturist, Nate.

"Are you calling about the stuff?" Lucy asks.

"What stuff?"

"The DVDs and clothes I left at Jason's place. You said you could pick them up for me."

"Oh, *that* stuff." *Crap, crap, crap! I'm really slipping!* I should have gotten Lucy's things back a week ago. I've been so preoccupied that I completely forgot. "Jason's still getting them together. I'll have them in another day or two," I lie. "I'm actually calling about a wedding."

"Who's getting married?"

"Jason's brother—"

"Forget it."

"You don't even know what I'm going to say!"

"Let me guess." She sighs. "Jason wants me to go to his brother's wedding with him, right?"

*How did she know that?* "How did you know that?"

"Because Jason is obsessed with that damn wedding. He's been talking about it for the past year. He and his brother have this horrible sibling-rivalry thing going."

"It would really mean a lot to him if you were there," I hint.

"Not a chance."

"Not even a tiny chance?"

"Danielle, I wasn't even planning to attend that wedding when we were dating. I hate weddings. Jason knows that. Weddings are oppressive and fake."

I always figured the only people who disliked weddings were those of us with a genuine fear of growing old alone. Lucy strikes me as one of those girls who's never been sans boyfriend for more than five minutes. "There's nothing I can say to convince you to go?"

"Nothing. Nate wouldn't be too happy if I went."

"Jason could really use another time seeing you to get over the relationship," I say, giving it one last-ditch effort. "He's taking this breakup pretty hard."

"All the more reason to say no. If I go, I'll be giving him false hope."

I see her point. I can also see she's not going to budge. "I understand."

"Give me a call when you get the stuff," Lucy says.

"I will," I promise. "Take care."

I hang up the phone. Looks like I'm going to have to do the job I was hired to do in the first place. I pick up the receiver to call Jason Dutwiler.

I'll arrange a time to get Lucy's things.

And I'll let him know that things are definitely, one hundred percent over.

# 12

# You Weren't This Fat When We Started Dating

I haven't seen or talked to my father since I met Gretchen four days ago.

Tonight's my mother's fifty-fifth birthday. We're celebrating by having dinner at my parents' house. This has been planned for a long time. I don't know how I'll face him, how I'll hug him hello, sit beside him and eat pasta. Can I talk to him without screaming or hitting him? Can I look at my mother without bursting into tears?

I arrive at five o'clock to find Father seated in the den, wrapping the Anne Klein shirt I helped him pick out during our shopping trip. It's telling that he waited so long to wrap it. It's obvious Mom isn't a priority in his life.

"Hey, honey!" he mumbles, struggling to get the paper even.

*Honey.* Is that his pet name for Gretchen, too? That would be really sickening.

Father tapes the paper and then shifts the box from his lap to the coffee table. "I hope you've come ready to eat, because we've got enough food to feed an army! I don't know how the four of us are going to manage."

*We could invite your mistress. That'd give us one more mouth to feed.*

"My appetite's fine," I say crisply, sailing past him into the kitchen. I set my gift bag for Mom down on the counter and reach into the refrigerator for a drink. I fix myself a Coke with ice and sit down on one of the stools. I take a few deep breaths and try to steady my nerves. My heart's racing and I feel shaky. Seeing my father was worse than I'd anticipated. I take a few sips of Coke and try to relax.

"Boo!" Sean says, sneaking up behind me.

I jump a mile, spilling half of my drink onto the countertop. I quickly grab the gift bag before the dark, fizzy liquid reaches it. "Don't ever do that to me again," I whisper hoarsely, grabbing a few paper towels and wiping up the mess.

"Well, excuse me," Sean says, picking up the soiled paper towels and depositing them in the trash. "How was I supposed to know you'd be so jumpy?"

"Of course I'm jumpy! Aren't you?"

"No, why would I be?"

I grab Sean's arm and pull him closer. "How can you look at that jerk without feeling sick to your stomach?"

"I've been looking at Dad for several days now, keeping an eye out for weird behavior."

"And?"

"Nothing." Sean sits down on a stool next to me. "Everything's copacetic."

"You're sure? I've been so worried I'd slip up in front of Mom tonight," I admit.

"There's nothing to slip up about. Everything's fine."

"Slip up about what in front of Mom?" my mother asks, strolling into the room.

I freeze. *How much did she hear? What does she know?*

"Your birthday present," Sean covers. "We got you something really special this year."

*We did?* I got Mom a pair of earrings. They're nice, but nothing that would require advance plotting and planning. I hope Sean's got a killer present I can go in on.

Mom grins. "I'll look forward to opening it after dinner."

"Oh, you can't open it tonight," Sean says, frantically looking at me for help.

"We ordered it from a specialty shop online. But it's on back order," I manage. My job has made me a pro in tight spots.

"Oh, I see." Mom seems nonplussed.

*Why* didn't *we think to order Mom some terrific gift?* I could kick myself. It might have helped ease the pain of Evil Cheating Bastard Father's affair. *If* he's having one . . .

Half an hour later, we sit down to eat.

The meal's good: rigatoni pasta with meat sauce; garlic bread; tomato and buffalo mozzarella with olive oil. We wash it down with merlot. The conversation is shockingly normal. My parents banter back and forth. Father tells funny stories about the Bruins game last night. Sean recounts the latest episode of *CSI*. Mom says after tonight, she'll be cutting desserts from her diet.

I freeze. "Since when are you concerned about your weight?" I ask, helping myself to a bite of tiramisu.

"I'm getting older, Dani," Mom says, picking at her dessert. "My metabolism's not what it used to be."

Father nods in agreement. I want to slug him. *Where does he get off insulting Mom's weight?*

"Yeah, but your body is perfect," I say. "What are you, a size two?"

"I just want to look the best I can," Mom says. "And let's leave it at that."

*Let's leave it at that? My God, she knows!* Maybe not about Gretchen, but she senses something's wrong. She knows Father's unhappy and she's desperate to win him back. I shoot Sean a pointed glance. "See?" I mouth. "She's doing this for Dad!"

Sean rolls his eyes. "So what?" he mouths back.

"They're falling apart!" I hiss under my breath.

Father leans forward. "Is something wrong, Dani?"

I shake my head.

"Beth and I were thinking," Father begins, "that maybe it's time to retire the old Thursday dinners."

I gasp. "We can't!"

"Sounds good to me," Sean says. "I hate missing *Survivor* and *CSI*."

"Who cares about stupid TV shows," I gripe. "Family should come first. Right, Mom?"

I'm expecting her to back me up. After all, just the other day, she was talking about how we never spend any time together. But Mom surprises me.

"We can still be together as a family," she says. "Even if we don't have dinner every other Thursday night. You and I are going to have a girls' night soon, remember?"

I nod solemnly, and Sean leans over and pats me on the arm. He smiles confidently as if everything is perfectly fine.

# 13

## STAGE TWO OF BREAKUP HELL:
### *Sour Grapes*

During this stage, many cracks are made about the former partner's appearance, sexual prowess (or lack thereof), and endless array of personality flaws. The dumpee cuts up photos of the not-so-dearly departed, burns relationship mementos, and trashes their ex-lover's reputation to anyone who'll listen.

"Asshole!"

I have just been awoken from a sound sleep by my ringing phone. It is 2:13 a.m., and I'm staring at the receiver—someone has just called me an asshole. *A prank call at 2:13 in the morning?* I'm about to hang up when I hear, "Dani, are you there?"

*Dani.* Okay, it's probably a disgruntled client who has somehow found out my home phone number. Which is kind of scary, considering I always follow rule #2 and *never* give out my last name. *Oh, God, I've got a nut on my hands.*

"Who the hell is this?" I demand, trying to sound forceful, menacing. If they think they're going to intimidate me, they've got another thing coming.

"It's me!"

That doesn't narrow it down much. "Excuse me?" I struggle to locate the lamp switch so I can flip it on and read the caller ID display. "Who is this?"

"Your brother! Dani, what's wrong with you?"

I rub the sleep out of my eyes. "Sean?"

"Yes, it's Sean! What other brother would it be?" He lets out a low whistle. "Wait, don't answer that. If Dad's illegitimate son came in to work today, I don't wanna know."

I'm wide awake. "What's up, Sean?"

"He's an asshole!"

"Who's an asshole?"

"Dad!"

I sit straight up in bed. "Did you find out Father is . . ." I can't quite bring myself to say the words *having an affair*.

There's a long silence on the other end of the line, and for a moment, I think Sean's hung up. "Yes. It's exactly what you thought. He's with *her*. Gretchen."

This isn't the response I wanted. "Are you sure?" I choke out.

"Dad has a girlfriend. Worse than that, he may have more than one. I found Match.com log-in info and a bunch of e-mails on his computer. I've been going through them for the last two hours. The e-mails date back almost six months."

This is the part of the conversation when I'm supposed to say, "I told you so." But I don't feel like gloating. I'm too stunned to even breathe. "How bad is it?" I finally ask in a voice barely above a whisper.

"Pretty bad. If this were *CSI*, we'd have enough evidence to convict."

My brother can act so over the top sometimes. "Convict him of what?"

"Adultery! There were tons of saved e-mails from Gretchen. Romantic and sexual in nature."

My father is a cybersex-obsessed pervert. "Son of a bitch!"

"I prefer asshole. Has more sting."

My heart's racing, my palms are sweating, and I'm dangerously close to passing out. "He just left them in a folder on the desktop? Right where *Mom could easily find them*?" I shout. I imagine poor Mom hopping online to look up a recipe and stumbling upon Dad's torrid love letters to another woman.

"Relax! The folder was password protected. I had to hack in."

"You know how to hack in to computers?" I ask, astonished. I knew my brother was a video-game aficionado. I didn't realize he was a hacker, too.

"I do now. I found a hacking guide online and I taught myself. Gotta love the Internet. You'd be amazed how easy it is. Once I got in, I found a virtual treasure trove, an orgy of evidence against Dad."

"Please don't use the word *orgy* in this context." I massage my temples, trying to make the image disappear.

"Sorry, I heard it on TV the other night. Anyway, Dad's folder was full of responses from personal ads. He's been placing them on websites for months now. He even frequents one chat room called Married, But Looking."

"Married, But Looking?" I say indignantly. "There's actually a chat room called Married, But Looking?"

"Yep. And worse," Sean says wryly. "Old Stallions for Young Fillies was another popular chat room."

"I think I'm gonna puke."

"It's pretty sick, isn't it?" Sean says. He lets out a harsh laugh. "I bet Gretchen isn't the first. I bet it's been going on for a long time."

"Ever since we moved to Massachusetts?" I swallow hard, trying to squelch the sour taste rising up my throat.

"Screw that! I bet this stretches back to New Orleans. Remember how Dad was always claiming to work late? I bet he was hitting up all those nudie bars on Bourbon Street."

A disturbing image pops into my mind: I see my father, cruising down Bourbon Street with a beer in one hand, Mardi Gras beads in the other. Every time a pert young girl passes by, he tosses them out in exchange for a little T&A action. It's like he's smack-dab in the middle of a *Girls Gone Wild* video. I sink back against my pillow, feeling the horror of it wash over me.

"Dani? Dani?"

I get the feeling Sean's been calling my name for a while. "Yeah?"

"You haven't even heard the worst part!"

I snuggle down against the mattress, praying it will swallow me whole. "It gets worse?"

"Much."

I don't know how much more I can handle. "I'd better go, Sean. I've got an early day tomorrow—"

"But I haven't even told you about the pictures!"

"Pictures?"

"I'm e-mailing them to you as we speak."

"What?" I shriek. "No! I don't want to see any pictures."

"You sure?"

"Yes! I'm absolutely positive. I have no interest in looking at photos of nude girls, thank you very much," I say indignantly. *What's wrong with Sean? Why the hell would he think I'd want to look at porn?*

"There's no nudes. Don't you want to see what Gretchen looks like?" Sean prods.

"I've already seen her, remember?"

"Oh, yeah. What am I thinking? Okay, I won't send you any photos. But I was pretty surprised when I saw her. Gretchen's an okay-looking woman."

"She has a big butt," I snap.

"Some men are into big butts." He launches into a quick verse of the Sir Mix-a-Lot song, "Baby Got Back." When I don't laugh, he adds, "I'm sorry, Dani. I'm trying to lighten the mood. This is all really depressing. I feel sick to my stomach right now. Imagine how Mom will feel when she finds out."

"Have you told her anything?" I ask.

"No. I'm going to dig through the rest of Dad's files, see what else I can find out. Once we've got all the available evidence, then we'll go to Mom."

"If you say so." I'm shaking. Part of me wants to stop right here, forget about what I already know.

"You have work tomorrow," Sean says. "I'll let you go to bed."

There's no way in hell I'll fall back asleep. But I'm grateful to get off the phone nonetheless. I'm too numb to listen to him anymore. As soon as we hang up, I feel desperately alone. I take a few deep breaths and, with shaking legs, climb out of bed.

I stare around my bedroom, trying to figure out what to do. My head is spinning; my heart is beating rapidly in my chest. So many things in my room remind me of my parents: the desk they bought me as high-school graduation present; the afghan throw my mother made me; the pair of amethyst earrings my parents gave me last Christmas.

My eyes travel to the photo album sitting on my bookshelf. It contains pictures of our family trip to France six years ago. Mom and Dad took me there as a college graduation present. I was twenty-two at the time. Most people that age would have dreaded a vacation with their parents, but I loved it. My father always worked such long hours that, growing up, I cherished every moment I got to spend with him. I never grew out of it. My brother was in the middle of finals, so he couldn't go. But Mom, Dad, and I had an amazing time.

I walk across the room and pull the photo album off the shelf. I flip through it, studying the various pictures: *Mom and Dad outside the glass pyramid entrance to the Louvre. Me and Dad in front of the Eiffel Tower. Me, Mom, and Dad taking a cruise along the Seine. Dad in the gardens of Versailles. Dad sipping wine in a Parisian café. Dad admiring the* Mona Lisa, *which had turned out to be disappointingly minuscule in person.*

The more I page through the album, the more I realize something. Dad—excuse me, *Father*—is in virtually every picture. Suddenly, this makes me furious. I never realized he was such a camera hog! Rather than snap a few shots of me and Mom for posterity, he insisted that his ugly mug be in every frame. Even back then, he was a selfish bastard.

My rage grows as I continue flipping through the album, finding page after page of his smug, irritating face. *Father strolling along the Champs-Elysees. Father trying on a beret in a tacky tourist shop. Father eating a croissant on our hotel balcony.*

It's bad enough the man has ruined my family. I'm not going to let him ruin my memories of Paris, too!

I dash over to my desk and grab a pair of scissors out of the top drawer. I start pulling the offending photos out of the album and dropping them in a pile on the bed. Once I've removed all the Father-tainted shots, I begin the arduous task of cutting him out while still salvaging the rest of the picture. It's tricky, but I manage. I slice the Eiffel Tower photo straight in half, keeping myself and tossing out the lying, cheating bastard. I crop Father out of the *Mona Lisa* photo—no sense letting him ruin good art. I remove him from the Champs-Elysees, the gardens of Versailles, the Arc de Triomphe.

I even tackle the croissant picture, cutting it down until all that's left is an unidentifiable hand holding a pastry.

When I'm finished, I slip the cropped pictures in the album and then lie back on my bed and admire my work. My photo book now contains a bizarre, scattered tour of France. To an outsider, it might appear as though these choppy prints were doctored by a psychopath. But I know better.

I toss Father's remains in the trash, feeling deeply satisfied.

# 14

# Trey's Tips

" 'Regretfully, I must tender my resignation,' " I read aloud.

"Are you quitting?" Amanda asks, coming into my office.

I jump. I didn't realize anyone was listening, and I'd prefer privacy.

"No, this is for a client."

"I thought Trey was in charge of job resignations?"

"Trey's in Wisconsin," I say for the thousandth time. *Why is it that no one but me seems to remember he's out?* "I'm handling his overflow." When I was a kid and having a bad day, my mother would say, "You can't crawl under your bed and hide when you have a problem." Today, I am truly wishing that I could crawl under my desk to hide. But I can't. I have to sit at it and pretend to be a normal person. I have to pretend that I never spoke to Sean, never cut up those pictures. I have to pretend that I didn't stay up until 4:00 a.m. last night, watching TV and trying not to cry.

"Dani, this letter you're writing sucks."

I have to pretend I don't want to strangle Amanda.

"It's a rough draft." I continue reading: " 'I have greatly enjoyed being in your employ these last three months. I feel my time at Morgan Keegan has allowed me to grow both personally and professionally.' "

Amanda grabs my spare chair and starts pulling it around my desk.

"Aren't you supposed to be in class right now?" I ask, giving her a pointed look. I'm on a tight deadline. It's 9:30 a.m., and this letter of resignation has to be signed, sealed, and delivered to the client within an hour.

"Nope. Summer term doesn't start for another two weeks."

"Shouldn't you be working on our website?"

She shakes her head. "Craig's got to approve the template I designed before I can move forward."

"Then don't you have some other work to do?" *Why won't she take the hint?*

"I've got nothing to do," she says, sitting down beside me, "so Craig wants me to shadow you for the day. He says it will be a great learning experience."

Just what I need. "Fine," I say with a tight smile. I get back to the letter. " 'However, at this stage in my career, I feel I need to refocus my efforts on obtaining an advanced business degree—' "

"Why are you reading it out loud?"

"To get a sense of the flow."

"I think it's too formal."

"I'm—I mean *he's*—resigning from a job. It's supposed to be formal."

"You can be professional without being formal," Amanda argues.

"Let's look at Trey's notes," I say firmly, searching through the papers on my desk. "He left instructions on job resignations."

"What makes Trey the be-all-end-all expert?"

"He used to work for a job placement firm," I tell her. "He rewrote people's résumés and cover letters, and coached them on interviewing skills. It's ironic. Trey spent three years helping people land jobs. Now he's helping people quit them."

Amanda shrugs. "It's a natural progression."

"I've written letters of resignation before," I assure her. "The problem with this guy is he only worked at Morgan Keegan for three months. Now he's bailing out to attend night school part-time. How do you spin that?"

"Just tell the truth." She reaches into her pocket and pulls out some Tootsie Rolls. "Want some?"

I shake my head. "No, thanks. It's not that simple. Our client doesn't want to burn bridges. If the MBA program doesn't work out, he might reapply for his old job."

She unwraps a Tootsie Roll and pops it into her mouth.

"Aha!" I exclaim, locating Trey's notes in the stack. "Now we're in business!"

"Or out of it," she cracks, "if you want to get technical."

I scan the page, which is a list of bulleted points.

### Trey's Tips for Letters of Resignation

- *Professionalism is key*

- *Be clear, concise, and, above all, confident*

- *Avoid emotionally charged phrases: I want, I must, I need, I feel*

- *Avoid doubtful phrases: I wish, I hope, I think, I fear*

- *Maintain a positive attitude*

- *If possible, word the letter in the third person*

- *Use the word "I" as infrequently as possible*

"What does it say?" Amanda asks, leaning over. I can smell the chocolate on her breath.

I hand her the piece of paper. "Third person?" I wonder aloud. "Is Trey kidding?"

Amanda laughs. "It'd sound bizarre, like people who talk about themselves in the third person. 'Amanda hates her job. Amanda is quitting. Amanda's boss is a pain in the ass!'"

"What?!" Craig screams, bursting through the door.

Sometimes I think he hangs around outside my office all day.

"Craig, I didn't mean it like that!" Her face is beet-red, and she looks to me for help.

"We're working on a job resignation letter for a client," I explain.

Craig's relief is visible.

"According to Trey, we're supposed to write it in the third person," I continue.

Craig nods, "That's basic business writing one-oh-one. You don't use *I*. But you don't have to stick to third person proper." He starts out the door, then stops. "Dani, I'm counting on you to give Amanda the tour of duty today."

*Tour of duty? This isn't a war zone.*

*Well, not on most days.*

"Will do," I promise.

Craig leaves, and I go back through the letter and clean it up, taking out some of the more emotionally charged phrases and cutting I's.

*Please accept this letter of resignation, effective immediately. Though brief, my time with Morgan Keegan has allowed for both personal and professional growth. At this stage, it is paramount to concentrate my efforts on obtaining an advanced business degree.*

I work diligently, addressing the three-months-on-the-job issue as best I can by placing emphasis on the importance of education. When I'm finished, I read the letter out loud. Amanda and I both agree that it does sound better. I print it out.

"Let's go," I say, rising from my desk. I place a copy of the resignation letter in a manila folder. "We've got a busy day ahead of us."

"Where are we going?" Amanda asks, hoisting herself up.

"To drop this off at Morgan Keegan," I say. "After that, I'm taking you to meet the biggest womanizer in all of Boston."

"The biggest womanizer in Boston?" She eats another Tootsie Roll. "Who's that?"

"His name's Evan Hirschbaum, and he's Your Big Break's number-one client."

"Number-one client, eh?" She raises an eyebrow. "This should be fun."

"Fun?" I repeat with a laugh. "Try baptism by fire."


"I thought I was going to meet a world-famous womanizer," Amanda gripes, shifting impatiently from one foot to the other.

"You are. But first I'm going to introduce you to an ex-girlfriend of his."

It's just past 11:30 a.m., and we're standing on the doorstep of Sophie Kennison's apartment building in Cambridge. "I live a few blocks from here," I muse, ringing the buzzer. "I didn't realize we were neighbors."

Amanda sighs. "I hope this doesn't take long. I'm hungry."

"You ate all those Tootsie Rolls," I point out.

"They're not *lunch*." She groans. "I need something more substantial."

I push the buzzer again. A weary voice calls, "Hello?"

"Sophie?"

Silence. Then, "Who's asking?"

"This is Danielle and Amanda from Your Big Break," I supply.

"And?"

"We'd like to come up and talk to you."

"No," she says sharply.

*Great, we're playing it this way.* I lean closer to the buzzer. "Sophie, it's really important that we see you."

"I'm busy."

"It will only take ten minutes," I try.

She pauses. "My apartment's a mess. I don't want any company."

"Why don't we go out for coffee?" I suggest. "Our treat." Technically, it's Evan's treat, since it'll be coming out of his retainer.

"I hate coffee."

"Soda?" I suggest.

"Not thirsty."

"You want to grab lunch?"

Amanda nods enthusiastically, but Sophie replies, "Not hungry."

"Picky, picky!" Amanda whispers in my ear, and I hope Sophie doesn't hear her.

"Is there anything you *are* in the mood for?" I ask, trying to hide my exasperation.

"Ice cream," she tells me. "I could go for some ice cream."

"Ice cream it is!" I say brightly.

"Let me throw on some clothes. I'll be down in five minutes." She clicks off.

Amanda nudges me. "I bet she's a porker. Who eats ice cream before noon?"

"Shhh! You shouldn't talk about people like that. Sophie is beautiful."

Amanda says coyly, "Beautiful as in big, beautiful woman?"

"Not even close. She probably weighs a hundred and five pounds soaking wet."

"Oh." Amanda seems genuinely disappointed. "Then why the ice cream?"

"Ice cream and chocolate are *the* biggest breakup comfort foods."

She smiles knowingly. "So, we're here to wallow?"

"Console. And convince."

"Convince?"

"We're going to convince her she's better off without Evan Hirschbaum."

"Exactly how do you plan to pull that off?" Amanda asks skeptically.

"Wait and see," I promise, winking slyly. Deep down, though, I'm starting to feel scared. Ever since the Gretchen fiasco, I've been feeling scared all the time. After Garrett dumped me last year, I was devastated. It took me so long to get to a place where I felt confident again. And now Gretchen has come along and crushed all of that.

When Sophie comes out a few minutes later, I'm taken aback by how gaunt she appears. Her skin is ghostly pale; her hair is limp; her eyes are framed by dark circles. Despite her promise to put on clothes, she appears to be wearing pajamas. She bears no resemblance to the stunning, vivacious sex kitten I broke up with two weeks ago. Back then, she looked like a model: strikingly tall, with huge, gray eyes, flawless flaxen skin, and white-blond hair. She looked exotic, Nordic. Today, she looks like a corpse. Or a college student in the middle of finals week, running on no sleep and propped up by coffee and junk food.

"There's a Ben and Jerry's around the corner," she says dully.

"Lead the way!"

We fall into step behind Sophie. "Did you have a nice vacation?"

"I was wondering about that. How did you know I went to Connecticut?" She stops dead in her tracks. "Did *he* tell you?"

*Uh-oh.* "No, your landlord did," I improvise.

"Nice try, but I don't have a landlord."

"Strike one," Amanda quips under her breath.

Sophie starts walking again. "It was Evan, wasn't it?" she asks.

"Yes, it was Evan," I admit.

"Well, I'm so *thrilled* Evan has time to talk to *you*!" She stops and puts her hands on her hips. "Because he's certainly made it a point of avoiding me," she shouts.

"Sophie, Evan's feelings have changed," I say gently. "He still cares about you, but he's got to focus on his career." This is

Evan's standard excuse. He insists that we use it. I don't know why. It never goes over well.

"Focus on his career," she scoffs. "Focus on some exotic dancer is more like it. Isn't that who he's dating this week?"

*That sounds about right.* "Evan's law practice is extremely important to him. He doesn't have time for a relationship."

She starts walking again. "But he has time for casual sex," she says.

We reach the Ben & Jerry's ice cream parlor and head inside.

"What are you having?" I ask, pulling out my wallet.

"Who's paying?" Sophie wants to know.

"I am."

"But *ultimately,* it's coming out of Evan's pocket, right?"

"Yup," Amanda pipes up. "Every cent."

"Maybe I'm hungrier than I thought." Sophie studies the menu. "I'll have two scoops of Cherry Garcia, three scoops of Phish Food, one scoop of Chubby Hubby, and one scoop of Chocolate Chip Cookie Dough. For here."

The acne-faced boy behind the counter bursts out laughing. "You serious, lady?"

"Lady? How old do I look to you?" she demands.

"Thirty-five?" he guesses.

She leans across the counter. "I am twenty-four! And I am not a lady, I'm a *girl*!"

I feel sorry for the clerk, and I understand his mistake. Ordinarily, Sophie looks her age, but today she's so run-down that even I would have pegged her for much older.

"You want the ice cream or not?" The counter boy isn't laughing anymore.

"Yes." She repeats her order. "Two scoops of Cherry Garcia, three scoops of Phish Food, one scoop of Chubby Hubby, and one scoop of Chocolate Chip Cookie Dough." I can't believe she remembered it.

"That's seven scoops, you know."

"I can add."

He smirks at her. "I'm going to put it in more than one container."

She stares him down. "I couldn't care less how it's prepared."

Amanda and I have been silently observing this exchange. We watch as the clerk fixes Sophie's massive ice cream order. When it's ready, he shoves a tray with all the containers at her.

"I'll snag us some seats," she says, trotting off with her enormous purchase. She stops in front of a small table in the corner and begins laying her cups of ice cream out in a circular formation. It looks ridiculous, as though she's ordered for a family of four.

Amanda settles on a vanilla shake, and I get a scoop of Cherry Garcia. Then I fish out my company Visa card and hand it over. I don't glance at the total. I'm not paying for it directly, but this feels extravagant, wrong.

We sit down across from Sophie, who is absentmindedly stirring a plastic spoon through her Chocolate Chip Cookie Dough. "I used to hate ice cream," she complains. "Evan was the one who turned me on to it. Of course, I wasn't the one doing the eating."

"I don't get it," Amanda says, slurping her shake.

I know where this is headed, but I'm powerless to stop it.

"Evan was an enthusiastic lover. He found very creative uses for ice cream."

"You mean, like, in bed?" Amanda asks, widening her eyes.

Sophie smiles coyly. "Evan and I used all kinds of foods during lovemaking: whipped cream, cantaloupe, strawberries, chocolate sauce . . ."

I wonder if Father uses these things with his mistress. *Don't go there. Do not go there. . . .*

Amanda is incredulous. "I didn't think people actually did that in real life."

"You've never mixed food with sex?" Sophie asks, looking surprised. "Never poured honey all over a lover's body, then licked it off?"

People are starting to stare. A young mother shoots us an angry glance as she yanks her son away from our table.

"No!"

"I guess I'm more adventurous than you."

"Speaking of being adventurous," I cut in, eager to change the subject, "did you have any fun adventures while you were visiting your parents?"

"In Connecticut?" she deadpans. "The trip sucked. Thanks for reminding me." Sophie gets up and tosses a half-eaten cup of ice cream into the trash.

"Strike two," Amanda whispers, *tsk tsk*ing me under her breath.

"What was so bad about your vacation?" I ask soothingly, as Sophie sits back down.

"All I did was mope around and think about Evan."

"That's the worst," Amanda butts in. "I hate when I can't get somebody out of my head."

"It's like I eat, breathe, and dream Evan." Sophie begins working on her three scoops of Phish Food. "When I was with him, life was perfect. It's so important that I win him back."

"Winning him back isn't an option," I say. "I know it's hard, Sophie, but you're going to have to let Evan go. You're going to have to move on."

"No can do," she says. "Evan loves me. He may not fully realize it yet, but he will."

"Don't you think that's a little—"

"I couldn't care less if you two think I'm pathetic! All that matters is that I win Evan back! I'll do it, too. Just watch me." She switches to Chubby Hubby.

"Sophie," I say in a very firm voice, "whatever you're thinking of won't work. Evan's made his decision. Trust me, I've known him a while. Once he makes up his mind, that's it."

She doesn't seem concerned. "I'm not above throwing myself at someone."

Amanda's jaw drops. "Why would you want to do that?"

"Because I love him."

I blurt, "But what about your dignity?"

"Dignity!" She laughs. "What dignity? I sold that down the river the day I met Evan. He's a jerk, a liar, and a cheat! I thought our relationship was real, and he treated it like a joke."

"If you think he's such a jerk, then why are you making a play to win him back?" Amanda points out, logically. I've gotta hand it to her—abrasive or not, she learns quickly.

"I'm in love with him, and you can't pick who you love."

She's right there. "You need to focus on the bad stuff Evan made you put up with," I say. "Then you won't want him."

"I'll always want him," Sophie says defiantly. "He's the biggest catch I've ever landed."

I pat her hand reassuringly. "You're drop-dead gorgeous. You'll meet someone else in no time."

"I don't want someone else; I want Evan!" she wails.

"Come on, he isn't *that* special," Amanda argues.

"He is! He always knows the exact right thing to say at the right time."

I think of Jason Dutwiler, who seems to have the opposite talent.

"Evan reels you in with compliments, then tosses you out when he gets bored."

Sophie's pretty much summed Evan up. "And you should remember those compliments, but forget the man." I eat a bite of Cherry Garcia. "You're a bright, energetic woman. You've got so much to offer."

"And no one to offer it to," she responds sadly.

We sit there in silence for a moment. "What can I do to make this easier on you?" I ask. "Is there anything you need? Someone to help clean your apartment, do your laundry?"

"I'm a big girl," she says sarcastically.

"If you keep eating all that ice cream, you will be," Amanda mutters under her breath. Fortunately, Sophie doesn't hear her.

"I can take care of myself," Sophie continues. She discards the Phish Food and Chubby Hubby, and begins nibbling from her container of Cherry Garcia.

"Okay, then how about a girlfriend to talk to, someone to unload on?" I suggest.

"I don't have any girlfriends. Women never like me."

"Well, Amanda and I both like you," I vow. I'm afraid Amanda's going to say something to the contrary, but, mercifully, she doesn't. "Consider *us* your new girlfriends. We're here when you need us, day or night."

Sophie reaches out and squeezes both of our hands. "I could use someone to help me move a few boxes to my place a week from Sunday. I got this apartment last month and haven't had time to transfer everything out of storage yet."

"I'm happy to help," I chime in. Amanda doesn't volunteer her services.

"Thanks, guys," she says, dropping our hands. "Or should I say gals?"

"You're welcome. It's no problem. But I need you to do one thing for me."

"Anything."

"For one week, I want you to have no contact with Evan. That means no phone calls, e-mails, or texts."

She shakes her head. "I can't do that."

"I'm only asking for a week." I look her straight in the eyes, showing that I mean business.

Sophie starts to tear up. "Why are you being so *mean*?"

"I'm not being mean. I'm asking you for a friendly favor. One week." Ideally, I'd like to get her to agree to two, but I figure it's best to start small. Sometimes the only way to help people is to wean them off their former lover one day at a time.

"All right," she says sadly. "You win. I'll try to leave Evan alone for a week. No promises, but I'll do my best."

I smile. "That's all I ask."

"Ice cream goes straight to my ass," Sophie declares, throwing her spoon down on the table. "You know what Evan used to say? He told me my ass should be declared a national treasure."

I suppress a laugh. Amanda's not so tactful. "I can't believe you bought a line like that!"

Sophie jumps up from the table. "Shut up!" she says. "It wasn't a line."

"Amanda didn't mean it like that." I want to throttle her.

"Oh, I'll bet she did. You know what, now I get it." Sophie narrows her eyes. "I can't believe I didn't see it from the start. You come in here, pretending to be my friends, when really, the two of you are jealous. You're probably both head over heels for

Evan, and that's why you're doing everything in your power to keep us apart!"

"Sophie, that's not true at all," I interrupt. "We're only trying to help."

"Yeah, help yourselves to Evan!"

"Sophie, I—"

"Leave me alone!" She whirls around and stalks out the door before I can stop her.

"Strike three," Amanda says, watching her go. "You're out."

# 15

## STAGE THREE OF BREAKUP HELL:
### *Rebounding*

In a misguided attempt to move on, the dumpee takes a flying
leap back into the dating pool. This phase includes blind dates,
casual hookups, and frequent visits to singles' hotspots.

"That meeting with Sophie was a total bust," Amanda says as
we walk into the lobby of Hirschbaum, Davis, and Klein thirty
minutes later. "In more ways than one." She squishes her boobs
together in an imitation of Sophie's.

"Par for the course," I tell Amanda, smoothing a wrinkle out
of my sleeve. I'm shaken, but I don't want Amanda to see that. I
want to keep up a strong front, show her that I'm still in control
of the situation. I knew it wouldn't be easy to persuade Sophie to
fall out of love with Evan, but I had been really eager to make
some inroads today. I was hoping that by the time we got to
Evan's office, I'd have some great news. We appear to have had
the opposite effect.

"I take it this guy's rich," Amanda says, "since he gets so
many women." Her eyes scan the law firm's impressive waiting
area.

"Rich as hell—a trust-fund baby turned high-paid lawyer."

We approach the front desk; the same receptionist from the other day is on duty, and I inform her that we're here to see Evan. She tells us to "go on back" and buzzes us in.

"What's the purpose of this meeting?" Amanda asks as we head down the hall.

"Evan's our number-one client; Sophie's become a thorn in his side, and I intend to take care of it."

"Take care of it how? She's going to keep harassing Evan until kingdom come."

"Not if I can help it."

"Good luck," Amanda says. "If you ask me, this is a losing battle."

"Don't give up so easily," I say. "We just need to approach this from a different angle."

"Like what?"

"That's what we're here to find out today. I'd hoped to have this settled before we came to Evan's office, but since we don't, I'm going to have to come clean with him. It's time to rethink the Sophie situation." I knock on Evan's door.

"Come in, come in," he beckons. "Who's this?" he asks upon seeing Amanda.

"Mr. Hirschbaum, I'd like you to meet Your Big Break's newest member, Amanda."

"You look young," he says, sizing her up.

"I'm twenty-two."

"Amanda's a senior at Boston University," I fill in.

He seems interested. "I used to date a girl over there."

"A professor?" Amanda asks. I want to kick her. Evan does not date professors. He dates nineteen-year-old coeds.

Evan cracks a small smile. "She was a drama major. Or was it dance? I don't remember. Anyway, Dani, give me an update. I've got precisely ten minutes."

I quickly bring him up to speed. "I apologize in advance, but you may still receive a few phone calls and e-mails until I can get this worked out."

"And when, exactly, do you plan to have it 'worked out'?"

"Soon. I've given this a lot of thought and I think we need a new strategy, something I could use to reach Sophie, to convince her to move on."

"You want to exploit a weakness," he says, nodding. He leans back in his chair and surveys us.

Put that way, it sounds brutal. "Right. Are there any things you and Sophie really disagreed on? Stuff I could use to make her see why this relationship wasn't meant to work out?"

Evan picks up a pen and taps it against his desk. "Sophie's somewhat of a purist. She doesn't drink, doesn't smoke, won't even take an aspirin when her head hurts. And she's dead set against recreational pharmaceuticals."

"You mean drugs," Amanda supplies.

"Right. And that's a big problem for me."

My eyes widen. Is he confessing an addiction?

"I'm not an addict," Evan says, as if reading my mind. "But I do enjoy fine wines and cigars. I need a woman who shares those loves."

I can feel the wheels turning. "I can work with this," I tell him, rising. "Thanks for your time."

We've just made it out into the hall when he stops me. "Dani, can I talk to you alone for a minute?"

Amanda gives me a little nudge. "I can find my own way out." She trots off toward the waiting room.

I step back into Evan's office. "Yes?"

"We need to arrange that lunch. I'm going out of town for a few days. But as soon as I come back, we should get together."

*Oh, shit.* It looks like I'm going to have to face this head-on. "Evan, may I call you Evan?"

"You know you may."

I bite my lip, summoning up my courage. Then I blurt it out in one rush: "As flattered as I am that you want to go out with me, I don't think it's a good idea."

The look on his face is one of pure shock. Then it turns to amusement. "You thought I was asking you out?" I nod. "Dani, you're not my type." He tips his head back and laughs. "No offense."

I blush. "None taken."

"Good. Now that we've cleared that up, when do you want to have lunch?"

I'm confused. "I thought you weren't asking me out?"

"I'm not." He heaves a sigh, then raises his eyebrows for emphasis. I lean back against the doorframe, inching my way out.

"I don't get it."

"I'm going to tell you something very personal, so I'd appreciate you not repeat it."

"Of course. You have total confidentiality." *Unless you tell me you want to tie me up and whip me. In which case, I'm filing a sexual harassment suit.*

"I don't have any sisters. My mother left when I was seven. I've never had any female friends. Other than dating, I associate with very few women."

"I follow," I lie. I have no idea where this is going.

"Lately, I've come to realize how little I understand women, and that's something I'd like to change. I've honestly never had a nonsexual relationship with a woman. I think it might be fun to have a female friend."

I stare at him blankly. "And you picked *me*?"

"I picked you."

"Why?"

"I'll be frank—I'm not good at seeing women for who they are as people. I tend to focus on how I can get them into bed."

I suppress the urge to gag.

"With you, there's no attraction on my end. I'm able to view you as a person, not a bed partner. That's why I'd like us to be friends. I know there's zero risk of it becoming romantic."

He's just told me I'm too ugly to sleep with. Talk about a giant slap in the face.

"Well, thanks, sir." I feel like an utter fool.

"So get back to me about that lunch date," Evan says as I try to make a clean exit.

"Definitely," I say, escaping down the hall. As soon as he's out of earshot, I add, "When hell freezes over."


"I wish he were dead."

"No you don't," Krista says, giving me a quick hug. "You're just angry."

"I never want to see my father again so long as I live."

I *should* be over at my parents' house, eating crawfish. But our Thursday family dinner is off, so I've invited Krista over to cheer me up. After the disastrous meeting with Sophie, and the huge embarrassment with Evan, I need the company.

"What your father is doing is awful," Krista says. "But is it truly unforgivable?"

"I don't know," I hedge, sitting down on a kitchen stool and crossing my legs. "That depends. We still don't know the extent of it, how long he's been cheating, if it's just Gretchen or if there are other women."

Krista sits down beside me. "Are you going to confront your dad?"

*"Father,"* I correct. "Not yet. Sean's going to do a little more digging, see what he can find out. Once we've got enough evidence to nail the bastard, we're going straight to Mom."

Krista's eyes widen. " 'Nail the bastard'? You sound like a TV detective."

"It's Sean. He's watched so much *CSI*, he thinks he's a crime scene investigator. It's starting to rub off on me."

"Your brother's too much. I forget he's twenty-five. He seems like a sixteen-year-old."

I run my fingers through my shoulder-length blonde hair, smoothing it into place. "You know how men are. They mature at half the rate of women."

"Let's get some food," she says.

"What are you in the mood for? Pizza, Thai, or Indian?"

"Indian." She picks up the menu and glances through it. "I'll take this Korma chicken curry meal. And do you want to split some garlic naan bread?"

"Sounds good." I pick up the phone and call in our order.

"So, how have you been dealing?" Krista asks softly. "I know this has been hard on you."

Hard doesn't begin to describe it. "I feel like I'm in a holding pattern," I tell her. "I feel stuck, like my world is about to end but I don't know when or why." I feel like Brady Simms, I realize.

"It's rough, I know."

"First Garrett, and now my father. I just don't know how I

can ever trust a man again." I get out two bottled waters and pass one to Krista.

"All men aren't like that," Krista says.

I ignore her. "It's the cheating that bothers me. Doesn't anyone value commitment anymore?"

"Of course they do."

"I mean, I think about all of my dumpees. Take Jason Dutwiler, for instance. He'd give anything to have a woman who loves him. But the poor guy keeps getting dumped. And he's such a nice person, to boot!"

Krista looks interested. "Jason who?"

"Jason Dutwiler," I repeat.

"And you said he's nice?"

*Uh-oh. I can see where this is going.* "He's not your type."

She looks surprised. "Since when is 'nice' not my type? I'm hardly the kind to chase after bad boys. So, is this Jason Dutwiler guy free?"

"He's free. Of course, he's also—"

"A serial killer? A leper?" she asks, raising an eyebrow.

"I was going to say 'kind of obsessive.' "

"Obsessive? How?"

I sip my water. "I don't know. I'm just going on what his ex-girlfriend told me."

Krista waves her hand dismissively. "You can't trust *her*. She's biased." She leans against the kitchen counter and smiles. "Jason Dutwiler," she repeats, running her fingers through her hair. "What does he look like?"

"Boyishly cute," I supply.

"Height? Build? Hair check?"

"Hair check?" I repeat, blinking.

"Full head of hair? Balding?"

I laugh. "He's got a full head of brown hair."

She nods approvingly.

"Jason's pretty cute. He's about five-eight," I say.

"Short guys are not a problem." Krista interjects. Krista's barely five feet tall.

"Medium build," I continue. "I think he played soccer in college."

She twists her hair into a ponytail at the back of her neck. "Sounds good. Give him my number."

*Oh, brother.* "I was *kidding.* I couldn't set you up with him."

"Why not?"

"It's against Your Big Break's policy."

She fiddles with her earrings, taking them off and sliding them back on.

A delivery guy arrives with our Indian food. I bring the piping-hot containers into the kitchen and set them down on the counter. "Come on, Dani," Krista says, pulling two plates out of the cupboard. "I could take the poor guy out, cheer him up."

"I'm not sure it would work." I get out knives and forks.

"Please." She bats her eyelashes playfully.

"Well, Jason *does* need a date for his brother's wedding." I don't mention that he wants to take Lucy. *Krista's cute; maybe it could work.*

"See, that's perfect. I love weddings!" She leans back against the fridge, her eyes glazing over. "They're so romantic."

I remember my promise to Craig. I swore I would stop meddling in our clients' lives. I swore I'd take Your Big Break Inc.'s cardinal rule more seriously: *Do not get personally involved.* But part of our job is to help people get over a breakup. Going on a date with Krista could really make Jason feel better. . . . I mull it over. *Maybe setting them up isn't such a bad idea. I can kill two birds with one stone: find Jason a date for his brother's wedding and find Krista a potential boyfriend. Who knows? It might work out. And it would be a great way for me to throw myself into my work again.* "I'll call Jason tomorrow," I say. "See if he's interested." I spoon rice onto my plate.

"Call him tonight." she prompts, clasping her hands together in a begging motion.

"It's after business hours."

"Great!" she says. "Then you'll probably catch him at home."

"All right, I'll call him." I heave a sigh and reach for my cordless. I dig Jason's number out of my purse. "But don't get your hopes up too high. He's still pretty hung up on his ex-girlfriend."

"I can take care of that," she says, tearing off a piece of naan bread and popping it into her mouth. "By the time I'm finished, Jason won't even remember her name."

I pick up the phone and dial his cell phone, pressing *67 to block my number from appearing on caller ID. He answers on the first ring.

"Can I speak to Jason Dutwiler?"

"Dani?" he says excitedly. "Any news on Lucy? Has she changed her mind about the wedding?"

"No, I'm afraid she hasn't." I take the plunge. "But I may have a solution. There's a girl I'd like you to meet. . . ."

# 16

It's time to launch Operation Dump Brady Simms.

All the key pieces are in place. I've got to drop everything in the mail today to ensure that it will arrive by this Thursday. I assembled his Breakup Recovery Kit over the weekend, and it's pretty nice. There's a mix CD, which includes a variety of songs downloaded from iTunes, a dark brown poetry journal, and a stash of stuff from Blockbuster. Sean really hooked me up—in addition to a stack of free rental coupons, he gave me a couple of boxes of microwave popcorn and a DVD of *Tomb Raider* that was "damaged during shipping." I wanted to include a card, but the greeting-card industry is seriously behind the times when it comes to cards meant specifically for getting over a breakup. The closest I've seen are sympathy cards, so I had to make one myself. I designed Brady a card in Quark. I used a clip-art drawing of a broken heart on the cover and included a poem inside:

*Roses are red*
*Violets are blue*
*Love really sucks*
*And Erin does, too*

I'm in major violation of Your Big Break Inc.'s rule #4: *You are an impartial observer*. But whatever. Erin does suck. Besides, it's not like Craig will ever find out what I wrote. At least, he probably won't. For added effect, I picked up a couple of scratch-off lottery tickets and stuffed them inside the card, along with this message: *Here's hoping your luck improves. Dani M., Your Big Break Inc.* Then I boxed up everything and wrote Brady's name and address on the front in bright purple marker.

All that's left to do is write him a Dear John letter.

I still have a copy of the original letter I wrote, the one I was going to give him that night at Barnes & Noble. I pull it up on my computer and reread it. It's not bad, but it lacks a certain amount of heart. I toil with it for nearly forty-five minutes, cutting and pasting, rewriting, rearranging. Finally, I hit print and read my efforts:

*Dear Brady,*

*This is one of the hardest letters I've ever had to write. I don't know where to begin, what to say. I guess I'll start with the truth. For a while now, things haven't been right between us. I know you've felt it, too.*

*Our conversations are strained, our times together awkward. I've done a lot of soul-searching, and I think the sad truth is that we just aren't compatible anymore. People change, and because they don't change together, they drift. The two years I had with you were among the best in my life, but I feel our relationship has run its course. Our lives are on different paths now. I think it's time we both move on.*

*I want you to know that I'll always love you. And maybe, someday in the future, we can be friends. But for now it's best if we go our separate ways. I'll be thinking of you often, but we probably shouldn't talk for a while. I need this time to get over you.*

*Sincerely,*

*Erin Foster-Ellis*

*P.S. Attached you will find a list of items I've left in your possession. Please return these to Danielle M. at Your Big Break Inc. Additionally, you're advised to contact Danielle M. with any questions or concerns.*

Unless the client requests otherwise, I always tuck a copy of my business card inside Dear John letters, along with a short cover letter explaining that Your Big Break Inc. will serve as a liaison between the dumper and the dumpee. I encourage people to call me when they have questions and concerns, to keep them from calling their ex. Sometimes this works (Jason Dutwiler); sometimes it doesn't (Sophie Kennison).

Every now and then, you meet a client who requests ambiguity. They don't want their ex to find out they hired Your Big Break Inc., so I ghostwrite the letter and deliver it to the client, who will in turn send it to the dumpee; job resignations are typically done this way.

I print out a clean copy of Brady's breakup letter, paper-clip one of my business cards to the top, and stick it in an envelope. I've just written his address on the front when it hits me: I can't send this. If I do, he'll think back to that night at Barnes & Noble when I introduced myself as a friend of Erin's. Once he learns I work for Your Big Break Inc., he'll put two and two together and realize I came to the poetry workshop that night to dump him. He'll realize Erin's been planning this for a while. It would completely defeat the purpose of having had her wait these two weeks to do the dumping.

I'll have to do this anonymously.

I rip the envelope in half and toss it in the trash. I go back to work on the letter, cutting out the P.S. I ask him to mail Erin's stuff back, rather than give it to communications specialist Dani M. Then I dig through my desk drawer and find a plain white envelope—the one I used before had our bright-red Your Big Break Inc. logo in the corner.

I also realize that I can't send him the Breakup Recovery Kit. Then I decide to mail it anonymously, in care of his school. With any luck, he'll think some cute single mom sent it over. I print out a new copy of the sympathy card and rewrite my greeting: *Here's hoping your luck improves. Signed, A Friend.*

I put a stamp on the letter to Brady and deposit it in the mailbox outside our building. I feel kind of guilty—Erin paid me to stop by Brady's and pick up her stuff in person. It's what I promised to do during our initial consultation. It seems kind of chintzy, just sending this letter and then doing no more. Then again, Erin was originally supposed to give me $110. She bargained the price down to thirty-five bucks.

You get what you pay for.


The storage facility is stifling hot and smells of mildew. "How long have you had your stuff in here?" I ask, wrinkling my nose.

Sophie doesn't answer. It's obvious she's still mad. After the disastrous ice cream outing, she doesn't trust me. But I'm here, just like I said I would be, giving up my Sunday afternoon to help her move boxes. We load up our cars and then I follow her back to Cambridge. I'm lucky to find a metered space in front of her building. I park and get out of the car.

"You can leave my stuff on the sidewalk if you want," Sophie says, coming up beside me. "I can take it from here."

"Don't be silly. I'll help you carry it upstairs."

She gives me a small smile. "Thanks."

It takes us nearly thirty minutes to move everything. We make trip after trip, carting boxes up the narrow stairwell to her apartment on the third floor. By the time we finish, I'm panting and drenched with sweat. The weather's unseasonably hot, made worse by the lack of ventilation in her apartment building.

Sophie and I lug the last of the boxes into her bedroom and plunk them down on the hardwood floor. I wipe the sweat off my brow. "What have you got in here? Rocks?"

"Books," she says.

"Nine boxes full?"

She nods. "A lot of them are left over from college. I was a lit major before I dropped out." She opens one of the boxes and begins pulling out texts, stacking them in a pile beside the bed. I'm amazed at her collection: Keats, T. S. Eliot, Oscar Wilde, Shakespeare, Hemingway, Thoreau.

"Have you read all these?" I ask, crouching down to sort through the pile.

"Most of them," she says. "We studied them in class. But I read a lot on my own, too."

Her modern books are just as impressive. I lift up a paperback copy of David Foster Wallace's *Infinite Jest*. "You've read *Infinite Jest*?" I ask, shocked.

"Off and on. I never finished it. I finally gave up on page seven hundred and something." She looks embarrassed.

"Don't sweat it. I think most people give up at page ten."

Sophie laughs. "I used to be an obsessive reader, but I don't have time anymore."

I lean back on my heels and stare at her. "Why did you drop out of school?"

"It didn't fit with my long-term career goal."

"Which is?"

"To be a dancer."

"Ballet?" I guess. She's certainly thin enough.

"Backup," she says. "I'd like to tour with Britney Spears or Madonna."

I eye her quizzically. "That's your life's dream?"

She stretches her arms above her head and twirls around gracefully. "Yes, but I'm probably too old to do it now."

"You're twenty-four!"

Sophie stops twirling. She sits down on the floor and stretches out her long, slender legs. "Dancing's like modeling. You're over the hill by the time you hit twenty-five."

I study her. "You've certainly still got the body for it."

"Thanks." She smiles sadly. "Evan used to say the exact same thing."

"So, if you weren't dancing, what would you do?"

"My secret dream is to own a bookstore." She grins. "That's pretty far-fetched. I've got a better chance of dancing for Janet Jackson."

"If it's what you really want to do, you should go for it. Go back to school and take some business courses."

"Maybe."

Sophie looks uncomfortable, so I change the subject. "How

have you been handling things? Have you kept up with our no-calls bargain?" I ask.

She nods. "Yes. Don't ask me how I've done it. I'm not even sure myself. But I haven't contacted Evan at all. Well, except for one little call to his office. But I hung up when he got on the line." She sighs. "I don't have any vices. It sucks sometimes." She flips through a book of Edwin Arlington Robinson's poems. "I don't crave drugs or cigarettes or anything like that. But it leaves me so few options."

This sounds like the perfect opening to work in the ammunition that Evan gave me. "You say that like it's a bad thing."

"I didn't used to think so, but now I'm not sure. If I had a weakness, then I could succumb to it in times of crisis. I could prop myself up with it, use it to get me through. Instead, I fall apart. I go crazy. I obsess about people and things—like with Evan."

I'm taken by how remarkably self-aware she is. I'm starting to think she is far smarter than people probably give her credit for. "You two were together for a month, right?"

"Five weeks," she confirms. "I guess I was his Miss April."

"Have you ever heard the breakup rule?" I ask. "That it takes one month to recover for every year you were together?"

She tucks her legs up to her chest and wraps her arms around them. "It takes me a year to recover from one month! I always have these brief, passionate affairs, and then I spend months agonizing over what went wrong."

I can't help smiling. "Same here."

"I don't know how people bounce back so quickly. I've never been like that."

"Me neither."

We sit there in silence for a moment, and then Sophie says,

"I know it's stupid to obsess over Evan." She hangs her head. "I want to move on, but I don't know how."

"I think I know a way to help you," I say. An idea's been forming in the back of my head for a while now, ever since we started going through Sophie's boxes.

"What?" She looks skeptical.

"How would you feel about a blind date?"

"Blind dates are for losers." She groans. "Everybody knows that."

"Not necessarily. I think I have a guy that will blow Evan out of the water." Sophie begins flipping through a book of essays. I can see her interest waning. "I know this guy named Brady. He's a lawyer turned high-school English teacher. He's well-read, and he's into poetry and writing."

She drops the book. "Okay, you've got my attention."

"Brady's new to the singles scene," I go on. *So new, in fact, he doesn't yet know it.* "He just got out of a long-term relationship."

She makes a face. "Sloppy seconds."

"It's perfect timing! You're newly single, he's newly single."

"I'll be catching him on the rebound."

"In this case, is that a bad thing?"

Sophie considers it. "I see what you mean. I'm not really in the market for something serious. Just a distraction, someone to take me out to dinner."

"And Brady can do that! No strings attached, just two people enjoying each other's company, helping each other through a rough time."

She smiles. "We can rebound *together*."

Part of me feels funny about setting them up. Jealous, almost. I try to picture Brady and Sophie together, and it makes me sad.

I push the feeling away. *I can do this. She's just a rebound girl. What do I care who Brady Simms dates? He obviously likes only drop-dead-gorgeous women like Erin Foster-Ellis. Sophie Kennison is in the same league. This is meant to be.*

We brainstorm for twenty minutes, coming up with a plan. We decide that on Friday, Sophie will pay an impromptu visit to Addington Academy, the school where Brady works. She'll show up around lunchtime, bearing a picnic basket full of treats.

"I'll tell him I'm a secret admirer," she says. "We'll eat lunch together, enjoy each other's company. Who knows where it will lead."

*Good places, I'm sure. What man could resist Sophie Kennison? It can't miss.*

# 17

# This Hurts Me As Much As It Hurts You

"What's this I hear about you turning away potential clients?" Craig demands, catching me as I come into the office the next morning.

I feign ignorance. "I don't know what you're talking about."

"Does the name Gretchen Monaghan ring any bells?"

I don't say anything for a minute. Then I mumble, "I had a consultation with her a few weeks ago."

"That's what I thought." Craig narrows his eyes. "You want to explain yourself here, Dani? Because I got a call from Ms. Monaghan early this morning. She wanted to know if our client load had eased up any, if we had enough 'free manpower' to take her case."

"What did you tell her?" I ask, staring down at my shoes.

"I told her you'd be more than happy to take her case."

I squeeze me eyes shut. "I can't do it, Craig."

"Why not?" he demands. "Is the boyfriend a rageaholic ex-con?"

"No, he's my father."

Craig bursts out laughing. "Good one, Dani. Don't play."

"I'm not playing. Gretchen wants to hire us to break up with *my father*."

He looks utterly perplexed. "I thought your parents were married."

"Craig, my father's having an affair!" I burst out. *Is he really this slow to catch on?*

"Morning!" Amanda comes sauntering in. Halfway to her desk, she turns and asks, "What's wrong with you guys?"

We must look pretty ridiculous. Craig's standing there, mouth agape, and I'm teetering, my lower lip quivering. "Dani's just told me a really funny story," Craig covers. His face is so red, it blots out his freckles.

"I love funny stories!" Amanda prances over to us.

"It's kind of personal," I explain.

"I don't mind."

I can't tell if she's too dumb to take a hint or just plain nosy. "I'd rather not talk about it."

"Talking about it might be the best medicine."

Craig recovers from his momentary stupor. "The time for talking's done. Back to work, peeps. Chop, chop!" he says, making a beeline for his office.

I head to my own office. I've just plopped down at my desk when an IM pops up on my computer screen.

**Bossman:** Sorry 'bout earlier. Didn't mean to bust your chops.

*Bossman? Craig's IM name is Bossman?* I quickly type a response.

**DaniM:** no problem. it's a nutty situation.

**Bossman:** Tell me about it. At first, I thought you were flodging.

**DaniM:** flodging?

**Bossman:** It means lying.

**DaniM:** oh. well, i'm not flodging. i'm telling the truth.

**Bossman:** That blows, Big D. My heart goes out to your family unit.

**DaniM:** thanks

**Bossman:** If you don't object, I'm gonna give the case to my main man, Trey.

*Object? I guess I don't object. . . .*

**Bossman:** Hate to lose the business.

**DaniM:** i understand.

**Bossman:** Thanks, Big D. You're Kool with a capital K.

He signs offline.

I didn't think it was possible, but Craig comes across even dorkier online than in person. I thought the Internet was supposed to have the opposite effect, making nerds into studs, losers into winners.

I don't dwell on this point too long. The real issue at hand is this: Your Big Break Inc. will be taking Gretchen's case after all. That means Father's about to get a Dear Paul letter, which might not be such a bad thing. At least their relationship will be over. But it's only a matter of time until he finds someone new. It's like that old saying: *Cheaters never change*. Or is it *Cheaters never win*?

Either way, the bottom line's the same.

My father's an adulterer. Always was, always will be.

Before I leave work, I place a quick follow-up call to Erin Foster-Ellis.

"Erin? It's Dani from Your Big Break," I say. "I was calling to see if you were satisfied with our job performance."

"Yes," she says simply, "I'm very satisfied."

"And you haven't had any troubles? Brady hasn't been contacting you?"

"No. It's a bit surprising." She's quiet for a minute. "I anticipated he wouldn't be able to *stop* calling me. But he's been oddly silent."

*What if he never got the letter?* "Did you receive your personal items?" I ask nervously.

"I did, thanks," Erin says. "They arrived this morning via FedEx."

"Great!" *Whew! That means Brady did receive his Dear John letter.* And since he sent Erin's stuff back without a fuss, and hasn't bothered calling her, I'd say he got the message loud and clear. I can forget about this case and move on. "Well, let me know if you have any problems."

"Oh, I will," Erin says. "First sign of trouble, I'll call you. Believe me."

# 18

**YBB INC. EMPLOYEE RULE #5**

Do *not* get personally involved. This is the **cardinal rule** and must be followed **above all others**!

"Sit! Stay!" I lurch forward. "No! Bad boy!"

It's Wednesday morning, and I'm being dragged down Boylston Street by an enormous Old English sheepdog named, quite appropriately, Magnus.

"Heel, Magnus! Heel! *Stay!*" I'm shouting out every dog command I can think of in an attempt to slow him down. Nothing's working. "Roll over!" I shriek helplessly. "Play dead!" He stops briefly, then takes off running again at top speed. "Down, boy!" I cling furiously to his leash, cursing myself for wearing my Coach pumps with two-inch heels. *Why didn't I put on flats this morning or, better yet, tennis shoes?*

He comes to an abrupt stop next to a red mailbox, squats, and . . . "*Magnuuuus*, no!"

I pull a plastic Baggie out of my tote and scoop up dog poop.

It's been a crazy day. I drove out to Norwood at the crack of dawn to pick up Magnus at his owner's ex-girlfriend's house.

"Take the filthy beast," the ex had said, showing me to the back-yard. "I never wanted him living here in the first place." Then she broke into sobs. I find "pet retrieval" one of our most difficult ser-vices. Magnus spent the twenty-five-minute drive back to Boston with his runny nose pressed up against the window in the backseat of my car. I wonder if he was watching for the ex-girlfriend.

I'm scheduled to meet Magnus's owner in front of Au Bon Pain at eight o'clock. I drop the soiled Baggie in a garbage bin and continue down Boylston. I tug on Magnus's leash, trying to get him to turn the corner. It's no use. We head across the street and go sailing past the turnoff for Au Bon Pain at a dead run. "Dani?" I hear someone yell. "Hey, wait up!"

I look over to see Brady Simms jogging along beside me.

Mercifully, Magnus stops right in front of the entrance to the Four Seasons. I struggle to catch my breath. Magnus sighs loudly and then hangs his head in gloom. "Poor baby," I say, massaging his ears. Sometimes pets have just as hard a time dealing with a breakup as their owners do.

Brady leans down to rub Magnus's head. "It's weird running into you like this. How've you been?"

"Good," I tell him, then want to smack myself. He's in the middle of a trauma. The last thing he wants to hear is how great I feel. "What are you doing in this neck of the woods?"

"My school—Addington Academy—is right around the corner."

"I see." We stand there awkwardly on the sidewalk, watching the guests move in and out of the Four Seasons Hotel. "I guess you heard about me and Erin. . . ." he says, his voice trailing off.

"I heard." *I wrote the letter and sent the Breakup Recovery Kit.* "I'm sorry."

He gives me a sad smile and I feel awful, as if it were me who broke his heart.

"On some level, I saw it coming," he admits.

Magnus sneezes loudly. "His nose has been running all morning. You wouldn't by chance have a Kleenex?"

Brady shakes his head and laughs. "I take it he's not your dog?"

"How'd you know?"

"Lucky guess." Brady continues to pet Magnus. "And it's a pretty safe bet you're not a professional dog walker, either."

"Is it that obvious?" I joke.

"Kind of." He stands up and looks at me. "Where'd you get the pooch?"

"He belongs to a . . . friend." I don't mention that the "friend" is a client.

"Do you need some help with him?"

"The friend?" I ask, startled.

Brady laughs. "No, the dog."

"I think I can manage, thanks." As if on cue, Magnus plops down on the sidewalk and makes himself comfortable. "Come on, boy, let's go." I tug at his leash, but he doesn't budge. The valet at the Four Seasons gives me an exasperated stare. "I've got to drop him off in front of Au Bon Pain"—I check my watch— "five minutes ago!"

"I have a way with animals," Brady says, winking. "I bet I can make him get up."

"That's a bet you'd lose. Magnus is cute," I tease, "but he's got a mind of his own."

"Sounds like someone else I know," Brady says. "The first part, anyway."

*Did Brady just call me cute?* I'm about to respond with something equally flirty, but Magnus chooses that exact moment to pass gas. Loudly.

I groan, moving away from the smell. "I'm sorry. This is so embarrassing."

"Don't be embarrassed," Brady says, smiling. "I grew up around dogs. Trust me, I've smelled worse. At least he didn't do it in your car."

"Good point." I laugh. "So, as you were saying before Magnus interrupted . . ."

"Ah, yes. We were negotiating a bet." Brady thinks it over. "How about the loser treats the winner to the Starbucks beverage of their choice? Might be a good chance to get to know each other."

"No!" I shriek. "I mean, no on the Starbucks, not the getting to know each other part."

"You hate coffee?"

"Something like that." I laugh. "Why don't we go somewhere else?"

"Okay. How about lunch, then?"

"Deal," I agree. He extends his hand and we shake on it.

Brady crouches down next to Magnus. "All right, boy, I need your help here." He scratches him behind the ears and takes hold of his leash. "Make me look good. Come on, Magnus!" The dog doesn't budge.

"Once he takes off, there's no stopping him," I caution.

"I noticed he was pulling you along pretty fast."

I laugh. "You'd have to be an Olympic track-and-field medalist to keep up with this dog."

"So you're not an Olympic runner and you're not a dog walker. What *do* you do for a living?"

When you have a lie already in place, it's easy to reach for it. "I write promotional copy for websites."

He stands up. "I thought Web designers died out with the Internet bust?"

I feel my face go red. "We're an endangered species, that's for sure."

"Speaking of species . . ." Brady reaches his arms around Magnus's midsection and attempts to lift him up again. It doesn't work.

"Ready to admit defeat?" I ask.

Brady nods. "Want to grab a quick breakfast?"

I glance at my watch and see that now it's ten past eight. "I'm really late. I was supposed to drop Magnus off ten minutes ago. I'd better call my friend and ask him to meet me here." I fish in my purse for my cell phone.

"No problem," Brady says. "I'm due at school soon myself. Why don't you give me your e-mail and I'll drop you a line this weekend?"

I'm not allowed to date clients. That's in definite violation of Your Big Break Inc.'s rule #5. Even if it weren't, Brady Simms is off-limits. He's Sophie Kennison's rebound guy. At least, he will be after this Friday. "Sure," I say, whipping out a pen and a piece of scrap paper. I can't give him my work addy, since it's registered to Your Big Break Inc.'s domain. I scrawl out my other e-mail address—DaniMyers@yahoo.com—and hand over the piece of paper. Now I've given him my last name, which breaks Your Big Break Inc.'s rule #2. *Oops.*

"Great! I'll e-mail you this week and we can get together."

"Bye, Brady." I smile, and he heads off down the street.

"We've gotta move quickly," Sean says when I call him that evening. "There's no telling what Dad will do when Gretchen dumps him. Whatever happens, we've got to be prepared. I don't want Mom caving in and staying with that creep. She's too good for him."

It's a harsh statement, but I've got to say I agree. "Have you finished your so-called investigation?" I ask.

"I'm close." Sean lowers his voice conspiratorially. "There are a lot of encrypted files on Dad's computer. Here's what I've found out so far: Dad placed a personal ad on Match.com last November. Between November and January, he got six responses."

"A whopping six responses. I guess Father's not too popular with the online ladies."

"This isn't a time to joke, Dani," Sean says, and for the first time I realize how hard all of this is hitting him. My brother has always been a goofball who cracks jokes and makes light of every situation. Now we seem to have switched places. I'm the one who's acting like a child, and Sean's the one being mature.

"From what I can tell, Gretchen is the youngest person who answered his ad."

*Typical. He went for the ripest piece he could find.* "What about the chat rooms?" I prod. "Did he meet many women there?"

"I don't think so. Ever since January, his efforts have been focused solely on Gretchen." Sean pauses. "I think he's in love with her."

I freeze. "No, that can't be right."

"Dani, I've read their e-mails. He calls her his soul mate."

This is much worse than I imagined. "You think he's being serious?"

"Yes."

"Then we've got to tell Mom. We can't wait any longer."

"I know."

It's as if someone's knocked the wind out of me, as though I've been run over by a truck. For a long moment, both of us are too depressed to speak. "How are we going to do it?" I finally ask.

"I'll confront Dad, and you come clean with Mom. That way, neither of them will feel like they're being ganged up on."

Confronting Father is arguably the tougher of the two tasks. "When would we do it?"

"The sooner the better," Sean says. "When's your coworker going to dump Dad?"

"Friday," I tell him. "Day after tomorrow."

"Then we do it tomorrow."

"But we're supposed to have our Thursday family dinner!" I say. "The first one in a whole month!"

"It's now or never, Dani."

"When you put it that way, never!"

Sean sighs. "I know you don't want to do this, but it's necessary."

"I know." I feel my eyes well up. "But part of me wishes we could just ignore this and hope it goes away."

"Life doesn't work that way. Besides, *after* Dad gets dumped, his whole demeanor may change. It'll be easier to deny the affair once he and Gretchen have officially broken up. We've got to reach Mom before it happens. She needs to have all the facts so she can make an informed decision about whether she wants to work to save their marriage."

"How are we going to tell them we found out?" I ask. "We can't mention Your Big Break Inc.!" I don't want to come clean about my job now. No way.

"We'll tell them I was on Dad's computer and I stumbled across the files."

*That's not bad.* "What were you doing on his computer? You've got one of your own."

"His Internet connection's faster. I'll say I was downloading med-school applications. Mom gets so excited whenever I talk about becoming a doctor."

"True." I lower my head, focusing on an invisible spot on the floor. "I can't believe we're going to do this. It would have been nice to have one last family dinner," I say. "Before the world as we know it comes crashing to an end."

"Trust me," Sean says, "it already has."

# 19

# Seeing Other People

I feel like a cop who knocks on someone's door and tells them their loved one has died.

I barely slept last night. I'm bogged down with second thoughts, sick with anxiety. *Why did I make this deal with Sean?* Initially, I thought I had come out on top, agreeing to have The Conversation with Mom. But the more I mull it over, the more I realize I got the short end of the stick. True, Sean has to confront Father. He has to tell him point blank that he knows about the affair. Not an easy task, but if you break it down, it's not so bad: Father will be shocked, angry, defensive. But he won't get hurt. He won't feel betrayed.

Mom, on the other hand, will be devastated.

She will totally break down. There's a good chance she'll become physically ill.

I grab a bottle of Pepto-Bismol on my way out the door and shove it into my purse. I arrive at the office forty minutes late.

Fortunately, no one's around to notice. That's good. I don't really feel like seeing anyone. I sit down at my desk and listen to my voicemail messages. The first one's from Evan Hirschbaum, informing me that he's got a new job for us. He's grown tired of his latest love, a nineteen-year-old salesgirl from Urban Outfitters. His taste is getting younger by the day. If his pattern holds, the next gal pal will be in junior high school, and he'll be beyond our help.

I have messages from other clients, and one from Krista. Normally, I'd take care of business first, personal calls second. But my mind's so scattered that I just don't care. I call Krista back.

"Fintane Catering, Krista speaking."

"Hi, it's me."

"Hi, Dani! Guess what?"

I massage my forehead in an effort to ward off a budding headache. I'm at a total loss. My brain is fried. "Honestly, Krista, I'm drawing a blank."

"Jason Dutwiler called this morning and asked me on a date!" she squeals. "We're going out this Saturday."

"That's great!" I say, leaning back in my desk chair. "Where's he taking you?"

"To see an exhibit at the Museum of Fine Arts. Afterwards, we're going for dinner in North Boston."

"Not bad, not bad at all." I'm impressed. Jason Dutwiler's stock just went up.

Her tone changes. "I'm almost afraid to ask you this."

"Ask away." I twirl the phone cord around my fingers, tangling and untangling it.

"I want you to give it to me straight: What's wrong with him?"

I'm exhausted. I need a giant cup of coffee. I look to see when my first breakup of the day is scheduled. Can I wait that long? Krista intrudes on my thoughts.

"He seems too good to be true," she says. "He's sweet, funny, smart. What am I missing here? Why is a great guy like Jason still on the market?"

"He's only been on the market a few weeks," I remind her.

"He's got a great job, he's well traveled, and he *recycles*," Krista argues.

"I didn't know you were so passionate about the environment," I say and stifle a yawn. "Look, Jason's a decent guy. There's nothing wrong with him."

"Are you *sure*?"

"He's clingy," I admit. "That's the extent of it, as far as I know."

"Dani," Krista hesitates, "there's something else. A favor I need to ask."

"Okay, shoot."

She gulps. "I like Jason a lot, and I want things to go well. We've gotten along on the phone, but sometimes it's different in person. What if we run out of stuff to talk about? What if we just sit there and stare at each other all night?"

"That's not going to happen," I assure her, rubbing my head.

"I just wish I knew a little bit more about him."

*Here we go.* I've got a pretty good feeling where this is headed. "Let me guess, you want me to give you an inside scoop?" I rub my temples harder. My head's killing me.

"Well, I know you've got a file on him—"

"It's confidential," I jump in. I reach into my desk and grab my bottle of Advil out of the top drawer. I take out two pills and pop them into my mouth, downing them without water.

"I know Jason's file is confidential," Krista says. "I don't want you to read it to me or anything. But I thought maybe you could casually glance at it and, you know, if your eyes just so *happen* to land on anything interesting, you could share it with me."

I don't say anything.

"Please, Dani! I *swear* I won't divulge where it came from."

On autopilot, I boot up my computer and open Jason's file. Krista's my best friend, but client confidentiality comes first. I'll just give her something innocent, harmless. I read over the notes from our first meeting. "Jason loves Red Sox baseball," I say. "And he's not into the New-Age, vegan lifestyle. That's the best I can do."

"Thanks, Dani!" she sounds genuinely pleased.

"I've got a lot of work to do."

"Is everything okay? You sound kind of down."

I debate whether or not to tell her about having The Conversation with my mom. I don't want to ruin her mood. "I'm tired," I lie. "That's all."

"How are you gonna do it?" I ask Trey later that afternoon.

"Do what?" Trey asks.

"You're handling Gretchen Monaghan's case, aren't you?"

Amanda abruptly stops typing. Trey motions to me, and we walk down the hall to his office. I follow him inside and shut the door behind me. "I thought you might want a little privacy," he says. "Amanda's been nosing around through all my client files."

I make a face. "That's annoying."

"She's eager. Craig likes that." Trey sits down on the corner of his desk. "So is it true? Is she really your father's girlfriend?"

"Mistress," I correct. "My parents are still married."

"That's what Craig said." He folds his hands in his lap. "Don't worry. Gretchen doesn't have any idea about the connection."

"Good. Keep it that way."

We stare at each other for a moment, and then Trey says, "I'll show up at Merriwether Payne Investments tomorrow afternoon and let him have it."

I wince. *Let him have it.* I shake the guilt out of my head. My father's getting only what he deserves.

"I'm going to be honest," Trey continues. "Tell him she's leaving because he's married."

I chew on the corner of my nail. "Are you going to be tough on him?"

He laughs. "No more than usual."

Trey and I have different philosophies when it comes to ending relationships. I try to let people down easy, sugarcoating the truth so it doesn't hurt so much. Trey doesn't hold any punches. He believes in being brutally honest. "People can spend their whole lives wondering why their lover left," he told me once. "If I'm in the position to give them the real reason, I've got an obligation to do it. People deserve to know the truth, no matter how ugly it is. That's the only way they can move on." I see where he's coming from, but I just don't have the heart to be so in-your-face honest.

"I wonder how my father will react," I say.

"No telling," Trey says. "Everyone's different."

"You've got that right." Being the bearer of bad news all the time wears you down. It's strange to see people's expressions when you dump them: shock, horror, anger, fear. Sometimes, it really depresses me.

"I'll go easy on him as much as possible, seeing how he's your dad," Trey promises.

I shake my head and walk out of the office. "Don't bother."

The day goes by in a blur. Before I know what's happening, I'm in the car on my way out to my parents' house. I can't believe how fast I get there; it feels like ten seconds. Then the instant I arrive on their doorstep, time slows down to a painstaking crawl.

"Hey, Mom," I say, greeting her in the living room. My heart's beating so forcibly that I'm afraid it's going to jump right out of my chest.

"Hi, hon." She gives me a quick kiss on the cheek. "Nice outfit."

I'm wearing a pair of black pants and a dark purple top from The Limited. "Thanks. You look great, too." Mom's in some gray slacks and a Gap button-down shirt. She looks classy, reminiscent of Diane Keaton. She grabs her purse and heads toward the door. "I'm so glad you invited me out for coffee and chocolates!" She stops to check her appearance in the hall mirror. "This is great, Dani! When you promised we'd have a girls' night out, I honestly didn't expect you to follow through with it." She smiles and puts her arm around my waist. "This means to so much to me. Do you know that?"

I nod solemnly and force a smile. I want to kick myself for being so cruel. *My God, why didn't I propose a* real *girls' night? Why didn't I invite her out to a movie last week or something?* Instead, I've opted to play grim reaper. I'm only hanging out with her because I have bad news.

"You ready to go yet?" I ask.

"Am I ever!" she enthuses. "Your dad and Sean are having

some sort of guys' movie marathon. They've been bugging me to get out of their hair all evening."

*Movie marathon.* I imagine what feature film Sean picked. What gets across the message: *You're Cheating on Mom, You Lying Jerk?*

The last thing I want is a run-in with Father, so I hightail it out the door and down the steps. Alone in the car with Mom, I'm so nervous I can't think of anything to say. The drive out to Back Bay seems to last for hours. Time is screwed up. *Why do uncomfortable silences stretch on endlessly, while amazing moments evaporate into thin air? Is this what Einstein meant when he said time was relative? I should have paid more attention in the Survey of Physics class I took freshman year.*

At long last, we arrive at Starbucks. "What do you want, Mom?" I ask as we make our way to the front door. "I'll go get our orders."

"Hmm . . . what's good?"

"Do you want iced or hot?"

"Iced."

I run through the list of items.

"My goodness, you're practically a walking, talking Starbucks menu."

I grimace. Maybe we should have gone somewhere else. But no, I have to stay in the right frame of mind. Technically, I'm dumping my mother. I need to view this as a business transaction or I'll never get through it.

A few minutes later, my mother and I are seated in the corner, sipping Iced Nonfat Mocha Lattes and eating a piece of chocolate cake. Or, more precisely, Mom's eating. I'm just picking at it with a fork. My stomach feels tense, nervous. I don't want to drag this out. I want to get it over with.

"I need to tell you something." I say.

"Tell me what?" She takes a sip of coffee.

I swallow hard. "It's about Dad."

"What about him?" she asks, stirring her drink with a straw.

I recite rule #4 in my mind: *You are an impartial observer.* I'm going to give her the facts. I'm not going to let this affect me personally. "Mom, you have to leave him," I blurt out.

"What are you talking about?" She looks uneasy.

*They're just words. Don't think about what they mean.* "You have to leave Dad. He has a girlfriend." I swallow hard, trying to force down the sickness that's building up in my throat. "Her name's Gretchen," I finish.

Mom's expression changes to one of horror. "Who told you?"

*Who told you?* I turn the words over in my mind. That's not the response I expected. *Why isn't she upset? Why isn't she demanding to know more about Gretchen? Why isn't she worried that her husband is an adulterer?* She's not shocked, she's not surprised. And then it hits me. Mom knows. Mom knows about Gretchen. *Oh my God, oh my God. Somehow, some way, she knows.*

"Did he tell you?" she asks. "Did Paul tell you about her?"

I stick to the story my brother and I came up with. "No, Sean found e-mails on Dad's computer."

"Your father shouldn't have been so careless."

*What the hell is going on here? Why is she so calm about this?*

"We were supposed to tell you together, when the time was right."

"What?" I ask. Any second now, I think I may pass out.

"Dani, I didn't want you to find out like this, but now you know half the story, so I'd better tell you the rest. Your father and I grew apart a long time ago. . . ." She keeps talking, telling me about how after she quit her job, she reevaluated her life, realized it wasn't working anymore. Her voice sounds distant, far away. I'm barely able to focus on what she's saying.

"When you marry as young as I did, when you only sleep with one man in your entire life, you reach a point where you just want more," Mom says. "It was my idea that we see other people, find out where it leads."

I'm stunned, nauseated. My mind flashes to the top ten biggest breakup excuses. I see right through Mom's story. The only time someone says they want to "see other people" is if they already have dates lined up.

"Who is he?" I ask, not sure I want to hear the answer.

"What makes you think there's someone else?"

"Isn't there?" I look her dead in the eyes, and she looks away.

"His name's Jude. He teaches my yoga class at the community center. We've been seeing each other off and on for six months."

I'm going to be sick. Right here, in the middle of all these Starbucks customers. I mentally measure the distance between the table and the bathroom—all the bodies I'll have to push past, all the tables, the coffee display, the baristas.

*I'll never make it.*

I lean down and vomit Iced Nonfat Mocha Latte all over my purse and the floor.


I'm cruising with my mother along the brightly lit streets of central Boston. This time Mom is driving, shifting the gears on my Volvo. *How did we get here?*

"Take this," she says as she pulls up to a stoplight. She hands me the bottle of Pepto-Bismol I'd stuffed in my purse earlier. "I wiped it off. It'll make you feel better."

I drink a few tentative sips of the thick, pink liquid.

I know, despite her assurances, that nothing will ever make me feel better again.

# 20

# In Another Time or Place, This Could've Worked Out

My eyes slowly open and I look around. I'm laying in a bed, but not my bed. My head feels fuzzy, thick, and it's difficult to concentrate. I fling back the floral bedspread and stare down at myself. *Why am I wearing clothes in bed?* I look down at my feet. *I went to bed with my shoes on?* My tongue feels as though it's stuck to the roof of my mouth. I climb out of bed and my knees buckle. Then it hits me: I'm in my parents' guest bedroom. Last night's events come flooding back. *Did Sean help me up here?* I think I'm going to be sick. Again.

I dash into the adjoining bathroom.

Fifteen minutes, a glass of Alka-Seltzer, and two Advils later, I feel somewhat better. What I really need are some ginger ale and saltines, like Mom used to serve whenever I had the flu. *Oh, God. Mom.* She's probably downstairs right now, watching Lifetime, Television for Women. Or is she out with some mystery man? I venture downstairs. "Hello?" I call out. No one answers.

I check the driveway. All three cars are gone. *I wonder where everyone is.* Dad, presumably, is at work. Sean may be, too. But Mom can't be at the office; she's retired (which I've now discovered is code for "sowing her wild oats").

I'm just grabbing my things to hightail it out the door when my cell phone rings. It's Sophie. "This has been one of the worst days of my life!" she complains, not bothering to say hello. "I went to Addington Academy."

*She's already been to Brady's school?* "Why didn't you wait till lunchtime?" I ask.

"Dani, it *is* lunchtime."

"It is?"

"Later, actually. It's two o'clock in the afternoon," Sophie informs me.

"Holy shit!" I shriek. *How can it be two o'clock? I've missed work!* Craig's bound to be freaking out. I'll call him the second I get off the phone with Sophie.

"What happened at the school?" I ask, sinking back down on the bed.

"I got arrested."

Obviously, I am still asleep. I must be dreaming. In fact, I'm starting to think the entire last month of my life has been one extended nightmare.

"Did you hear what I just said?" Sophie demands, sounding indignant. "I got *arrested*. Sort of."

"I heard you," I answer. "Why did you get arrested?"

"I had some trouble finding Brady's classroom. Some teacher saw me wandering around and asked me for a hall pass. I couldn't produce one, so she dragged my ass down to the principal's office!"

I'm speechless. I finally ask, "What did the principal do?"

"She said visitors aren't allowed on school property without prior permission."

"Did you see Brady?" I ask.

"The principal was making such a big stink, I was worried I might get Brady in trouble, too. So when she asked who I was there to see, I refused to answer."

*Uh-oh.* "What happened then?"

"They called the cops on me for trespassing!"

"Sophie, I'm so sorry. I never meant to get you"—I swallow hard—"arrested," I whisper.

"*Almost* arrested," she corrects. "The school didn't *actually* press charges. They just had the cops take down a file on me, and I was warned to never again come on school property unless I had prior permission."

That's far less dramatic than what she initially told me. "Still, I feel terrible. I should have never suggested you surprise Brady at school. We can arrange another way—"

"I'm done," she says. "At least for the time being. I've had enough."

I realize I'm a tiny bit glad things didn't work out. Now that I think about it, they don't seem like such a good match. "Again, I'm sorry," I apologize. "If there's any way I can make it up to you, let me know."

"I'm rearranging my apartment tomorrow evening. I could use some help. You up for it?"

"I'd love to," I say, and I mean it. Krista's going out with Jason Dutwiler tomorrow, which means my Saturday night is free. The last thing I want to do is sit around all weekend and think about the situation with my parents. It'll be good to take my mind off things for a while.

"Can't wait," she says, and clicks off the line abruptly.

I check my cell phone. There are eight calls from Craig. *Not good*. I call him back and apologize for missing work. He's surprisingly understanding. "Problem with the parental units?" he asks.

"How'd you know?"

"Trey heard from Gretchen. She called off the breakup. Guess she's staying with your old man."

"Guess so." I honestly have no idea what's happening. I need to talk to Sean, find out what transpired between him and Father. *Or should I go back to Dad? Since this isn't entirely his fault.* "I'll stop by the office for a few hours."

"Don't worry about it," Craig says. "Take a sick day. No biggie."


I call Blockbuster as soon as I get back to my apartment.

"Can I speak to Sean Myers?" I ask the girl who answers. She puts me on hold. A minute later, my brother picks up the phone.

"Welcome to the Apocalypse," he says, instead of hello.

"That's not funny."

"It's not meant to be."

"So, how did it go with Dad?" I ask.

"Not good."

"Did he tell you about Mom's yoga instructor boyfriend?" I ask.

"No, but she did."

I gasp. "When?"

"When she brought you home last night. You were completely out of it. I had to help you upstairs and put you in bed! Don't you remember?"

I grimace; I feel so humiliated. "I can't believe Mom told you."

"I knew something was up anyway," he explains. "When I confronted Dad about Gretchen, he got really quiet and then he said that was a topic for me to discuss with Mom."

*This situation is so surreal, so bizarre.* "I'm in shock."

"Tell me about it." He groans. "I feel like a first-class moron. I've been living under the same roof with them and I never even realized any of this was going on!"

"They did a good job of hiding it," I say.

"Dani, I've gotta get back to work. I'm stuck here until midnight, but give me a call tomorrow and we can figure out what to do, how to patch up our family."

"Okay," I agree, but I'm pretty sure we've run out of options.


I walk over to Sophie's about five the next evening. It's a beautiful night, and I enjoy the stroll. It's nice knowing someone else in the neighborhood. Sophie buzzes me up and answers the door looking peppy and bright-eyed. Her mousy, sullen, post-breakup frumpiness is completely gone. She's back to her former goddess state.

"Thanks for helping me with this." She smiles.

"No problem."

We work diligently to rearrange her apartment, scooting couches across the floor, hanging up new curtains, moving bookshelves and dressers. It's hard work, but we pass the time talking, jabbering about clothes and men and books. A few times, she runs across items that remind her of Evan: matchbooks from restaurants, earrings he gave her "just because," a small teddy bear from FAO Schwarz, postcards from a trip they took to Martha's Vineyard. Sophie's eyes tear up when she finds the postcards. "I fought so hard to get him to take that vacation. He did not want to go, but once we got there, he cut loose. He was like a big kid again, building sandcastles, collecting seashells."

I almost laugh at the mental image of Evan Hirschbaum trotting along the beach, poking around in the sand for dainty shells. "You shouldn't keep it," I advise her. "Any of it. They'll only serve as bitter reminders."

"You're right." She sinks down on the floor, postcards in hand. She wipes her eyes. "I think I'm over it, that I've moved on. I haven't even called him in weeks. But then I see something that reminds me of him and I fall to pieces. I've managed to collect more mementos from this than from all my other relationships combined."

I fold my arms across my chest. "He's not coming back," I say with a conviction that surprises even me. I sound like Trey.

"The way you said that"—Sophie bursts into tears—"it sounds so final."

I move down on the floor beside her and wrap my arms around her in a hug. "I've known Evan for a year. This is who he *is*. He doesn't get involved, he doesn't get hurt. He takes nothing personally. People are just possessions to him."

Craig would flip if he heard me bashing our number-one client like this. But I feel bad for Sophie, and I want to help her.

"It's so hard," she says, drying her eyes on her sleeve. "You lose a part of yourself when you lose a relationship."

"I know. Believe me, I know."

We sit there, side by side on the floor, for a long time. We talk about relationships, about Evan. I tell her about my dumped-on-the-radio horror story.

"Is he still on WBCN?" she asks.

"No." I stand and stretch. "He moved to California, last I heard."

"Good riddance," she says. "At least you've got him out of your hair. There's no hiding from Evan."

"Boston's a big city," I point out, turning to pick up my purse.

"Don't leave," Sophie says. "We could hang out for a while. Order a pie or something?" She gives me a shy smile. "It'd be nice to have the company."

"Sure," I tell her. "Should we rent a movie, too?"

"Yeah!" she says enthusiastically. "We can pick up a pizza on the way back." She scoops her car keys off the end table and heads toward the door. "I don't have a Blockbuster card. Are you a member?"

"Don't worry," I say, putting my arm around her shoulder. "I've got the hookup." I realize that Craig is rubbing off on me.

I take Sophie to Sean's Blockbuster on Commonwealth Avenue in Boston.

It's a bit of a haul from Cambridge, but the rentals will be free. We crank the stereo up and sing along to U2 as we cruise down Massachusetts Avenue. I'm surprised to discover that Sophie and I have the same taste in music.

"You can't live in Boston and not love U2," Sophie screams over the blare of *Mysterious Ways*. "This is practically their second home, next to Dublin."

The traffic's surprisingly light for a Saturday night, and we arrive in record time. Sophie drives around for a few minutes and locates a parking spot on the street. We hop out of the car and head into the store. "We can get our videos free here; my brother's one of the assistant managers," I tell her as we walk through the front door.

"Older or younger?"

"Younger. He's twenty-five." We make our way over to the

front counter, where Sean's busily sorting through a stack of DVDs.

"Hi, Dani," he says. His eyes widen as he takes in Sophie.

"Sean, this is Sophie. Sophie, my brother, Sean."

Sophie leans across the counter and shakes his hand. "Nice to meet you."

His face goes bright red and he drops her hand like a hot potato. "Can I, uh, help you, uh, find something?" My brother's hardly a smooth operator. He's only dated three girls in his life, and most of his free time is spent in front of the TV or the computer. The last time he got up close and personal with a woman as striking as Sophie was probably while watching *General Hospital*.

"We'll have a look around and let you know," Sophie tells him, flashing a friendly grin.

"Why don't you browse by yourself for a minute?" I suggest. "I need to talk to my brother."

"No problem." She trots off toward the new arrivals section.

"Where'd you meet the supermodel?" Sean asks, his eyes trained on Sophie.

"Work. Anyway, about Mom's boyfriend—"

"She must be a real heartbreaker."

"*Mom?*"

"No, not *Mom*, you idiot." He guffaws. "*Sophie!* Man, she's hot!"

"Actually, Sophie was the dumpee, not the dumper."

Sean lets out a low whistle. "What kind of man would let her get away?"

"A man who has five more women just like her lined up outside his door."

A customer needs Sean's attention, so I go join Sophie, who's moved on from new arrivals and is now browsing in the center aisle of older movies. "What are you in the mood for?" I ask, sidling up to her.

"Something intriguing," she says. "But not too serious."

After some deliberation, we settle on the latest James Bond flick.

We head to the counter and wait in line. When we get to the front, Sean comes over to ring us up on his account. Thankfully, he's much more composed this time. "You know who you look like?" he asks as he scans our videos.

She shakes her head.

"Irène Jacob."

"Who?"

"She's a beautiful French actress. You look exactly like her, except her hair's a lot darker."

"Sorry, I don't know who she is."

"Trust me, it's a compliment," Sean says. He turns to me. "Dani, have you heard of Irène Jacob?"

"No."

"Come on, you two must have heard of her. She played the starring role in *Trois Couleurs: Rouge*. It's an incredible film. It has some of the best cinematography I've ever seen. And the dialogue is brilliant." Sean rattles off a few lines in French.

"You speak French?" Sophie asks.

He laughs. "Only what I've picked up from movies, but I'm thinking of taking a course in it. I'd love to learn conversational French. There are so many amazing French films, especially the *Trois Couleurs* trilogy."

I stare at him blankly. *Is this really my little brother, the dorky guy who loves* CSI *and* General Hospital? *Since when has he developed a taste for fine cinema?*

Sophie smiles, obviously impressed. And, much as it surprises me to admit it, I am, too.

"Hang on, I think we've got a copy in the foreign film section." He runs around the counter and hurries across the store. A minute later, he resurfaces with the video. "Let me know what you think." He finishes scanning the movies and places them in a bag.

"Okay," she agrees, giving him a little wave as we make our way out of the store. "Nice meeting you, Sean."

"Nice meeting you, too," he says, blushing. "And thanks for making it a Blockbuster night!"

# 21

**STAGE FOUR OF BREAKUP HELL:**
*Backsliding*

After sampling the dismal dating scene, the dumpee concludes that no one could possibly be as smart, witty, charming, and attractive as his or her ex. Desperate and obsessed, the dumpee attempts to win the former lover back using any means necessary.

Sunday night, the phone rings. I quickly grab it. "Hello?"

It's Sean. "I just had a heart-to-heart conversation with Mom, and I have some great news!"

"You did?" I ask. "And you do?"

"Yeah, isn't that amazing? Just when things seemed bleakest, Mom and I went out for coffee and conversation."

I groan inwardly. Looks like my coffee habit is spreading to the whole family. "How did it go?"

"It was awkward, but I have to admit it was also kind of nice. I don't feel like I've ever really gotten to know Mom as a person, if that makes sense. She's always just been my mother. But I feel like we're really starting to communicate as adults."

I blink in surprise. My brother never used to talk like this. He sounds mature. I guess a family fiasco will do that to you. "So, what did you talk about?"

"Oh, everything. Work, career goals, life, true love."

"True love," I say, feeling like a bashful teenager. "You and Mom talked about true love?"

"Yeah. We talked about her relationship with Dad versus her relationship with Jude."

I'm in shock. "Was it weird?"

"Not as weird as you might think. It was good to be so honest for once."

*Honest.* I gulp. That's one area where I have a real problem.

"Mom says her relationship with Jude is nice, but it lacks passion! We can make this work to our advantage."

*That* is *good news.* "So all we have to do is convince her to go back with Dad and our problems are solved?" I'm twenty-eight, and maybe it's wrong of me to be depressed about the possibility of my parents splitting up. But I don't want to face two Christmases, two Thanksgivings. If I was twelve, it might make more sense. But I *do* care, and it *is* depressing. I want everything to remain the same.

"Now for the bad news." He pauses. "And before I tell you this, I just want you to remember, things are really looking up for Mom. So don't get too discouraged by this downturn. We'll just consider it a bump in the road, okay? Unpleasant, yes, but our family can overcome it."

I take a deep breath. "Okay, I'm ready."

"I found some pretty upsetting e-mails on Dad's computer."

My brother's turning into a regular sneak. "What did you find?"

"Dad erased the folder of Gretchen's e-mails off the desktop. But I managed to run a recovery and pull up all the messages he tried to delete. I'm forwarding you the e-mails."

"I don't want them," I jump in.

"Too late. Message sent."

"I'll delete them," I warn, playing with the phone cord anxiously.

"No, you won't."

He's right. I won't. I pull the phone closer to me. "I don't want to read Dad's pornographic e-mails."

"It's not porn, but it's pretty bad. I thought you should see them for yourself. Dad mentions us a bunch. Not by name, but he talks about his 'daughter and son.' He talks about wanting to introduce us to Gretchen. He also talks about . . ." Sean's voice trails off. "Never mind, you've gotta read them for yourself."

We chat for a few more minutes, and then I hang up the phone.

I wander into the living room and survey my surroundings. The refrigerator hums from the kitchen, and I consider digging into yesterday's Chinese takeout but decide against it. There's nothing I can eat, or read, or watch, or do that will change things. My laptop computer sits on my desk, taunting me to switch it on and read the recovered e-mails. Before I can change my mind, I sit down at my desk and turn it on. It hums to life. I log on to my Yahoo account and go to my inbox. Thirteen new messages. Three of them are advertisements for penile enlargement, Prozac, and loan-consolidation schemes, one's from Krista, and all the rest are from Sean. My hand wavers for a second. I'm about to open the first of Sean's e-mails when a new message pops into my account. When I see who it's from, my heart skips a beat. Brady wrote! It's only been a couple of days. I didn't think I'd hear from him so soon.

**From:** "Brady K. Simms" <brady_simms@hotmail.com>
**To:** DaniMyers@yahoo.com
**Sent:** Monday, June 6, 2:35 a.m.
**Subject:** Testing, testing . . . 1, 2, 3

Hi, Dani.

I'm an idiot. I meant to get in touch with you over the weekend, but I lost your e-mail address. Actually, I didn't lose it, I washed it. It was in my pants pocket when I threw them in the machine. Oops. Long story short, the ink got smeared and my khakis got ruined. Even worse, all I could make out was **s@yah**. But never fear! My keen memory (and the yahoo directory) led me back to you. Let me know when you want to grab that meal sometime. . . .

~Brady Simms

I quickly type a reply and hit send.

**From:** "Danielle Myers" <DaniMyers@yahoo.com>
**To:** brady_simms@hotmail.com
**Sent:** Monday, June 6, 2:41 a.m.
**Subject:** RE: Testing, testing . . . 1, 2, 3
And here I thought you'd reneged on our bet, in which case I would have had to hunt you down. In light of the fact that Magnus did NOT move, you owe me one lunch. Seriously, I'll check my schedule and let you know when I'm free.
Dani
P.S. Sorry about the pants. I'll remember to use waterproof ink next time.

I don't want to appear overeager, so I don't suggest a firm date for us to get together. I'm not expecting to hear back from him, but a few minutes later, another e-mail comes through. I decide to focus my attention on Brady and ignore Sean's e-mails of impending doom.

**From:** "Brady K. Simms" <brady_simms@hotmail.com>
**To:** DaniMyers@yahoo.com
**Sent:** Monday, June 6, 2:47 a.m.
**Subject:** RE: RE: Testing, testing . . . 1, 2, 3
Wow! Another night owl. I'm an incurable insomniac. What's
your excuse?
~Brady

**From:** "Danielle Myers" <DaniMyers@yahoo.com>
**To:** brady_simms@hotmail.com
**Sent:** Monday, June 6, 2:53 a.m.
**Subject:** RE: RE: RE: Testing, testing . . . 1, 2, 3
There's an all-night Ted Danson marathon on TV. I couldn't
resist.
Dani

**From:** "Brady K. Simms" <brady_simms@hotmail.com>
**To:** DaniMyers@yahoo.com
**Sent:** Monday, June 6, 2:59 a.m.
**Subject:** RE: RE: RE: RE: Testing, testing . . . 1, 2, 3
Ted Danson, eh? I didn't know you were such a big fan. Ha,
ha! You made me laugh so hard I spewed Coke out of my nose.
The drink, not the drug. I don't do drugs. Not that the image
of me spewing Coca-Cola is all that pleasant. Now, on a much
more appealing topic—have you got an ETA for our food
date yet?
~B

I note how his signature has evolved from Brady Simms to Brady
to B. I'm doubly glad things didn't work out with Sophie. . . .

**From:** "Danielle Myers" <DaniMyers@yahoo.com>
**To:** brady_simms@hotmail.com
**Sent:** Monday, June 6, 3:03 a.m.
**Subject:** RE: RE: RE: RE: RE: Testing, testing . . . 1, 2, 3
So it's a food DATE now? Interesting. How about tomorrow?
D

I hit send and immediately start second-guessing myself. *Am I being too forward? Was it a mistake to comment about the "date"? And why did I capitalize the word?* That's like screaming out: "I'm so desperate for a DATE that I'm latching on and not letting go!" *And what was I thinking, suggesting tomorrow? What is that saying? Absence makes the heart grow fonder. In that vein, shouldn't I be putting him off for five days or something?* As I debate this in my head, nearly twenty minutes pass and there's no return e-mail from Brady. I refresh my inbox several times a minute, hoping to see a new message. At long last, he responds.

**From:** "Brady K. Simms" <brady_simms@hotmail.com>
**To:** DaniMyers@yahoo.com
**Sent:** Monday, June 6, 3:22 a.m.
**Subject:** (No subject)
Sorry, got sick of all the RE: RE:s. Yes, tomorrow sounds great. Name the time and place.
~Brady
P.S. Finished reading *High Fidelity* the other day. Terrific book. Thanks for the tip.

*Hmm . . . first the long response time, then he completely ignores my "date" question. And now he's back to signing his e-mails Brady instead of B. Well. If he's signing his e-mails*

*"Brady,"* then I'm signing mine *"Dani."* Wait, screw that. *"Danielle."* Maybe he thinks I'm really hard up, suggesting we go out tomorrow. Of course, he's free, too, which says something about *him. Am I overanalyzing this?* I type out a response but decide to hold off on sending it. I wait ten minutes, then press send.

---

**From:** "Danielle Myers" <DaniMyers@yahoo.com>
**To:** brady_simms@hotmail.com
**Sent:** Monday, June 6, 3:33 a.m.
**Subject:** Lunch
What do you say, should we go with tried-and-true? If yes, how about we meet at Au Bon Pain near the Four Seasons around 1:30? Glad you enjoyed *High Fidelity*.
Danielle
P.S. What does the "K" stand for?

**From:** "Brady K. Simms" <brady_simms@hotmail.com>
**To:** DaniMyers@yahoo.com
**Sent:** Monday, June 6, 3:38 a.m.
**Subject:** Great!
I'll see you there.
~Brady
P.S. I could tell you, but then I'd have to kill you.

---

I log out of my Yahoo account and shut down my computer. I was online for an hour and I managed to ignore Sean's e-mails the whole time. My lying, cheating father can wait until tomorrow. I'm going to grab a few hours of sleep before work. As I crawl into bed and snuggle down beneath the covers, I can't help smiling. I have a Sort-of Date tomorrow with Brady Simms.

Maybe things aren't so bad after all.

# 22

# SODs, SOBs, and SOS

Sort-of Dates—SODs for short—have their advantages. Unlike an Actual Date, which generally includes some kind of ceremonial activity—dinner and movie, dinner and a play, etc.—SODs are easy to get out of. The guy doesn't pick you up; you meet him there. There's no time limit to how long the date should last, so you can duck out if things get hairy. SODs never take place during the weekend, and the guy is under no obligation to pay. The two most typical SODs are quickie lunches and casual coffees.

The downside to Sort-of Dates is that they tend to produce Sort-of Boyfriends—guys who sometimes call, sometimes don't; who take you out on a Friday night, then wait three weeks before asking you out again; who are happy to hang out with you, sleep with you if you'll let them, but who don't feel the need to give you gifts on Valentine's Day or introduce you to their parents. It's no coincidence that the abbreviation for Sort-of Boyfriend is SOB.

I hope that my SOD with Brady won't lead to SOS—Sort-of Sex. The more I think about it, the more worried I become. If he really liked me, he'd ask me out on an Actual Date, wouldn't he? What if Brady really wants to get together so he can pump me for info on Erin Foster-Ellis? What if he's backsliding, trying to get with her again?

I'm careful not to let news of my SOD leak to Craig; he'd flip. He'd also kill me if he found out about Krista and Jason Dutwiler.

However, I rationalize, the particular rule he cautioned me to start following was rule #5: Do *not* get personally involved. This is the cardinal rule and must be followed above all others! That rule doesn't really cover my situation, does it? I mean, it isn't like the rule reads: *Do not give your e-mail address out to a hot ex in the hopes that he'll ask you out for a Sort-of Date.*

*Technically, I've done nothing wrong.*


I make it through the first part of the morning without succumbing to temptation. Except for a quick check to see if Brady had written—he hadn't—I've stayed out of my Yahoo account. Work keeps me pretty busy. Work, and thinking about my SOD. Even though it's not an Actual Date, I'm still pretty excited. I'm wearing a pair of black pants and a brand-new pink sleeveless top with a pretty pale pink scarf. I hope Brady doesn't think I dressed up for this occasion. Even though I did.

By the time twelve-forty-five rolls around, I'm starting to get antsy. I need to leave the office at one to meet Brady. But there's no way I can concentrate between now and then. I'm like a kid counting down the last fifteen minutes until Christmas vacation. I could go chat with Trey or Craig. Or I could take a peek at

Sean's e-mails. I decide to go for it. I call up the Yahoo homepage and type in my e-mail addy and password. Then, with a nauseous feeling settling in my stomach, I open the first of Sean's messages.

**From:** "Sean Myers" <CSIfan411@yahoo.com>
**To:** DaniMyers@yahoo.com
**Sent:** Monday, June 6, 2:01 a.m.
**Subject:** Read 'em and weep
dani—
here it is, all the proof u need. call me when u get this.—your bro

Attached is an e-mail message from Gretchen Monaghan to my father. It's dated two days ago.

Paul,
How is it that you can go through thirty-five years of your life before meeting your soul mate? Fifty-seven years in your case. The days stretch on forever while I wait till six o'clock comes and we can be together. I keep myself sane with fantasies. Fantasies of things we've done, of things we've yet to do. As soon as your divorce is final, we'll make our love official. Speaking of the D, have you gone to see a lawyer yet?
Kisses,
Gretch

*Gretch? Who the hell goes by a stupid nickname like Gretch? She might as well go ahead and drop the G and be honest.*
*This letter makes no sense.*
Gretchen came to Your Big Break Inc.—not once but twice— in an attempt to dump my father. Now she's back together with

him, anticipating the day he'll divorce my mom? *Not gonna happen, sweetie.* Married men always say they'll leave their wives; they never do. Something else is bothering me. She mentions waiting until six o'clock at night to be together. My dad has always been a major workaholic. How is it that he's suddenly getting off work at six o'clock like a normal person?

I pick up the phone and dial Sean's cell.

"Have you read them?" he asks.

"One of them. This is bad."

"I know. I'm starting to think we're fighting a losing battle."

I pop a piece of gum into my mouth and chomp down on it angrily. "I just want our family to be normal again."

"That prick Jude dropped by last night."

My heartbeat quickens. *Jude dropped by?* "You mean you've met him?"

"I spied on them from the landing. Look, Dani, I've gotta run. I'm in the middle of my shift."

"Sure, no problem."

"I'll call you later," he promises. "Read the rest of the e-mails."

"I will."

We say good-bye and get off the phone. I glance at two more e-mails from Gretchen and, while they aren't easy to take, I manage to keep my composure. *So far, so good.*

Then I open the last one.

Paul,
I can't wait until we can be a real family. Me, you, your daughter and son. We can spend Christmas together. Wrap presents. Hang stockings. Set out milk and cookies for Santa. Or are your kids too old for that stuff? We'll have to wait until we have children of our own!

The last sentence of the e-mail hits me like a punch in the gut.

*Children of their own? Gretchen wants to have children with my father? What if they've already started trying to get pregnant?* I read the letter again, and my insides turn over. I slowly rise from my desk, put one foot in front of the other, and stumble down the hall. I make it to the bathroom without a second to spare. I fall into the stall, lean forward, and once again toss the contents of my stomach into the toilet.


I should have gotten Brady's cell number.

I'm twenty minutes late meeting him. I had to stop by CVS and pick up a few emergency items: Crest, a toothbrush, breath mints, and a bottle of Pepto-Bismol. I'm beginning to think I should carry a bottle in my purse at all times. I ran back to the office and cleaned myself up. Physically, I feel brand-new. My stomach has settled, and my mouth is minty-fresh. I even fixed my makeup and applied some lip gloss.

But all of this has put me behind schedule.

I dash into Au Bon Pain at ten till two. I spy Brady sitting down at the window counter with a cup of coffee. "Hi Dani," he calls, standing to greet me. "What can I get you to eat?"

"I'm not very hungry. A warm herbal tea would be nice, though."

He looks surprised. "Is everything all right?"

"My stomach's been a bit off today. Tea might settle it."

Brady eyes me curiously. "You look kind of pale. Are you sure you're up for this?"

"Definitely. I'm feeling much better now." It's the truth. Just seeing him has perked me up. For the next little while, I will avoid thinking about my bastard jackass father and his biological clock–

obsessed mistress. I will focus on enjoying a soothing drink with a new friend. I get up and move to a table so we can face each other.

Brady returns with my drink and two small turkey sandwiches. "In case you change your mind about eating." He also sets down a few sugar packets on the table. He sits across from me.

I empty a few packets of sugar into my drink.

"You're not from Boston, are you?" he asks.

I stir the sugar in my drink. "How'd you guess?"

"Your accent. You don't sound like a native Bostonian."

"My family moved here from New Orleans about ten years ago. It was kind of a rough time, actually. We moved right at the start of my senior year of high school."

"That must have been hard." Brady takes a sip of his coffee and a quick bite of his sandwich. "The culture shock of coming to Boston's pretty alarming, isn't it?"

"I think the strangest thing was getting used to the weather," I admit. "The only time you see snow in New Orleans is on TV. I'm used to warm winters, and summers that boil with heat. The second you step outside, you're drenched with sweat. My dad and I used to joke about it all the time, how wimpy everyone up here is. How they start running their ceiling fans the second it hits seventy degrees."

Brady laughs. "Bostonians don't know how good they have it. They should try dealing with some real heat."

"I'm guessing you're not from around here either," I venture.

"Nope, I grew up in Arizona. Came out to Boston six years ago for law school. My plan was to move back west once I graduated, but I wound up with a great job offer here. And then I met Erin, which changed everything."

"You guys were together for two years?" I ask, even though I already know the answer.

"Two years last March." Brady gets quiet for a minute, then says, "But enough about Erin. I didn't come here to rehash my old relationship." Brady runs his fingers through his short, dark hair. He really is cute in a sweet, college professor kind of way. He looks as though he should be hanging around Boston University, teaching an introductory lit class. We sit there in silence for a few. "So," I begin, and Brady nods encouragingly. "What does the K in your name stand for?"

"No way." He laughs. "Too embarrassing."

I take a drink of tea and pick at my sandwich. "It can't be that bad."

"Guess."

"Kevin? Keith?"

"Uh-uh."

"Kyle? Kurt?"

"Not even close."

"Is it a girl's name, like Karen or Katie?"

"Nope, it's not a girl's name." He takes a small bite of his sandwich into his mouth. "It's nothing traditional, nothing you've heard of."

"Kilimanjaro?" I joke.

Brady laughs. "I'm guessing you've heard of Mount Kilimanjaro."

"That I have." I take a quick sip of tea.

"Kryptonite?"

"You're not going to give up, are you?" He grins.

"Not a chance."

He thinks about it for a minute. "I guess it wouldn't hurt anything," he says, scooting his chair closer. "But this stays between you and me. Got that?"

"Got it."

He lowers his voice. "My middle name's Koogan."

"What?" I struggle not to laugh. "Brady *Koogan* Simms?"

"It's my mother's maiden name." He's smiling now—a really sweet, flirty grin. "So, since I told you my secret, now you've got to tell me one."

"What do you wanna know?" I ask coyly.

"Since we're on the topic of names, how about you tell me the most embarrassing nickname you've ever been given?"

I think about it. "Pumpkin Legs."

"*Pumpkin* Legs?" Brady raises an eyebrow. "There's bound to be a good story behind that one."

"When I was growing up in New Orleans, the hot thing was to be really tanned. Since I'm only capable of burning"—I run a finger along my pale skin for emphasis—"I tried to use one of those fake-bake tanners the day before the junior class prom. I put on too much, and my skin turned orange. For the rest of the school year, everybody called me Pumpkin Legs."

"That was almost worth giving up Koogan for. *Almost*," he teases.

We sit in silence for a few moments. But it's a comfortable, friendly silence, like we're old friends. "So, I was wondering," Brady says. "would you like to go to a movie with me sometime?"

*An Actual Date. He's asking me for an Actual Date! This is definitely against rule #5. Oh, who cares? My life's been stressful lately. I deserve a little fun.* "Love to," I say, trying to remain calm. Like Sean, I'm not exactly a smooth operator. I guess it runs in the family.

"I was thinking we could catch a matinee one weekend," Brady continues.

Looks like I jumped the gun when I declared it an Actual Date. An afternoon matinee definitely classifies as an SOD. And he didn't suggest a specific time.

We finish our drinks and sandwiches, exchange phone numbers, and go our separate ways with a plan to get together again soon. I'm not really sure what the lunch meant, but I enjoyed myself nonetheless. It was nice to take my mind off things for a while.

"Bye, Brady *Koogan* Simms," I say as he heads out the door.

"Bye, Pumpkin Legs," he calls, winking at me.

# 23

# I Think We Should Date Other People

I haven't talked to my mother since that fateful night of The Conversation. It's been nearly three weeks. She hasn't called me, and I see no point in calling her. I haven't spoken to my father, either. We were supposed to have a family meal last week, but Thursday passed and no one mentioned it. I guess we're all mutually avoiding one another. I get my news through Sean, who keeps me updated on a regular basis. *Jude took Mom to the movies tonight. Jude brought Mom flowers.* And I hear stuff about Father, too. *Dad was on the phone with Gretchen for an hour last night. Dad didn't come home until 2 a.m. I think he was with Gretchen.*

Krista's been spending virtually every free moment with Jason Dutwiler; I barely see her anymore. Brady Simms has also been MIA. He hasn't called or e-mailed since our semi-date. It's weird, but talking to my brother has now become the highlight of my day. In the past, we were never very close. We always got along, but you couldn't really call us "friends." Now I view him as a trusted confidant.

"I've got a plan," Sean says when he phones me at work Tuesday afternoon.

I'm in the middle of writing a breakup letter for Evan Hirschbaum's latest castoff. "I'm all ears."

"Brace yourself: It involves porn."

"What?" I exclaim, dropping my pen.

"*Gay* porn, to be specific."

"What the hell are you talking about?"

"Okay, this is gonna sound nuts, but hear me out before you make your decision."

"I'm skeptical, but I'm listening."

"*Mom's* the one who wanted to see other people, right?"

"Uh-huh."

"Dad was merely following *Mom's* orders. He wanted to stay faithful to her, wanted to keep his marriage intact. But he felt he had no choice but to do what she asked. So he turned to Gretchen Monaghan out of desperation, because he couldn't be with the woman he really wanted. This exact same thing happened on *Days of Our Lives* when Bo hooked up with Billie because he thought his true love, Hope, had drowned in a vat of acid."

"I thought you watched *General Hospital,* not *Days of Our Lives.*"

"I kind of watch them both," he says sheepishly. "Back to what I was saying. Dad's only with Gretchen because he can't have Mom. If Mom dumps Jude and offers to take Dad back, he'll go in a heartbeat!"

I'm not so sure. "He called Gretchen his soul mate."

"He can't have meant it," Sean argues. "Judging by their

e-mails, Gretchen said it first. It's kind of like when someone says 'I love you.' You just *have* to say it back."

"Mom doesn't want Dad. She wants Jude," I point out.

"She only *thinks* she wants Jude. All we've got to do is convince her otherwise."

"How are we going to do that?"

"We have to convince Mom that Jude is gay. She'll toss him out on his ass."

I burst out laughing. "Sean, you've lost it. There's no way we can do that."

"We can," he insists. "Mom *said* her relationship with Jude doesn't have any passion."

I frown. "It sounds too far-fetched, too risky."

"All good plans are risky," Sean counters. "It'll work."

I'm still reluctant. Part of me thinks we should just butt out, leave well enough alone.

"Look," Sean says, "every time Jude's come over here, he's brought his yoga bag. All we have to do is hide some gay porn in it and then make sure Mom finds it. That'll plant enough seeds of doubt to have her running back to Dad's arms." When I don't say anything, he adds, "Dani, I'm going to do this with or without your help. Though, if you'll remember, we formed a coalition, we agreed to work together to keep our family from falling apart."

I let out a sigh. "All right, I'll help. Tell me what I need to do."


A few days pass, and Brady still doesn't call to ask me to a movie. But Sophie Kennison does.

"I was wondering if you want to rent some DVDs and hang out at my place tonight?" she offers on Friday afternoon. I don't have any plans, so I say yes.

I arrive to find her waiting for me outside her apartment. "I was thinking we could go to your brother's Blockbuster on Comm. Ave.," she suggests. "They have a really good selection."

"Sure," I say. We arrive at the store, and Sophie heads straight for new arrivals.

"I'll catch up with you in a minute," I say, scouting the store for Sean. I spy him stocking videos by the register and hurry over.

"What are you doing here?" he asks.

"I'm having a movie night with Sophie. We dropped by to get a few flicks."

"Sophie's here?" His eyes begin scanning the store.

"Yeah, she's picking out some movies. Anyway, update me on what's going on at home?" I ask.

"It's depressing. After that one great talk, now we barely speak to each other. Mom left me a note on the kitchen table this morning." He reaches into the pocket of his khaki pants and pulls out a wadded-up napkin. "Here, read it for yourself."

S—
*How about dinner at the house this Tuesday? Me, you, Dani, &*
*Jude. Could be a good bonding opportunity. I'll cook. Ask*
*your sister if she's free.*
*Mom*

"I can't believe she left you a note on a napkin," I say, as soon as my eyes have finished scanning the message.

"I told you, we don't talk. What do you want to do about this?"

"We should probably go for it. This might be our big chance."

"I know," Sean says. "I'll tell her we can be there." He snorts.

"Maybe I'll write an acceptance note on a square of toilet paper."

I feel badly for him, living in that house of tension. "So, we'll implement Operation Gay Porn this Tuesday, and see where it leads?"

"For my sanity's sake, I hope it works. At the very least, I'd like us to all start talking again. It's too quiet at home." Sean picks up a few videos and heads to the end counter, away from the line of customers. "I'm so spaced-out, Dani," he says, setting them down. "These haven't even been checked back in yet, and I was about to restock them." He shakes his head. "I'm losing my mind."

I pat him on the back. "It's been a rough couple of weeks."

"So, about the porn," Sean says, lowering his voice. "I was thinking it would be best to go with magazines. Porno movies might be too obvious. Besides, it'd be easier to connect them back to me, since I work in a video store."

"I doubt she'd even think about it. It's not like Blockbuster specializes in porn."

"Mom doesn't necessarily know that."

"I guess you're right."

"What are you guys talking about?" Sophie asks, strolling over to us. She leans up against the counter.

"You really wanna know?" I say.

She grins. "I asked, didn't I?"

*Fair enough.* "Gay porn."

"Is Blockbuster looking to expand their collection?" she asks.

"Not exactly," Sean says, looking embarrassed. "We were, uh, asking for ourselves."

"Oh." She seems rightly alarmed.

"We need the porn for our mom's boyfriend," I explain. *There's a sentence I never thought I'd say.*

"Like lesbian stuff?" Sophie asks.

This conversation is getting more embarrassing by the second. Apparently, Sean agrees. "Let's continue this discussion outside," he says, coming around from behind the counter and making a beeline for the door. Once we're outside the building and away from the prying eyes of his coworkers, Sean says, "We want a couple of magazines."

I briefly fill her in on the plan to plant the incriminating evidence in Jude's yoga bag.

Sophie bursts out laughing. "You guys are insane. That'll never work."

"It might," I argue. "And we have to try. It's our only hope."

"Well, if you're dead set on doing it, I might be able to help. Would a few issues of *Playgirl* work? They feature naked men. It would probably be pretty disturbing if a straight guy had them in his yoga bag."

"*Playgirl* would be perfect," I say.

"Okay. I have a couple of issues at my apartment. They're yours."

"Really?" Sean and I say in unison.

"Do you mind if I ask why?"

She shrugs. "Evan used to buy them. He left a few at my place."

I draw in a sharp breath. "Evan Hirschbaum's gay?!"

"No."

"Then why *Playgirl*?" I ask. "And don't tell me he bought it for the articles!"

Sean's standing there with his mouth hanging open.

"He said he liked studying the male form—the closer to perfection, the better. It gave him something to strive for." Sophie's expression shifts as she talks. "Now that I think about it, I guess it *was* slightly weird." She shudders. "Anyway, I'll be glad to have the things out of my apartment. I should have thrown them in the garbage weeks ago."

Sean shakes his head. "We can't take them." He looks uncomfortable. "They're *used*."

"So?" I ask.

"So," Sean says pointedly. "The pages might be . . . stuck together."

"Guys, Evan didn't . . . they're not." Sophie frowns. "Let's just say the magazines are in pristine condition and leave it at that. Now, do you want them or not?"

"We'll take them," I say. "Thanks."

I hang out with Sophie until three in the morning and, as a result, don't get out of bed until noon the next day. Ordinarily, this wouldn't be a problem—I love sleeping late and do it virtually every chance I get—but today I've got a packed schedule. In addition to a host of errands—I've got to do two loads of laundry, pick up shirts at the dry cleaner, go grocery shopping—I promised Craig I'd come into the office for a few hours and catch up on work. I'm seriously falling behind.

Plus, I'm meeting Krista and Jason for an early dinner at an Indian restaurant in Jamaica Plain. It's bring-your-own-wine, and I've offered to pick up a bottle of merlot. I grab a shower and then quickly get dressed. Before I head out the door, I stop and check my e-mail. I'm pleasantly surprised to find a message from Brady Simms. It's been a while, but he finally wrote!

**From:** "Brady K. Simms" <brady_simms@hotmail.com>
**To:** DaniMyers@yahoo.com

**Sent:** Saturday, June 25, 10:12 a.m.
**Subject:** Long time, no speak
Hi Dani,

Greetings from Arizona! That's right, I've flown the coop and headed out west. What can I say? The frigid Boston summer finally got to me—I was craving scalding sun and 110-degree temperatures. Seriously, my mother had some unexpected legal issues and needed me to fly out here and take care of them. I'll be heading back your way in a few days, and I was hoping we could still have that movie date. I've been thinking about you a lot, and I'd really love to see you. How about my place, this Wednesday night at 8 p.m.? I'll make dinner; you bring a DVD.
~Brady Simms
P.S. Is Italian cool?

Well. This is interesting for several reasons. First, not only does he suggest we hook up for a dinner-and-a-movie *date*, but he thinks we should do it *at his place*. That's a far cry from meeting at the theater for a Sunday matinee. And he suggested a firm time, which proves he's able to commit. If that doesn't classify as an Actual Date, I don't know what does. I decide to stop overanalyzing his e-mail and just answer the damn thing.

**From:** "Danielle Myers" <DaniMyers@yahoo.com>
**To:** brady_simms@hotmail.com
**Sent:** Saturday, June 25, 1:09 p.m.
**Subject:** RE: Long time, no speak
Hello, stranger! Good to hear from you. Hope the Southwest is treating you well. I'm checking my schedule for this Wednesday. Let's see, I've got brain surgery at four, trapeze

lessons at six, dog walking at seven . . . okay, eight works.
Italian is very cool. I assume you mean the food, not the
language. But in case you were wondering, I love the language,
too. Very sexy. Never mind. I'll shut up now.
Dani
P.S. What kind of movies do you like?

I read over the e-mail. *Am I being too cheesy? Should I even
be using the word* sexy? *Is he going to think that means I want
to sleep with him? (Maybe I do, but down the road.)* I shake my
head, read over my reply one last time. *Ah, fuck it.* I solemnly
vow to stop second-guessing myself. I hit send.

**From:** "Brady K. Simms" <brady_simms@hotmail.com>
**To:** DaniMyers@yahoo.com
**Sent:** Saturday, June 25, 1:22 p.m.
**Subject:** Parli Italiano?
Ciao Dani,
Come sta? Bene grazie. And that's about the extent of my
Italian. I spent a semester there in high school, and the only
thing I learned how to say was "Prego!" I used it
approximately 500 times per day while living in Florence,
though I'm still not quite sure what it translates to. I think
it's an all-purpose greeting, much like "Aloha" in Hawaii. But I
digress. FYI, I didn't mean the food OR the language. I meant
the people. I was thinking we could invite a family of Italians
to join us for dinner.
~Brady
P.S. I like all kinds of movies, although if you bring a slasher
flick, I'll have to sleep with my nightlight on.

P.P.S. Brain surgery and trapeze lessons I'd believe, but dog walking? Nah. You made that up.

P.P.P.S. Have you ever noticed how we always seem to be online at the same time? It's Kismet.

P.P.P.P.S. I lied. I know how to say a few other things in Italian. . . . I'll tell you, if you're good.

# 24

# The Male-Female Friendship Parameters

Even though it's Saturday, Your Big Break Inc.'s office is buzzing with activity. The phones are ringing, the fax machine's whirring, and the printer is humming. We used to be closed on the weekends, but lately Trey and Craig have both been working Saturday shifts to keep up with rising demands.

"Look at this!" Craig exclaims, waving a fistful of papers at me as I walk through the door. "We're famous!"

"The Salon.com article came out!" I say. I scan the first paragraph. *"Niiiice."*

"It's better than nice. We've been fielding calls all morning." Craig beams. "I'm taking out a half-page ad in *The Boston Globe* magazine to coincide with the launch of the new website Amanda's designing. And I'm going to have ten thousand fliers made up and distributed around the city. Can you draft some copy for the flier? Nothing much, just a paragraph teaser to get people interested. I'd need it by the end of this week."

"Sure, I can do that."

Craig slaps my back. "See what you can come up with. Think clever! Think cute!"

"I'll get working right away."

"This is a key moment for us, Dani. If business keeps booming the way I expect, I'm going to have to hire more staff. This is the big time, baby!" Craig rubs his hands together in anticipation and heads to his office.

Two men are milling around our waiting room, presumably here to see about off-loading their girlfriends. And standing in the corner by the window is . . . I blink. *It can't be.*

"Erin?" I ask tentatively.

She whirls around. "Oh. Danielle."

"Can I help you with something?" *What if she's talked to Brady? What if she told him who I really am?*

"I have an appointment."

"You do?" Did she call and book an appointment and no one bothered to tell me? "I'm so sorry. How long have you been waiting?"

"Actually, my appointment's with your colleague, Trey." She turns her back to me and stares out the window.

I'm taken aback. "Is it . . . is it something I did?" I ask. "I mean, were you unhappy with the level of service you received?"

She doesn't answer me.

There's only one conclusion. "I'm sorry you weren't satisfied with the job I did."

"Honestly, Danielle," she says, turning around to face me. "You're so insecure. You didn't do anything wrong. I'm here to see Trey S. because I have another uncomfortable personal

situation I'd like to take care of. And I prefer workin~~g~~
I assume that's permitted." She folds her arms across
as if daring me to challenge her.

I don't. "Of course," I say. "You're free to work with w~~h~~
you choose."

I walk into my office and then stop in my tracks. *Another*
Is she ditching the PBS producer already? I make a mental ~~n~~
to ask Trey about it later. I spend most of the afternoon retu~~rn~~
ing phone calls, answering e-mails, and writing breakup lette~~r~~
for clients. I attempt to come up with some advertising copy, but
I draw a blank. It'll have to wait until later.

Just as I'm finishing up, Evan Hirschbaum calls.

"I was going to leave a message. I didn't think you'd be in on
a Saturday," he says approvingly. "If you add in Sundays and
holidays, you could come work for my law firm."

"I think I'll stick with Your Big Break," I say. "But thanks."

Evan tells me he's got a new case for me to handle. I get her vi-
tal stats: Michelle, twenty-seven, dance instructor, they've been
dating for five weeks. I'm relieved to see Evan's switching back
to older women again. I never thought I'd consider a twenty-
seven-year-old an "older woman." I note how long they've been
together: five weeks.

"I see you're overlapping," I say. "Juggling more than one
woman at a time."

"How do you figure?"

"Well, you were with Quinn until a few weeks ago."

"Ah, yes, Quinn, that little redhead from Urban Outfitters."

"Actually, she was a brunette."

"A brunette?"

"Yes."

"I should develop a system to keep them all straight." He cackles. "I'm starting to worry myself."

*Just starting?* "Did you tell Quinn and Michelle about each other?" I can't help asking.

He says, "A little tip for you, Dani: Unless a man says otherwise, always assume he's got more than one girlfriend, that he's sampling more than one dish at a time."

*Ew.* I tell Evan I'll get in touch with Michelle on Monday and make an appointment to break up with her.

"Speaking of appointments . . ."

*Uh-oh, here it comes.*

". . . I'm going to have my secretary fax over a list of guidelines for our lunch."

*Excuse me, what lunch?* Last I checked, we didn't have a firm date for that, and I've been avoiding making one. *And what guidelines? Is this a business meeting?* "I'm sorry, I don't understand," I say.

"I'd like us to meet, go over the male-female friendship parameters."

*Male-female friendship parameters? Are we negotiating a contract?* "Evan, I'm really not following."

"My secretary will fill you in," he says. "I'm going out of town next week, but I'll speak to you when I get back."

I spend the rest of the afternoon updating my files. Before I leave, I pop into Trey's office. "I understand you've inherited Erin Foster-Ellis as a client," I comment.

"Sorry about that. Didn't mean to poach her from you." Trey looks up from his computer. "She went to Craig and requested not to work with you."

*Ouch.* "She actually did that?" I feel a tinge of guilt; I probably deserve it. I didn't exactly do a very thorough job for her.

Trey nods. "She said she didn't like your personality. She was pleased with the job you did, though."

Boy, Trey doesn't miss a beat when it comes to brutal honesty.

"Sorry, don't mean to be harsh."

"No, it's fine. So, is she ditching the PBS guy?" I ask.

Trey nods. "Apparently, he works too hard, doesn't spend enough time with her. That woman is a pain in the butt," he says, as if reading my thoughts. "You're lucky to be done with her."

"Oh, baby," Krista says, brushing her fingers over Jason Dutwiler's hand. "*You're* the cutie pie."

"No, *you* are."

"No, *you*!"

*Great. Couple talk.* I gulp down my glass of merlot while they trade sickly sweet pet names. I wish the food would hurry up and get here. We've been sitting for more than thirty minutes, and I'm starting to get crabby. A few bites of lamb biryani would really cheer me up.

"I'm sorry, Dani." Krista says. "Are we making you feel like a third wheel?"

*Yes!* "No."

Krista and Jason exchange glances. "I think I left something in the car," he says, rising from the table. "Be back in a sec."

"I know we can be a little overwhelming sometimes," she says once he's gone. "We've just hit it off so well."

I play with my napkin, folding it and unfolding it in my lap. "It's weird seeing you together. When I set you up, I never imagined you'd be joined at the hip."

"I've never clicked with anyone like this before. When I

introduced him to my mother last night, she was totally blown away by how well we got along."

"You introduced Jason to your parents?" *Whoa, this is serious.*

"He hasn't met my dad," Krista says, picking up her water glass. "But soon."

I'm happy for Krista, but I also feel left out. Things between us are changing. A few weeks ago, we were best friends, hanging out every weekend. Now I see Sophie and Sean more than I do her. We only exchange brief e-mails these days.

"How are things going with your parents?" Krista asks softly.

I sigh. "Not so good." I fill her in on what's been happening. "I'm trying to push it out of my mind," I conclude.

"Then let's talk about something more pleasant. Any news on the Brady front?" Krista asks, taking a quick sip of water.

"As a matter of fact, yes." I fill her in on what's been happening.

"That's so exciting!" Krista says, clasping her hands. "Dinner and a movie at his place sounds very romantic."

"I worry it's too soon," I confess, shifting nervously in my seat.

"Too soon for what?"

"Brady lost his father and his long-term girlfriend in a one-month period. Is he ready for a serious relationship?"

Krista seems unfazed. "People are always ready for relationships. The only time they claim otherwise is if they haven't met the right person. Take Jason, for example. He's completely over Lucy," she declares. "For a long time, he didn't think he'd be able to let go. But meeting me changed everything."

"You really think so?" I ask uncertainly. "I mean, he was pretty hung up on her."

"I *know* so." She thumps the table emphatically. "Jason and I are rock-solid. And I'm sure it'll be the same way with Brady. You'll see."

Jason reappears in the doorway of the restaurant. "Isn't this ironic?" Krista asks, catching sight of him. "You and I are both going out with castoffs from Your Big Break. Did you ever imagine your job would hold such a hotbed of potential dates?"

"I've got access to one of the largest singles pools in the city of Boston," I say, grinning. "It's better than working for a matchmaking service." I take another sip of wine. "The problem is, they're all rebound guys."

"You worry too much." Krista leans back in her chair and motions for Jason to rejoin us. "The whole rebound thing—it's a myth. Like Bigfoot or the Loch Ness Monster."

"I hope you're right."

# 25

# I Sound Like My Parents

"I'm going back to school!" Sophie announces as she walks into my office Monday morning.

I look up from the stack of paperwork on my desk. I wasn't expecting Sophie to drop by, and I certainly wasn't expecting her to tell me this. "Are you serious?"

"I start this fall," she says, sitting down across from my desk. She's decked out in a gorgeous black pantsuit and stylish Marc Jacobs pumps. Every time I see her, she looks more stunning than before.

"Congratulations!" I say. "That's awesome. When did this happen?"

"I enrolled this morning. I've been thinking about it ever since that day you helped me move the boxes and we had our talk."

I had no idea our discussion had such an impact on her. "Where are you going?"

"Northeastern. I missed the deadline for fall enrollment, but

I'm going to audit a few courses. In the spring, I'll start full-time."

I smile. I'm genuinely happy for her.

"Anyway, I brought these," she says, reaching into her tote bag and passing me three *Playgirls*.

I note that they're in pristine condition, newsstand-fresh, and I take them from her hands. "So, are you excited?" I ask, setting the magazines down on my desk.

"Excited and nervous. I hope I made the right choice in selecting Northeastern."

"My brother graduated from Northeastern. It's a fantastic school."

"Really?" She looks surprised. "I had no idea. What did he study?"

"Biochemistry."

"Sean has a biochemistry degree from Northeastern and he's working at *Blockbuster*?" she exclaims.

"I know. My parents have been trying to convince him to go to medical school for two years. He claims he wants to be a doctor, but as far as I know, he's never applied to med school."

"Do you think he's worried he won't be accepted? It's incredibly tough to get in."

"That could be part of it," I agree, playing with a pencil on my desk. "But his undergrad GPA was a three-point-eight, and he did pretty well on his MCATs—that's the med-school entrance exam."

"Then there's no reason he shouldn't apply. Have you asked him why he's reluctant?"

"A couple of times," I say, folding my hands in my lap. "He brushes it off, or cracks a joke about having too much fun shelving DVDs. I don't know. . . . He's smart, yet he spends all his free time watching TV and playing video games." *I sound like my parents.*

"Want me to talk to him?"

I'm taken aback. "That's okay. I don't think he'd appreciate me sending my friends to pester him about his career." As soon as the words have left my mouth, I realize what I've said. *Friends. Can I call her that? Have we reached that stage? Or is she still Evan's ex?* We've hung out so many times, talked about our personal lives, watched movies together. I'd definitely say that qualifies. *Is being friends with a client's former girlfriend in violation of Your Big Break Inc.'s rule #5?*

I decide that it's not.

"I could find out what he wants to do with his life in a round-about way," Sophie says. "We'd just talk, like friends."

*There's that word again.*

"Maybe the doctor thing isn't his dream anymore?" She gives me an imploring look. "Your brother's so adorable and sweet. I'd hate to see him pass up the chance to make something really great out of his life."

I study her face. Ever since the topic switched to Sean, Sophie has been grinning from ear to ear. She sure is interested in my brother's med-school plight. Come to think of it, it was her idea to drive all the way out to Sean's Blockbuster the other night, too. I remember her remarking, ever so casually, that his location had the best selection.

*Could a girl like Sophie Kennison be interested in my brother? Nah, not possible.*

"You could give me Sean's cell number, and I could call him up sometime."

*Okay, it's definitely possible.*

"Do you want to go out with my brother?" I ask. No sense beating around the bush.

She doesn't hesitate. "Yes."

I stare at her incredulously. *"Really?"*

"Geez, Dani, you make Sean sound like such a catch," she says.

"It's not that. I just never imagined you'd like someone like Sean."

"Why are you so surprised?"

"He's doesn't seem like your type."

"I don't have a type," she says. "I've dated all sorts of guys. Rich, poor. Different races. It doesn't matter. I base it on whether or not I like the person. And I think Sean's charming." She pauses. "Do you think he would go for me?"

"Do I think Sean would go for you?" I ask, laughing. "Yes, I think Sean would go for you."

She giggles. "Fabulous! I was so nervous about this! Deep down, I'm just this big dork." She smiles.

"If you want, I can talk to Sean," I offer. "I'll even set up a date for you two, if you'd like."

"Would you?" Sophie jumps up and rushes around the side of the desk. She bends down and gives me a quick hug. "That'd be fantastic."

I hug her back. "Of course. I'd be happy to."

"Thanks, Dani," she says. "You've been so great to me. I feel awful the way I treated you the first time we met. And then the way I stormed out of Ben and Jerry's that day—"

I wave my hand. "Don't sweat it! The first time we met, I was dumping you. Of course you weren't going to welcome me with open arms."

"This is so nice . . . having you as a friend, and now maybe having a date with Sean. I feel lucky."

"Me, too. Things have been rough with my family lately," I confess. "I think it would really cheer Sean up to go out on a date."

"I was sorry to hear about your parent troubles. If there's anything I can do to help . . ."

"Thanks," I say, holding up the issues of *Playgirl*. "But you've already gone above and beyond the call of duty."


I stop by Sean's Blockbuster on my way home from work. I need to give him the *Playgirl* magazines. We've decided the best strategy is for Sean to sneak them into Jude's yoga bag. Since he lives at home, he has much easier access. My job will be to "discover" them tomorrow night. I'm not sure exactly how I'm going to accomplish this. I'm sure I'll think of something between now and then.

Sean's helping a customer when I arrive, so I spend a few minutes browsing.

"Have you got the stash?" he asks, sidling up to me. He glances around nervously, making sure no one's within earshot.

"Right here." I pull them out of my bag.

He immediately stuffs them under his shirt. "I can't believe I have to hang on to these for the rest of the night." He groans. "If any of my coworkers see them, I'm toast."

"Can't you hide them in the break room?" I ask.

"That's what I'm planning to do," he says, nodding. "The way my luck's been going, my manager will stumble across them while she's taking her coffee break." He looks really stressed-out. I feel awful for my brother. There are bags under his eyes, and he can't stop fidgeting. "I have some news that's guaranteed to cheer you up," I say, slinging my arm over his shoulder.

"Dani, nothing could cheer me up right about now."

"How about a date with Sophie Kennison?"

"Sophie?" he sputters. "As in your majorly hot friend Sophie?"

"The same."

His eyes bulge. "Don't tease me, Dani. It's not nice."

"I'm not teasing," I say. "Sophie wants to go out with you."

Sean smiles slowly. "Well, I'll be damned. You were right. There *was* something that could cheer me up!"

# 26

# Hey, Jude

Sometimes I wish I were a smoker, so I could suck down a few cigarettes and let the nicotine soothe me. They say it performs miracles on shot nerves. Until it kills you.

As I turn into the driveway, I catch sight of my brother, crouched down by the side of the house. I do a double take. He's lying in wait like a prowler.

I pull the car to a stop at the edge of the driveway, parking behind Mom's Ford Explorer. I've just climbed out when Sean comes running toward me. "What are you doing lurking out here?" I ask, staring at him in surprise.

"We've got a big problem," Sean hisses in my ear.

"Words I'm not fond of hearing," I say wearily. "What is it?" I don't know if I can handle any roadblocks. This is already too complicated.

"Jude didn't bring his yoga bag."

"Oh, no." I groan. "You said Jude and that yoga bag were joined at the hip."

"Apparently, he gave it the night off."

"So much for Operation Gay Porn."

"Gotcha," Sean says wickedly. "He brought it. It's in the closet, and I've tucked in the magazines."

I blink in surprise. "So the plan is a go?"

"Yes. Sometime during the course of dinner, you've got to unearth the stash." Tugging at my sleeve, he adds, "Come on, we'd better go inside."

I grab his arm. "I can't just go digging around in his personal bag."

Sean throws up his hands. "You'll figure out something."

*I'm glad one of us is confident.* We walk inside the house. I can smell dinner wafting in from the kitchen as we head into the living room. "Prepare to enter hell," Sean whispers.

I walk into the room. "Hello!" Mom calls out.

"Hi," I answer.

Mom and Jude are sitting on the couch, holding hands and drinking white wine. "Jude, this is my daughter, Danielle. Dani, this is Jude," Mom says. She's positively glowing.

"Nice to meet you," I say. Jude nods in my direction.

I perch awkwardly on the couch beside them. Jude looks nothing like how I pictured him. I was expecting some artsy-fartsy, ponytailed hippie who walks around the house barefoot chanting "Ommmmmm" and striking yoga poses. But Jude's as normal-looking as they come. He has short, gray hair and is lightly tanned. He's wearing khaki pants and a white polo shirt with loafers. He seems more like a retired banker than a yoga instructor.

"Dani, would you like some wine?" Mom asks.

"Yes, I'd love a drink." *Morphine would be nice, too.*

"I'll get Dani a glass," Sean says, scooting off to the kitchen. I'm left alone with Mom and Jude. The silence is so deafening I can actually hear the second hand ticking on Jude's watch. So I know it is exactly one minute later when Sean returns with my drink. "Enjoy," he says, clinking glasses with only me.

"Dani, why don't you tell us what's been going on at work?" Mom prompts.

Sean plops down on a chair opposite us. "Yes, Dani, update us on the fascinating world of writing promotional copy for websites."

I glare at him. "Dani?" Mom asks. "I think Jude would really like to hear about your job."

I turn to face Jude. "Are you interested in my work?" I ask him.

Jude smiles brightly. "I'd love to hear about it! What Web design programs do you use? Microsoft Frontpage?"

"What do you care," I snap.

Jude looks genuinely hurt.

"Dani!" Mom gasps. "Why are you acting like this?"

"Because I don't want to talk about work," I say stubbornly.

"I was merely trying to make conversation," Mom says. After that, she doesn't try so hard. The four of us sit there in silence for what feels like an eternity but is probably closer to five minutes.

"So, Sean, Beth tells me you work in the film industry?" Jude prompts.

I snort. "He works at Blockbuster. It's hardly Hollywood." I'm being mean, and as soon as the words leave my mouth, I regret them. I'm scared Sean will take offense, but he plays along.

"Dani's right. I'm a video clerk. In fact, I only make ten dollars an hour, so I hope if you and Mom get married, you'll be willing to support me," he says.

"Oh, I don't know about that," Mom quips.

"I'm your child," Sean says. "It's not like you can throw me out on the street."

"Children have to grow up sometime," Jude points out, and we lapse back into silence.

"How about I get us some munchies?" Sean asks. He's smiling so tightly that his teeth are clenched.

"I'll come with you." I spring up and stalk into the kitchen before Mom can stop me. "This is a nightmare," I say as soon as we're out of earshot.

He pulls open the oven door. "Do you think if I stuck my head in here anyone would notice?"

I swat him on the arm. "I'd notice. And I'd kill you for deserting me."

Sean sighs, slamming the oven shut.

I reach into the fridge and pull out a container of hummus. "What are we having for dinner?" I ask.

"I have no clue," Sean says, opening the oven again. "Looks like some sort of casserole."

I look down at the hummus. "I doubt this goes with casserole."

"Who cares? Serve it anyway." He shuts the oven again and turns to look at me. "As a matter of fact, I think we've got some sardines in the cabinet." He stands on tiptoe and begins digging around.

"Sardines?" I ask, wrinkling my nose. "Don't tell me you're going to serve those."

"Yup," he says. "And jelly and crackers. This is going to be the suckiest dinner ever. Get me anything else weird you can find," Sean instructs. He locates the sardines and proceeds to open the can.

I search through the refrigerator and retrieve a packet of tofu and a jar of pickles. "Together?" I ask, holding them up.

Sean nods his approval. "Mix 'em."

I get out a bowl and concoct a tofu/pickle dish guaranteed to make even a pregnant woman cringe. "This reminds me of when we were kids. You remember how we used to mix up all sorts of food and make vomit-worthy creations?"

"Sure do," Sean says, a look of intense concentration on his face. He grins devilishly. "I just had an idea. Put the sardines in with that."

"Really?"

"We're kicking the plan up a notch."

I continue to stir while he passes over ingredients: jelly, peanut butter, raisins, paprika. Once I'm finished, Sean grabs the bowl. "Here goes nothing," he says. Using an oven mitt, he takes the casserole out of the oven. Then he dumps the horrendous-looking concoction over it.

I gasp. "What the hell are you doing?"

"Sprucing up dinner," he says.

"We can't eat that!"

"We're not going to eat it." He grins. "Mom wanted a bonding dinner with Jude. Well, this is what I think of her damn dinner."

I burst out laughing. "You're too much."

"What's taking you two so long?" Mom asks, sailing into the kitchen. Her gaze zeroes in on the ruined casserole in Sean's hands. "What did you do to this?" she demands, waving her finger at the demolished dish.

"We added a few ingredients," Sean says seriously. "To improve the flavor."

"Bullshit," Mom says, and I wince. Mom never cusses. I've heard

her swear a few times in my life. "I can't believe this," she scolds.
"Here I thought you two were in your late twenties. But, apparently, you're five years old. My children are five years old!"
she yells, turning on her heel and stomping out of the kitchen.
"Fine then, fuck dinner!" she calls from the other room. "Tonight,
we starve."

Sean and I look at each other. Sean dumps the soiled casserole
in the sink. "I'll order a pizza," he says, red-faced. He picks up
the phone and dials. "Go find out what Jude likes on his."

"Who cares," I say, not bothering to move.

"*Dani,*" Sean says, nudging me toward the door. "We've already screwed up enough as it is. The least we can do is spring
for some food."

"Oh, all right," I huff, heading into the living room. I can't
believe I have to speak to Jude. "Hey, Jude," I ask, and then I
can't stop thinking of the Beatles song. "We're getting a pizza.
Do you have any requests?"

"No." Jude stands up. "I have no intention of eating pizza."

*Here it comes,* I think, *the big blowup that will end their relationship. Jude's about to reveal what a snob he is.*

"Your mother worked very hard on that casserole, and the
two of you went in there like spoiled brats and destroyed it."
Jude shakes his head sadly. "I was hoping we could all be adult
about this and have a nice dinner, but apparently that's not the
case." He turns to my mother. "Come on, Beth. I'm taking you
out. The children"—he nods toward me and Sean—"can eat
pizza."

"It's now or never," Sean whispers, nudging me hard. "Go
find those mags!"

I'm not sure if I can go through with this. *Wasn't sabotaging*

*Mom's casserole enough? Do we really need to sabotage her re-lationship, too?* Maybe we should give Jude a fair chance. We ought to at least get to know him before we decide to hate him. I look at Sean, and can tell by his face that it's too late to back out now. I dash out of the room and into the hall. I fling open the closet door just as Jude and Mom get there. I make a grab for the yoga bag, which Jude has placed on the shelf over the coats, in-stead of on the floor like a normal person. I snatch it. It's heavier than it looks, and as I pull it toward me, I hear a small ruffling noise. I watch as a few copies of *Playgirl* slide out and onto the floor.

"Dani!" Mom says, spying the *Playgirl*s. "Why on earth do you have a bunch of magazines with half-naked men on the cover?"

"The guys inside are completely naked!" I blurt.

"Yes, but why do *you* have them?"

"They were, uh, in Jude's bag," I mumble.

Jude stares at me. "No they weren't."

Mom sighs. "Dani, exploring one's sexuality is a perfectly normal thing." She comes over and strokes my hair. "If you want to look at naked men, there's nothing wrong with that."

"But I wasn't looking at naked men!" I shriek. "Jude was!" Even to my own ears, this sounds ludicrous. I see Sean appear in the hallway and then quickly duck out of view. I'm going to kill him for coming up with this asinine plan. *Why did I ever think it would work?*

"Those aren't mine," Jude says again.

Mom winks at me. "A healthy interest in sex is perfectly nor-mal."

*Please, God, let me sink through the floor.*

Mom and Jude go out to dinner, and Sean and I are left alone. We order a pizza, and it's cold and soggy by the time it arrives. We sit in the kitchen—the scene of the crime—and pick at it.

"We've blown it," Sean says. "We acted like two-year-olds."

I feel horrified, ashamed. "I know," I tell him.

For a long time neither of us says anything, and then I ask, "Do you think things will ever be okay again?"

He shrugs. "I don't know. But I can't keep living like this."

# 27

# Here's Hoping He's Not: a Psycho, a Nerd, or "a Little Out of Shape"

Brady owns a trendy, spacious studio in Kenmore Square, near the Boston University campus. I arrive at his building at exactly five minutes past eight. I've timed my entrance perfectly. I don't want to seem rude, but I don't want to appear overeager. Brady buzzes me in and I take the elevator up to the ninth floor. "Hi, Dani! You look great," he says as he ushers me into his apartment.

I'm wearing a charcoal pencil skirt, a dark blue camisole top, and low, black heels. I was afraid I might be overdressed, but I'm glad to see Brady's wearing nice black slacks and a smooth, button-down, French-cuffed shirt. I'm carrying a bottle of red wine and two DVDs: *About a Boy* and *Jerry Maguire,* both of which were suggested by Sean. "You want the film to be romantic,

but you don't want to bludgeon him over the head with something like *An Affair to Remember*. Not on the first date, anyway," Sean had said. As we walk into the makeshift living room,
Brady glances at the movies in my hand. "Good choices," he
says.

"Oh, have you already seen them?" I ask.

"I own *Jerry Maguire*, but I've never seen *About a Boy*.
Should I pour us some wine?" he asks, taking the bottle from my
hands.

"That'd be nice," I say.

He goes over to the kitchen, a sprawling alcove with a gorgeous granite-topped island and grill-top stove. There's a small
wineglass rack, which holds a dozen or so glasses, hanging from
the ceiling. Brady gets a corkscrew out of the drawer and then
grabs two glasses from the rack. He proceeds to uncork the bottle of Chianti.

"Dinner smells wonderful," I say. "What are we having?"

"Hazelnut pesto lasagna," he says, "with salad and some
bruschetta pomodoro to start."

I blink in surprise. "You know how to cook all that?"

"*Si*," he says, bowing playfully. "Well, I made the bruschetta
and the salad," he admits. "The lasagna's from Masetti's. I am a
master when it comes to ordering in." He takes a small dish of
gourmet pitted olives out of the fridge. "Dinner will be ready in
about twenty minutes. Why don't we sit and relax?"

I follow him over to the living room. He sets down the olives
on the coffee table and sits on the couch; I ease down on the opposite end, leaving one couch cushion between us.

"So, how have you been lately?" I ask.

"Busy. As soon as school let out, I flew to Scottsdale."

"You said you were out there on legal business?" I say, picking up an olive.

He nods. "There were some concerns over my dad's will."

"You're licensed to practice in Arizona?" I'm amazed.

"No." Brady laughs. "But my mother wanted me to look over the paperwork anyway, to make sure the attorney wasn't 'screwing her over.' "

"Lawyers have a reputation for doing that kind of thing, huh?"

"Oh, yeah." He runs his fingers through his dark hair. "I want to hear about *your* job. What's it like being a Web designer? Do you use Dreamweaver and Adobe GoLive? Have you done any sites I might have seen?"

"Uh, I'm not that involved with the design end of things," I say, feeling my skin flush pink. "My job mainly consists of writing promotional copy," I clarify, "the text you see on websites." *Why can't I just tell him the truth?* I curse myself for not having the courage to be honest. The closer I get to it, the harder it is for me to be myself. I want to pull away, to hide. Anything to avoid being hurt, anything to maintain control.

"So, you're a writer," he says, leaning forward and picking up an olive.

"Not exactly. I mean, I write a lot of letters." I feel my face flame up. *What am I doing?* I might as well just come right out and tell him about the Dear Brady note.

"Letters?" He looks confused.

"Uh, yeah. You know . . . letters of the alphabet. A, B, C, D. All the usual suspects."

It's a lame joke, a poor attempt to save face, and it falls flat. "It's more like advertising. I have to be really flattering toward the client," I improvise.

He chews on the olive for a minute and then swallows. "So you get a chance to be creative. And there's lots of variety, which I bet is nice."

I nod. "It has its moments."

"What did you study in college?" Brady asks.

"I've got a journalism degree from the University of Massachusetts and a master's in communications from Tulane. What about you? Where'd you go to law school?"

Brady finishes his glass of wine and pours himself a fresh one before answering. "Harvard."

Brady went to Harvard Law? "Very impressive!"

He shrugs. "I had every intention of becoming an English teacher when I graduated from college. That was always my passion."

"Why didn't you?"

"My father was dead set against it," he answers, looking uncomfortable. "He thought I was throwing my life away. . . ." His voice trails off and he shifts positions on the couch.

"So instead you went to Harvard Law?" I ask, trying to draw him out.

"Yeah." He looks me in the eyes. "And for a long time, I thought I'd made the right decision. From the outside, my life seemed perfect. But when you fool yourself into taking the wrong path, eventually you reach a point where nothing in life makes sense anymore. You can't keep up the act. I just didn't want to do it anymore."

"Was it hard leaving your law practice?"

"It was the best day of my life. The hard part was finding a teaching job. There aren't a lot of openings in late April. That's why I wound up at Addington. Private schools have more leeway on when they can bring in new staff."

"It wasn't your first choice?" I ask, surprised.

"I'd prefer to teach public school. I think there's more potential to make an impact. I'll start looking to move in a year or two." He gets a faraway look in his eyes. "I'm sorry, I'm rambling." He leans across the couch and quickly squeezes my hand. I feel a small rush. "Tell me about your hobbies."

"Making things," I tell him. "Like homemade cards and gifts." *Also known as breakup letters and recovery kits.*

"Really?" Brady asks, interested.

I nod. "I made this terrific card in Quark for my best friend, Krista, not too long ago. On the front cover it said: "Good luck meeting your Internet boyfriend!" Then, inside were three clip-art pictures: a scary guy holding a meat cleaver, a dorky scientist with huge glasses, and an enormous beer-bellied trucker. I wrote: "Here's hoping he's not a psycho, a nerd, or 'a little out of shape.' "

Brady smiles. "So how'd the date turn out?"

"It didn't. He never showed up."

Brady sets down his wineglass on the coffee table. "That's probably a good thing. Who knows? He might have matched the description in your card to a tee." He rises from the couch. "Let me check on dinner."

I stand up and stretch as he heads over to the kitchen and begins tinkering around in the oven. I feel comfortable, relaxed. Brady's "dining room" is actually a small table in the far corner of the loft. He's already set it with nice dinnerware and a few candles.

"This looks about ready. Have a seat, Dani. I'll bring everything over."

"You want some help?"

"Don't be silly. You're the guest," he says. "I'll wait on you."

*A modern man. I like it.* I arrange myself in one of the chairs. A few minutes later, Brady comes over with a platter of bruschetta topped with tomatoes. He shuffles back and forth to the kitchen, bringing in the large salad bowl, a basket of bread, and then, finally, the hazelnut pesto lasagna. I've never had pesto lasagna before; it smells divine.

Brady sits down across from me. "I hope it's good!" he says.

I sample the hazelnut pesto lasagna. "It's fabulous," I say, and he beams. "I love your apartment, too," I add. "How long have you lived here?"

"I bought this place a year ago," he says, spearing a forkful of salad. "I love the area."

The conversation shifts to architecture, and then to art. Brady's not afraid to share his opinions, but he's open to new ideas as well. By the time we've finished dinner, coffee, and dessert—tiramisu from a local bakery—we've bantered about everything from European travel to shopping to politics. We've just begun a discussion about movies when Brady says, "Speaking of which, maybe we ought to put on one of the DVDs? It's getting late."

I glance at my watch. "I can't believe it's already ten-forty-five!"

"Time flies when you're having fun." Brady smiles and begins clearing the table.

I pick up our empty coffee mugs and follow him to the kitchen. "Which one do you want to watch?" I ask, setting the dishes in the sink.

"Since I've seen *Jerry Maguire* fifteen times, why don't we go with *About a Boy*?"

"Works for me."

"It's based on a Nick Hornby book, isn't it? You helped me pick out *High Fidelity* when we first met. I really loved it."

Brady and I settle down on the couch to watch *About a Boy*. He sits closer to me this time, with one cheek on the middle cushion. *About a Boy* turns out to be a good choice. Brady laughs at all the right places, gets all the same jokes I do.

When I leave that night, around one in the morning, Brady walks me downstairs to my car. As we stroll through the apartment's parking garage, he tells me what a wonderful time he's had and thanks me for coming over. "Or, should I say *grazie*?"

"Ah, yes," I say. "I almost forgot you're fluent in Italian."

He laughs. "I know ten words. That's hardly fluent."

"So what are they?" I ask. "That P.S. in your last e-mail got me wondering."

Brady blushes. "It seemed clever at the time. Now I feel kind of funny telling you."

"You told me about Koogan," I say playfully. "You can tell me anything."

He smiles shyly at me. "One of the Italian phrases I know is *La donna è bella*. It means 'The girl is beautiful.' I was going to say that about you."

I don't respond for a minute. I'm speechless, breathless, and he takes it the wrong way.

"I hope that doesn't sound like some cheesy line. I didn't mean it that way!"

It's not every day a man tells me I'm beautiful, and in Italian, no less. I feel my face flush with pleasure. I wish I knew some kick-ass Italian phrase I could use to impress him. "Thanks, that's sweet," I say, embarrassed.

"We'll do this again soon," he promises, handing me the

DVDs as I unlock the driver's-side door. I get in the car and strap on my seatbelt.

"Take care, Dani," Brady says as I shut the door and place the key in the ignition. I start my car and drive out onto the street, waving at him as I go, a huge, goofy grin on my face.

# 28

# You Were Just Being Honest

"What's the verdict? Are you and Sean giving up the fight?" Krista asks the next morning over a prework breakfast at De-Salle's Diner. I take a sip of orange juice. She dumps a few packets of Equal into her coffee.

I sigh. "There is no fight. We've already lost the battle and the war."

"So you aren't going to try to reunite them?"

I shrug. "How are things going with Jason?" I ask to change the subject.

"Jason talks about Lucy. A lot," Krista says. "We get into these long, drawn-out conversations about her. Everything from where Lucy was born—Topeka, Kansas—to what kind of toothpaste she prefers—Aquafresh. I know Lucy Dooley better than I know some of my closest friends."

"Everyone talks about their exes. It's normal. It's part of the healing process."

"Does Brady do it?" She sips her drink.

"Well, no. He thinks I'm friends with Erin. He doesn't want to badmouth her."

"But wouldn't that make him *more* likely to talk to you about her? Wouldn't he be concerned with what she's told you about him?"

*A great point. Why* isn't *Brady trying to pump me for info about Erin?*

"Are you guys going for a round two?" Krista asks.

"He said he'd call." I sigh again, and shove a bite of omelet into my mouth.

"For the love of God, Dani," Krista says, shaking her fork at me, "join the twenty-first century and call the guy first!"

"I guess I could," I hedge. "I'm just afraid of coming off as too eager."

"No, you're afraid of taking a chance, afraid of putting your feelings on the line."

"You really think?"

"Yes, I do." She sets down her knife and fork. "Dani, ever since you and Garrett broke up last year, you haven't been the same. You rushed to move on, you laughed off what he did as a joke. But it's changed you."

I don't say anything. *Of course it's changed me!* It's impossible to get your heart smashed into pieces by someone you love and stay the same person you were before.

"You and Garrett were *engaged*," Krista continues. "He left you for a waitress. He treated your relationship like a joke."

*Engaged.* I never think about that part. I block it out, push it to the back of my mind. It's the part of the story I never share. "I didn't have a ring," I argue.

"It was at the jeweler's being resized when he left," she reminds me.

Remembering this fact makes me feel bitter all over again. I didn't get the ring, but I desperately wanted it. I'm not sure what I would have done with it. *Pawnshop? Garbage disposal? Hawk it on eBay?* I didn't hold on to anything else from our relationship. I threw out all the mementos: the photos, the CDs he'd pinched from WBCN, the presents he'd given me on Christmas, birthdays, anniversaries. I went through such a horrific time when he left me. But I worked through it, dealt with it. I never tell people this, but Garrett's the reason I started working at Your Big Break Inc. I read about the company after he dumped me. And I saw an opportunity, a chance to make sure no one else was ever blindsided the way I was.

I take another sip of orange juice and try to steady my nerves.

I think of all the lies I've told since I've taken this job. When you lie, you distance yourself from other people. You create walls. *Why haven't I just come clean? To my parents about my job? Or to Brady, about Erin? Would it really be that difficult?*

"I've got to get to the office soon," Krista says, glancing at her watch. "Give me a call later if you need to talk."

I don't respond.

"Hey, I'm sorry," she says gently. "I didn't mean to upset you."

"No, it's okay," I say. "You were just being honest."


"Hi Dani, this is your dad. I was wondering if you'd like to come over for a Fourth of July cookout Monday night. I'll make my world-famous burgers with bread crumbs. Your brother's working late that night, so he can't make it. But I'd really love for you to be here. Call me back and let me know either way."

And then he leaves his phone number on my answering machine, as though I don't have it. As though I haven't dialed his cell a thousand times. I can't believe he's called me. It's been a long day at work, and I don't want to speak to him—not yet.

But he's making the effort to reach out to me.

And I know I have to meet him halfway. I could avoid my parents indefinitely. Or I could face this situation head-on. It's better to get this over with, I reason. Just like ripping off a Band-Aid. Isn't that what I always tell my clients? I pull my cell phone out of my purse and text Dad a short, two-word message: *I'll go.* Then I decide to get in touch with Brady and see if he wants to go out again. Krista's right, I can't just sit around and wait for him to call. I hop online and compose a brief message.

**From:** "Danielle Myers" <DaniMyers@yahoo.com>
**To:** brady_simms@hotmail.com
**Sent:** Thursday, June 30, 6:42 p.m.
**Subject:** thanks
Brady,
What's Italian for "I had a great time last night and hope we can do it again soon"? Seriously, I did have a great time—no, make that an amazing time. And I do hope we can get do it again soon.
Dani

A few hours later, he writes back.

**From:** "Brady K. Simms" <brady_simms@hotmail.com>
**To:** DaniMyers@yahoo.com

**Sent:** Thursday, June 30, 9:51 p.m.
**Subject:** RE: thanks
Dani,

I'll have to check my Italian/English dictionary and get back to you. My language skills are pretty limited to hi, bye, and "Can I have another slice of pizza?" Plus that thing I said the other night. . . . Speaking of the other night, I had a great time, too! And I'd love to see you again. Name the time and place and I'm there.

~Brady

**From:** "Danielle Myers" <DaniMyers@yahoo.com>
**To:** brady_simms@hotmail.com
**Sent:** Thursday, June 30, 10:22 p.m.
**Subject:** How about next weekend?

I'm working Saturday, but my schedule's wide open next Sunday if you want to grab lunch or dinner.

Dani

**From:** "Brady K. Simms" <brady_simms@hotmail.com>
**To:** DaniMyers@yahoo.com
**Sent:** Thursday, June 30, 10:46 p.m.
**Subject:** RE: How about next weekend?

Dani,

Here's what I'm thinking: you, me, and a picnic lunch in the Public Garden next Sunday at 1 p.m. I'll bring the main course and side dishes (I make a mean turkey sandwich and an even meaner potato salad). You take care of drinks and dessert. You game?

~Brady

**From:** "Danielle Myers" <DaniMyers@yahoo.com>
**To:** brady_simms@hotmail.com
**Sent:** Thursday, June 30, 11:01 p.m.
**Subject:** Picnic

I am so game.

Dani

# 29

Tired of your boring relationship?
Longing to wash that man or woman right out of your hair?
Then let us be your shampoo!
Call **Your Big Break Inc**. today—
We'll dump that dead weight so you don't have to!

I scroll the cursor across the screen, highlight, and hit delete. I could kick myself. It's Friday morning, and I promised Craig I'd have this copy to him by the end of the day. I've had a week to write one measly paragraph for a flier, yet I've put it off until the last minute. Craig wants something "clever and cute." All I have is "cheesy and convoluted." I start humming that old Neil Sedaka classic, *Breaking Up Is Hard to Do*. It doesn't inspire me. *Writing* about breaking up is even harder than *doing*—

I put my hands on the keyboard and quickly type:

**Breaking up is hard to do? Not anymore . . .**
**Your Big Break Inc. can help!**
*It's not you, it's us!*

Property Retrieval • Dear John Letters • Counseling Phone Calls •
Breakup Recovery Kits

We do it all! Let us let them down easy for you.

Call (617) 55-LEAVE

Because breaking up doesn't have to give you a breakdown.


I tag on a couple of sentences about our prices and our web-site address and then hit print. I think Craig will be pleased. I know I am. I think it sounds clever, smart. I leave the mock-up on his desk and then run right into Amanda as I head back to my office. "Fax for you," she says, waving a piece of paper in the air.

"Thanks," I say, taking it. I can see the letterhead of Hirschbaum, Davis, and Klein: Attorneys at Law printed across the top. My eyes catch sight of the date. "This came in last Saturday!" I yelp. "It's nearly a week old. Why didn't you give it to me sooner?"

She shrugs. "It got mixed in with my faxes. I didn't notice it until today."

"Great," I snap. "Just great. Evan Hirschbaum is top priority," I scold her.

Without saying anything, Amanda turns on her heel and stalks away.

I scan the fax.

## Hirschbaum, Davis, and Klein
## Attorneys at Law

# FAX

**To:** Danielle M. of Your Big Break Inc.
**From:** Martha Rowe, assistant to Evan Hirschbaum
**Date:** Saturday, June 25
**Re:** Lunch Arrangements
**Comments:**
Mr. Evan Hirschbaum, Esq. would like to invite you to lunch at The Ritz-Carlton Hotel, date TBD. Please be advised that the following conditions apply:

- Mr. Hirschbaum will not provide you with monetary compensation.
- Mr. Hirschbaum *will* pay for all dining expenses.
- You will be responsible for your own transportation.

Please contact me at your earliest convenience to confirm that you've read and understood these conditions.
EH/mr

I sit there with my mouth gaping open. *"Mr. Hirschbaum will not provide you with monetary compensation?"* What am I, a prostitute? *I'm not after his money! I'm not after anything. I don't even want to go to this stupid lunch!*

I'm indignant! Outraged!

Over the past year, I've put up with a lot of crap from Evan Hirschbaum—no more. I've finally reached my limit. With shaking hands, I pick up the phone and dial his office. His assistant answers on the second ring.

"Hirschbaum, Davis, and Klein. Martha speaking, may I help you?"

"Put me through to Evan Hirschbaum, please."

"He's in a meeting right now. May I take a message?"

"Yes, you certainly may," I say haughtily. "Tell Evan that Danielle from Your Big Break Inc. called. I got his fax—"

"What does your schedule look like? Mr. Hirschbaum's wide open next Tuesday, if you want to have lunch then."

"I'm all booked up," I say, and then I let out a loud, exaggerated laugh. "In fact, you can tell Evan that I will be booked up for the rest of my life. He can take his lunch date and shove it up his ass!" I slam down the phone before she has time to respond.

Thirty minutes later, Evan calls.

"I can shove our lunch date up my ass, can I?"

As soon as I'd hung up, I'd felt a twinge of remorse. Maybe I'd been too harsh? Maybe I'd gotten carried away? And, most troubling of all, maybe I'll get fired when Craig discovers what I've done. "Yes, about that," I begin. "I was a little put off when I read your fax."

"You took things the wrong way," he says matter-of-factly. Then he says, "You know, Dani, it's important I get to know you." He continues, "You'll allow me to broaden my horizons, see women in a different context."

*Could it be possible that his intentions are good?*

"An insider's view of what makes women tick. I'll be able to utilize what you teach me to my advantage in numerous ways."

*No, he's just a shallow pig, looking to manipulate women.*

"I don't know how much I'll be able to help you with that," I say.

"It all remains to be seen. Now, switching gears, I trust Sophie is doing better?"

"Much. She's pulled her life together over the past couple of weeks. She's found a new man." This is only half true. Sophie and Sean's first date is tonight, so technically he's not "her man." But they've been talking on the phone constantly, and they seem to be hitting it off well. "And she's going back to college in the fall."

"College," Evan scoffs. "She should enroll in cosmetology school. Though even that might be a bit too cerebral for our Sophie."

"*Our Sophie.*" This phrase bugs me. As though Evan can lay claim to her, as though she belongs to him. "I think she'll hold her own," I say diplomatically. "Sophie's a smart cookie."

# 30

# I'm Still Getting to Know Myself, Finding Out Who I Am As a Person

I've promised to help Sean get ready for his big date tonight, so I drive out to my parents' house after work. I time things wrong and show up before Sean's made it home from Blockbuster. I'm hoping I can sneak through the door and up the stairs without running into anyone, but no such luck. I've just let myself into the entrance hall when a voice calls out, "Dani? Is that you?"

It's my mother. She's sitting in the living room with all the lights out.

"Can you come in here a sec? You can turn on the light if you want."

My hands fumble for the switch. *Why is she sitting in the dark?* I flip on the lights.

"Sit down," Mom says.

I perch gingerly on the couch beside her. Mom's face is blotchy, and her eyes are swollen. She's surrounded by a mountain of Kleenex. "What's wrong?" I ask.

"Jude broke up with me today."

"He did?" I ask, shocked. "Did he give you a reason?"

"Apparently, he's not ready to make a serious commitment." She hugs the box of Kleenex close to her chest. "He said he's still getting to know himself, finding out who he is as a person."

I nearly fall off the couch. My *mom* has just received one of the ten biggest breakup excuses! Excuse: I'm still getting to know myself, finding out who I am as a person. Translation: I'm gay. I can't believe it. Jude really is gay. "He's gay, isn't he?" I ask.

"Good grief!" Mom looks stricken. "Where do you come up with these things, Dani?"

"You said your relationship didn't have any passion." I stop as I realize that she told that to Sean, not me. "At least, that's what Sean told me."

Mom looks annoyed. "Do you really want to have this conversation? Because if you're curious about whether or not Jude and I slept together, then come right out and ask. I'm not shy."

"I just can't believe he broke up with you," I say, shaking my head in surprise.

"That makes two of us."

"Don't worry about him. He wasn't worth it."

She blows her nose in a Kleenex. "But he *was* worth it. It's always worth it when you love someone."

I raise my eyebrows. "You loved Jude?"

"I don't know. I think I loved the change in me. I could be a different person when I was around him."

I stare at her. "You want to be a different person?" I can't believe we're talking so candidly.

Mom pulls the blanket tighter. "I already *am* different. You try to stay the same, you try to hold on to who you've always been. But when I was laid off from my job last year . . ." She stops and hangs her head.

This is the first time I've ever heard Mom use the words "laid off." Up until this point, she's made it sound voluntary, even though we all knew she didn't leave by choice.

"When I lost my job, I lost a part of my identity. I started to reexamine things, see all the ways my life was lacking. I got married so young. I never saw the world, never knew any other men." And by "knew," I know she means "slept with." Mom and I exchange a significant look. "I don't regret the decisions I've made in life, but I've reached a point where I want to experience new things."

I swallow hard. I can't believe this is really happening.

"Don't seem so down, Dani." She leans over and pats my leg. "I'm looking forward to this weekend."

"This weekend?"

"The cookout on Monday. Didn't your father tell you? He's making hamburgers and hotdogs for July Fourth. Sean's got to work, but he's hoping you can make it. It will be nice, for old time's sake."

"I'll be there," I say, struggling to keep my tone even.

"You know I'll always have strong feelings—" Mom says, and then stops as Sean arrives, whistling as he comes in through the front door.

I want her to finish the sentence, but she never does.

When Brady phones later that night, he catches me off guard. I didn't expect to hear from him; I figured he'd be out. I thought I was the only one dorky enough to be stuck home on weekends. While I'm happy that I've matched up Jason and Krista and Sophie and Sean, there's a definite downside. I've matched myself right out of having available friends.

"Hi, Dani," Brady says when I answer. "I hope I'm not calling too late."

"Well, I do normally turn in at seven-thirty. . . . What's going on?"

"Not much. I just got back from the movies."

*Movies? As in "I just got back from escorting some really hot girl to the movies?"*

"Oh, how was that?" I say casually.

"Kind of dull. It was just me, my buddy Andrew, and his girlfriend. I wound up being the third wheel. I spent most of the night wishing you were there."

My breath catches. "You should have invited me."

"I didn't know we were going until the last minute. I assumed you'd already have plans."

Little does he know that my evening consisted of helping my brother prep for his date and then camping out in front of the television with take-out Thai food. "Next time, try me anyway," I advise, walking into my bedroom and closing the door.

"I will," he says. "So are you looking to forward to our picnic next Sunday?"

I kick off my shoes and climb into bed. "Yeah! I think it'll be great. Maybe we can go for a walk after we eat. The Public Garden is so gorgeous this time of year."

"Have you ever been on the Swan Boats?" Brady asks.

"About ten years ago. When we first moved here, my family did all kinds of touristy stuff. We even took one of those cheesy duck-boat rides with the costumed tour guides."

"Don't laugh," Brady says in a mock whisper, "but I love cheesy tourist stuff. I never got the chance to do any of it when I was growing up."

"Really?" I pull the covers around me.

"Yeah. My family was more into visiting museums or architecturally significant houses and buildings. When we traveled, we never went to places like Sea World or Graceland."

"Hey, Graceland's an 'architecturally significant house,'" I point out, propping a few pillows behind my head. "Elvis lived there."

"My parents veered more toward Frank Lloyd Wright than the King."

"Sounds like you've got a lot of lost time to make up for. Should we start on Sunday, with a fun-filled ride on one of the Swan Boats?"

"That'd be fun," he says.

I'm surprised he didn't take Erin; they dated for two years. We wind up talking late into the night, chatting about our favorite foods, TV shows, music, vacations. Brady's well traveled. He's visited more than thirty U.S. states and has been to Europe a handful of times.

"This is fun," I say rolling over onto my stomach. "It reminds me of being fifteen years old. You know, when you stay up on the phone all night talking to your—" I stop abruptly. I was going to say "boyfriend." "Friends," I substitute.

When we finally get off the phone, it's nearly 3 a.m.

"I'll see you next Sunday," Brady says.

I can't wait.

Even though it's July Fourth, I envy Sean for having to work. I wish I'd been able to say I was working. But after my talk with

Mom the other day, I feel better about the whole situation. It's still weird, knowing I'll be dining with two cheaters, but I'm learning to accept it.

"Hi," I call out, sailing into the living room.

"There's someone I want to introduce you to!" Dad says, beaming. "Gretchen, you've already met my son, Sean. This is my daughter. I'm sorry I've kept you from each other."

*Oh fuck, oh fuck, oh fuck! Why didn't anybody tell me Dad's girlfriend was coming?*

"I know her," Gretchen jumps in, snapping her fingers. "That's Danielle."

"Did you two go to college together?" Mom cracks. I open my mouth to speak, but nothing comes out. There has to be a way to salvage the situation, to stop her before—

"She's the breakup girl," Gretchen announces.

*Too late.* My cover's officially blown.

My parents stare at both of us as realization continues to dawn on Gretchen. "Paul, I tried to *hire* your *daughter* to end things with you!"

"What are you talking about?" Dad looks at Gretchen as though she's lost her mind.

I have no idea what to do. *Should I feign innocence and pretend Gretchen is crazy? Should I act like the whole thing is one giant misunderstanding? Should I come clean?*

Before I can make a decision, Gretchen blurts out the story. "When I first found out you were married, I wanted to end things, so I hired that company, Your Big Break Incorporated. I read about them in the newspaper. They dump people for you."

Dad looks stunned. "You were planning to dump me?" he says.

"It was before we had our big talk," she says, walking over to Dad. She wraps her arms around his waist. I was going to pay her"—she points at me—"to handle everything."

"Why on earth would you involve Dani?" he asks. "How did you two even meet?"

"Dani's the *breakup girl,*" Gretchen says again, with emphasis.

"I don't get it," Dad says. "What's she talking about?"

Mom's quicker on the uptake. "So *that's* how you found out. It wasn't the computer files after all." And then, addressing Gretchen, she says, "Let me see if I've got this straight. Dani— *our Dani*—does freelance work for some sort of relationship-wrecking firm? She makes money ending happy unions? Is that even legal?"

*Yep. And it's surprisingly profitable, too.* I take a deep breath and say, "It's not freelance, Mom. It's my full-time job."

"How do you manage to juggle two full-time jobs?" Dad asks.

Gretchen looks nervous now, worried. "I'll go touch up my makeup," she says, darting out of the room.

"I was never a Web designer," I say, my voice quavering. "I made that up."

His jaw drops. "You made it up?"

I nod sheepishly. "Yes."

Mom whirls around to face me. "You lied to us?"

"You lied, too," I point out. "You lied about Gretchen and Jude!"

At the sound of her name, Gretchen resurfaces. "Are you talking about me?" she asks, slipping her arm through Dad's.

Mom ignores her. "Yes, we lied. But that's different."

"It's different because it's *you,*" I tell her.

"I don't know what to say." Mom sighs. She looks really sad. "This family is—" she stops. "It's not even a family anymore. I'm sorry I started this."

My father walks toward the back door. "Dinner's off," he says, going outside to shut off the grill. "I've just lost my appetite."

# 31

# The Five Stages of Breakup Hell

It's one of those perfect Sunday afternoons. The weather's gorgeous, cool and breezy with a glorious sun. Brady picks me up from my house at 1 p.m. and we drive into downtown Boston. He manages to find a vacant spot on Boylston Street a few blocks down from the Public Garden, the Holy Grail of parking places.

We walk side by side, Brady clutching a large wicker picnic basket. When we reach the gardens, he finds a shady spot near the lake and sets up camp, laying out blankets and pillows.

The picnic is amazing. We eat turkey sandwiches and German-style potato salad made with mustard. I've brought apple juice and bottled water, plus apricot tarts courtesy of the chef at Fintane Catering.

"So, you've never told me about your family," Brady says. "What are they like?"

I shove a bite of apricot tart into my mouth. "My parents

aren't exactly my favorite people at the moment. Their marriage is breaking up," I tell him.

"I'm sorry. That's rough."

"I feel so stupid that I'm upset about it. What am I, ten years old?"

"I don't think it's stupid," Brady says. "You seem to be coping pretty well."

"When I first found out my father was having an affair, I was devastated. I had a virtual meltdown. Then I got murderously angry. I destroyed a bunch of pictures of him."

As I continue with the story, something occurs to me.

The *nervous breakdown* I had when I found out. The *sour grapes* anger I'd felt toward my father. I'd wanted my mother to move on, to *rebound* and find joy in her life. And then, when I discovered the truth about Jude, the desperate push to reunite my parents at all costs—the *backslide*. I can't believe I didn't see it before: I've been going through the five stages of breakup hell.

Well, the first four at least—and with my parents, no less!

I didn't think that was possible. I wasn't even the one who got dumped. . . .

"Are you okay?" Brady asks, interrupting my thoughts.

I tug at a loose string on the picnic blanket. "I wish I could learn to let go, to butt out."

"Easier said than done."

"I have a hard time accepting when things are out of my control." I brush a few crumbs off the blanket, throwing them to a waiting pool of ants. "Whenever I see a situation where I think I can fix things, I get too involved."

Brady stares at me, his eyes focusing on mine. "My father did a lot of things I didn't agree with. He was bullheaded, he was a workaholic, and he was never satisfied with me, no matter what I did. But he was my *father*. And now that he's gone . . . all those things we argued about seem shallow, insignificant. I'm sorry about your mom and dad, and I can understand why you'd be upset. But you have to accept their choices, much in the same way they have to accept yours."

"Were you close to your dad?" I ask softly.

He shakes his head. "Not really. We were civil toward one another, but we were never friends. And that's one of the things I regret. I wish I could have understood him better; I wish he could have understood me. It was like we were on different wavelengths from the moment I was born. And now he's gone. Just like that. And no matter how much it hurts sometimes, no matter how I want to change things, I can't. It's awful, and I have to accept it." He takes a deep breath. "I don't have a choice."

We're quiet for a minute.

Brady sits up beside me and runs his fingers lightly over my back. "I love talking to you, Dani," he says softly. "It always makes me feel better."

The way he's looking at me I wonder, for a second, if he's about to kiss me.

But the moment passes and he doesn't.

"So, what do you say we go for that Swan Boat ride?" Brady asks. We get up, dust ourselves off, and head over to the lake.


"He called me Lucy!"

Krista's standing on my doorstep, staring up at me through mascara-stained lashes. It's eleven-thirty on Sunday night, and I'm still high off my afternoon with Brady. I note the backpack slung over her shoulder. Her face is red and puffy, and it's obvious she's been crying.

"Come in." I pull her through the door, and she deposits her backpack on the floor. "You want something to drink?"

She shakes her head miserably.

"Here, sit down." I guide her to the couch and she collapses on the center cushion.

"It's over with Jason."

"Oh, no." I wrap my arms around her in a quick hug. "What happened?"

She embraces me for a minute and then pulls away. "I told you, he called me Lucy."

"I assume you mean he did it—"

"During sex," Krista finishes.

"That's the worst," I say, though I have never experienced this horror. *Thank God.*

Her ears flush pink. "I feel so stupid talking about this."

"You don't have to feel stupid. It's just me."

"All right. I was . . . going down on Jason tonight." She looks really embarrassed. I'm not sure why. It's not as though we haven't discussed these kinds of things before. "And he was getting really into it and he said"—she grimaces—" 'Oh, Lucy, that feels so good!' "

"I bet that stopped things cold."

"At first I tried to ignore it, but he just kept saying it. 'Lucy! Oh, God, Lucy! Oh, God!' " she mimics. "So I had to stop."

"Did you call him on it?"

"Yeah," she mumbles. "And that's when he asked it." Her face goes pale.

"Asked what?"

"If it would be okay if he did something."

I tense up, anticipating what's about to follow, anticipating the part of the story where I'm going to discover what a gigantic freak Jason Dutwiler is in bed. "Go on, tell me," I urge.

"He wondered if I would mind if he fantasized about Lucy during sex!" Krista shouts.

"He actually asked your permission to fantasize about his ex-girlfriend?"

Krista groans. "There were warning signs all along. The way he dwelled on Lucy, the way he talked about her too much, the way he compared me to her constantly. But I liked him so much that I pushed it out of my mind. But tonight, things went too far." Krista's shoulders slump. "I've seen it coming for a while, but this was the last straw. The biggest thing we had going for us was mutual loneliness. We both wanted to be in love so badly. We were in love with the idea, not the reality."

"Are you sure?" I ask.

She rolls her eyes. "He was seriously on the rebound. You were so right. Guys who are fresh out of relationships don't make good boyfriends."

I groan. That doesn't bode well for me and Brady.

I pat her on the shoulder. "I'm sorry things didn't work out. What did he say when you told him it was over?"

"Uh, I haven't exactly done it yet."

"When are you going to tell him?"

"I was thinking . . ."

*Uh-oh.*

". . . since you've broken up with Jason once before."

"Krista, I can't."

She looks me in the eyes, pleadingly. "He'll take it better coming from you!"

"I can't."

Krista squeezes her eyes shut. "Dani, please! His brother's wedding is in a week and he's dying for me to go. He's gonna *freak* when I break things off."

"I'll think about it," I promise. "I can't give you an answer now."

She opens her eyes and turns to face me. "You know, Jason was obsessed with that damn wedding. He talked about it almost as often as he talked about Lucy." Krista pauses. "I really don't want to be alone tonight. You mind if I sleep over?"

"No, of course not." A few minutes later, we grab her backpack and head into my bedroom. "I'm sorry you had such a sucky time tonight," I tell her.

Krista bursts out laughing. "No pun intended, right?"

# 32

# Everybody Lies

"Come on in," Brady says, leading me into the living room, where I set down my purse and take a seat on the couch. It's a couple of nights later and he's invited me for dinner at his place. "The chicken's taking longer than I'd thought to finish roasting."

"How are things?" I ask.

"They're okay."

We sit in silence for a moment. I feel awkward, unsure of myself. The situation with my family, with Krista and Jason—combined with the memories of Garrett—is making me uncomfortable. I feel like my life is spiraling out of control.

"Do you ever think about Erin?" I blurt out, unable to stop myself.

Brady nods. "Of course I do."

*That's normal, right? I still think about Garrett. Jason still thinks about Lucy.*

"I'm not in love with her, if that's what you're asking."

For a moment, I feel relieved. *But is he lying?* "Not that I don't believe you," I say, "but it seems kind of soon. How can you be over your broken heart already?"

He thinks about it. "The truth is, Erin and I grew apart a long time ago. I was clinging to her because I'd been with her for years, and suddenly my entire world was changing and I didn't want any more change. But I'd fallen out of love; we were just going through the motions."

I'm surprised by this. "I thought Erin meant the world to you."

He takes a sip of wine. "She did mean the world to me. But the Erin you see now isn't the same Erin I fell in love with. The old Erin was a sweet, friendly girl who cared about charity work and about making a difference in the world—at least, that's what I wanted to believe. But the longer we dated, the more I got to know her. And I realized all she cared about was money. And I could never be rich enough for her." He laughs. "Donald Trump wouldn't be rich enough for her."

I choose my words carefully. "Erin says you haven't called her. She was . . . surprised you weren't heartbroken."

"I always forget you and Erin are friends," Brady says, reaching for my hand. "You two seem so different." He turns my hand over in his, stroking my palm with his fingertips. "When two people aren't in love anymore, it makes sense to call it quits."

I think about the breakup of my parents' marriage. *Was it meant to happen, and I just didn't notice the signs? No, it coundn't have been.* My father has always worked long hours, and my parents have never been the lovey-dovey type. When their marriage first went on the rocks, they didn't let it show. No one in my family is very good at letting things show, it seems. We hide behind work, or lies, or television. "I guess that's like my last boyfriend," I say instead, then stop and rephrase it: "My fiancé."

"You were engaged?" Brady asks, surprised.

I tell him about Garrett, about my radio breakup.

"What an asshole!" Brady exclaims. "People like that make me sick."

"People like that?"

"Liars, cheaters. There's never a good excuse to hurt someone that way."

I brush it off. "Oh, everybody lies," I say meekly, trying to soften the blow. "Even me sometimes."

"Yeah, but you've never told a lie like that. You've never cheated on anyone."

"No, I've never cheated. But I have lied from time to time."

"Okay, then what's the biggest lie you've ever told?" Brady asks.

*Keeping Your Big Break Inc. a secret.* I try to say the words, but I can't. "Lying to my mom about my father's affair."

"That must have been hard."

"Hard doesn't even begin to describe it."

Brady looks at me for a long time. I love that moment when you can feel the landscape shift and you know, beyond a shadow of a doubt, what's about to happen. "Can I kiss you?" he asks. I nod and he takes my face in his hands, traces his thumb over my lower lip. He pulls me toward him and our lips meet softly. Brady squeezes me in his arms. "I've wanted to do that for so long."

I lay my head against his shoulder. I feel dizzy, light-headed. *If there's such a thing as a perfect first kiss,* I think, *that was certainly it.* I try to focus my mind, to think rationally. I move my lips up and kiss Brady again. He's an incredible kisser, soft and gentle but passionate. He kisses my upper lip, my lower lip, the corners of my mouth . . . I feel his hands working on the buttons of my shirt and the thought of stopping him doesn't even cross my mind.

Brady's just taken my shirt off when the doorbell rings.

"Ignore it," I whisper.

He does and keeps kissing me, moving on to my neck.

Someone's knocking loudly on the front door. Brady continues to ignore it, but the knocking turns into pounding. "Brady! I know you're in there!" says a shrill voice. It's familiar, but I can't place it.

Exasperated, he untangles himself from me and jumps up off the couch. "Talk about a colossal case of bad timing," he says. "Hold that thought." He winks. "I'll be right back."

"Sure," I say. I feel drunk, weak-kneed.

"I need to get my pink Jimmy Choos," a voice says. "The twit forgot them."

I realize who it is and I scoop my shirt off the floor—but not in time.

"Danielle!" Her jaw drops. "What the hell's going on here?"

"I, well, we—"

"I recall you offer sympathy gifts and phone calls. I had no idea Your Big Break Inc. offered sympathy fucks!"

I pull on my shirt, rapidly buttoning it.

"Erin," Brady says, "Dani and I never meant to hurt you."

She sneers at me. "Brady, did you pay for a night with communications specialist Danielle M.? Or did you instruct them to bill *me* for it?"

Brady stares at her in disgust. "Get out," he says sharply.

She stalks into the bedroom and retrieves her Jimmy Choos. "Ta-ta," she says, waving them and heading toward the door.

"Apologize to Dani," Brady says, blocking her path.

"Keep dreaming," Erin says, trying to move around him.

"I'm embarrassed, truly embarrassed, by the way you treat people." Brady glares at her. "You dump me the month after my father passes away. Then you come over here and call Dani a prostitute? I'm sorry if you can't handle me dating your friend, but—"

"My *friend*?" Erin asks. Suddenly, the realization dawns on her. She turns to me. "You haven't told him, have you?"

I feel the color drain from my face.

"Brady, do you know how Danielle makes her living?"

"She works on websites."

Erin snorts. "You want to clue him in, Danielle, or must I?"

When I don't say anything, she announces, "Your *girlfriend* here works for a breakup company called Your Big Break Inc."

"A breakup company?" Brady's eyes try to catch mine. "What's she talking about?"

I clear my throat. "We provide, um, a service to people looking to end relationships."

"She dumps people," Erin clarifies. "Breaks their hearts for a buck."

"People actually pay for that?" He looks stunned.

"They certainly do," Erin tells him. "She makes money off of people's misery."

If I had a feather, I could knock Brady with it and test out that old saying; he looks ready to topple over. "What about that breakup letter you mailed me?" Brady begins.

"Dani wrote you that breakup letter," Erin continues. "*She* hurt you. And she knows you're vulnerable and weak right now."

And there it is, the reason people come to us. We allow them to transfer their guilt, to ease their conscience. They're no longer responsible; *we are*. They didn't dump anyone; *we did*. They don't have to feel bad about anything; *we do*. Amazingly, I never saw it this clearly before.

"It's better that you know," Erin says, touching Brady's arm. She squeezes around him. "Call me if you need a sympathetic ear." *Sympathetic ear?* Last time I checked, Erin hated Brady's guts. But I guess it's true, the quickest way to make a person want something is to rub their face in the fact that they can't have it. As soon as Erin's out the door, Brady heads to the kitchen. I follow him. He shuts off the oven and takes out the chicken. He sets it in the sink.

"Brady?"

"I think you should go."

"Don't you want to talk about this?"

"Not really." He opens the refrigerator and takes out a Coke. "I want to be alone."

I touch his arm and he jerks it away. "Maybe if I explain things—"

"I don't want to hear it." Brady walks back into the living room and shows me to the door. "I really think you should go. I'll call you."

"I'll call you?" I repeat. "You're not doing that typical guy thing where you say you'll call but you really won't, are you?" It's meant to be a joke, but Brady doesn't laugh. And he doesn't answer me, either.

"Do you want me to walk you to your car?"

"No, it's right downstairs. I can manage."

He seems relieved. "I'll see you later, Dani," he says, practically booting me out the door.

I stumble down the stairs and make my way to my car. The

whole thing went down so fast, my mind can't fully process it. My night went from perfect bliss to utter hell in no time flat. As I climb into my Volvo and pull out of the parking garage, I glance up at Brady's apartment. I see him watching through the window, checking to make sure I made it to my car safely. Even after everything, he's still a perfect gentleman.

He's a perfect gentleman, and I've lost him.

As soon as I get home, I write an e-mail. I keep it short and sweet.

**From:** "Danielle Myers" <DaniMyers@yahoo.com>
**To:** brady_simms@hotmail.com
**Sent:** Friday, July 15, 9:13 p.m.
**Subject:** Hi
Brady,
I feel really bad about what happened tonight. I'd like to explain things.
Sincerely,
Dani

I hope I'll hear back from him before I go to bed. I surf the Web for an hour, periodically checking my Yahoo inbox. Nothing. After another thirty minutes online, I'm going stir-crazy. I need a distraction. I drag myself away from the computer and make microwave popcorn. Then I settle down on the couch and turn on the TV. Nothing's on, so I dig out a couple of DVDs. Exactly one and a half Sandra Bullock movies later, I get back online. I'm 99.9 percent certain I'll have a return e-mail from Brady.

Point-one percent wins out.

*Damn.* I come up with a new e-mail.

**From:** "Danielle Myers" <DaniMyers@yahoo.com>
**To:** brady_simms@hotmail.com
**Sent:** Friday, July 15, 12:47 p.m.
**Subject:** all night long
Dear Brady,
I'm turning into an incurable insomniac, too! And there
weren't even any Ted Danson marathons on to keep me
company. I'll be up for a while. Call or write if you want some
company.
Dani

I finish the second Sandra Bullock movie and then flip off the
TV and change into my pajamas. I check my e-mail one last time
before I crawl into bed.

My inbox is empty.

A few days later, he sends this e-mail:

**From:** "Brady K. Simms" <brady_simms@hotmail.com>
**To:** DaniMyers@yahoo.com
**Sent:** Monday, July 18, 12:08 a.m.
**Subject:** Leaving town
Dani,
I'm going away for a few days. I need some time to think. I'll
call you when I get back.
~Brady Simms

An entire week goes by and I never hear back from Brady. His
"I'm going away for a few days" line was a lie. I've got to talk to

him, plead my case. I have to come clean to him, apologize for lying, and beg his forgiveness. Why couldn't I have been honest with him from day one? If I'd told him the truth about Your Big Break, the truth about my job and myself, none of this would ever have happened. True, he might not have dated me, but that was a choice I had to let him make. I tried to take control of everything, and it backfired. I need to explain.

But how, since he won't see me willingly? I run through the options in my mind. There's the poetry workshop. *No, that's where I went to break up with him.* His school? *No way. I don't have a hall pass; I don't want to end up in the principal's office.* After Erin spilled my beans, Brady's apartment is off-limits, too. I can't come up with a winning scenario.

What I need is one of those movie-perfect moments. Something romantic. Like if Brady were to inexplicably tumble into icy-cold water and I had to strip naked and revive him with my body heat. Once his base temperature returned to a healthy 98.6 degrees, he'd be so grateful I saved him from hypothermia that he'd forget all about the breakup service. I heave a sigh. This has no chance of coming true. *I guess I could shove Brady into the Charles River and hope for the best. . . .*

I'll have to come up with something else.

# 33

# Dumping Jason Dutwiler, Part 2

"I wasn't expecting *you*," Jason says warily, looking to see if anyone's behind me.

It's Saturday morning and the stage is set for Dumping Jason Dutwiler, Part 2.

I smile and slide into the seat across from him. I'm carrying a duffel bag, which I place beside my feet. This time a letter from Krista is inside it. I clear my throat. "Krista asked me to talk to you."

"This can't be happening!" Jason wails, banging his head on the table. "Not again!"

"Krista doesn't feel things are working out."

"She hates me!" he shrieks.

"Krista doesn't hate you," I reassure him. "But she does think you two have no chemistry." *Actually, she thinks you're freakishly obsessed with your ex-girlfriend.*

"Does this mean the wedding's off?" he asks, his face racked with desperation.

"Krista doesn't think it would be appropriate to go as your date."

"Noooo!" Jason cries. "I can't show up *alone*."

I motion for him to keep it down. Other Starbucks patrons are staring at us.

"My brother Mark's wedding is *tomorrow*," he hisses. "Don't you have another friend I could take?"

"No. I'm all friended out," I tell him. "Sorry." I pick up the duffel bag from the floor. "Krista wanted me to give these to you." I hand it to him.

"I can't believe I've already ruined another relationship. I'm destined to die alone."

"No, you're not, Jason."

"*Yes*, I am."

I open my mouth, knowing I'll be breaking rule #3: Avoid cheesy euphemisms. "You'll find the right girl soon."

Jason juts out his lower lip. "Right now, I'm not concerned about finding the *right* girl. I'm concerned about finding *a* girl. I cannot show up at my brother's wedding alone."

"Don't you have any friends you could ask?"

He shakes his head. "Dani, you're my only hope."

"Jason, I'd love to help you, but I honestly don't know anyone you could take."

"That's not true. There is one person."

"I already told you, Krista's mind is made up."

"I wasn't talking about Krista."

*Uh-oh. He can't mean . . .*

"We're practically friends now. You could *pretend* to be my girlfriend."

"Jason, I can't."

"Please, Dani!" He eyes me pleadingly. "If you do this, my brother and parents will stay off my back. And I'll never ask you for another favor again. I swear!"

I sigh. I know I shouldn't do this. It's against the rules. But I'm wracked with guilt and regret over what I did to Brady, over the way I've been lying to him and to everyone else. Going out with Jason won't make up for that, but it could be a start. I can turn over a new leaf. "What time is the wedding?"

The following afternoon I'm wearing a pale blue dress with spaghetti straps and a soft, billowy skirt—the same one I wore to my cousin's wedding last spring. I'm cruising with Jason along Route 3 South toward Hyannis, Massachusetts. It will be nearly a two-hour drive down the Cape.

It's a beautiful day, and the traffic is thick. We arrive just as the ceremony is getting underway. The wedding is being held on the grounds of a beautiful inn. A huge reception tent has been erected next to the makeshift pews. Rather than head up front to sit with the groom's family, Jason and I slide onto a bench in the second-to-last row.

"Don't you want to sit up front?" I whisper.

"No," Jason leans over and whispers back. "I'm sure my family didn't save me a seat."

I look. He's right.

After the ceremony, we make our way over to the reception tent. Jason is holding my hand in a death grip. "You're cutting off my circulation," I say, which causes him to squeeze harder.

"This is when the going gets tough," he cautions. "When I introduce you to my family, be on your best behavior."

I shoot him an annoyed glare. "I'm doing you a favor. I don't *have* to be here."

His tone softens. "I'm sorry, Dani. I'm really stressed-out."

I force a smile. "All right, I'll be on my best behavior."

"By the way," Jason says as we walk into the reception tent, "you're a literary agent."

I stop dead in my tracks. "I'm a what?"

"A literary agent," he repeats. "I couldn't tell my family you're a breakup artist."

*No, I guess not.* We continue walking.

"I can't keep up a lie like that," I say. "Do literary agents even live in Boston?"

"Just do me this one little favor."

"Being here is favor enough!"

"I already told them you were a literary agent from New York!" Jason looks so desperate, so pathetic.

"Oh, all right. I'll do my best!"

He lowers his voice as we near our table. "I said we met when I was down there on business. And, a few weeks from now, when we 'break up,' I'll say it was because I couldn't handle the strain of a long-distance relationship." He beams. "See, I've thought of everything."

Everything except the most important thing.

"Who do you represent?" Jason's mother asks, as soon as we're seated at the family table. There are eight spaces in all, but so far only Jason's parents have joined us.

"Represent?" I repeat.

"Yes," she says, taking a sip of wine. "Have you sold any books we'd have heard of?"

*Oh fuck.* I stare at at Jason. "I don't like to talk about my clients."

"Why on earth not?" she demands.

"I have so many. If I mention one, the others feel left out."
*Lame!*

"She's kidding," Jason says, flashing a big, fake smile. "Dani
doesn't like to brag."

"C'mon," Jason's dad chides. "Give us one name."

The only book I can think of is *High Fidelity*, which depresses
me. I miss Brady.

"Just one name," Jason's dad prompts.

I'm about to make up a title when Jason blurts out, "*The Da
Vinci Code*!"

I stare at him in horror. *The Da Vinci Code*? He could have
said anything, and he picked *The Da Vinci Code*?

"Are you serious?" his mother asks, eyeing me skeptically.

I'm about to tell her that it's a joke, that I represent textbooks,
when Jason says, "Absolutely. Dani's a huge, *huge* agent. She
knows everybody on the New York scene."

"Wow!" his dad says. "That's incredible!"

"I'm going to grab Rebecca," his mother says. "*The Da Vinci
Code*'s her all-time favorite book. Becks!" She jumps up and
jogs off across the yard.

Jason's father lets out a low whistle. "I've gotta hand it to you,
son. When Lucy left, I figured that was it for you, sport. It was
all downhill from there. But I can see I was wrong. You've traded
up." His dad gives him an exaggerated wink.

"I'm really lucky to have found Dani." Jason slips an arm
around my shoulders. The look on his face nearly breaks my
heart. It's like he's about to burst from happiness. At long last,
he's finally made it in the eyes of his family.

I have two choices. I can blow this for him, or I can play
along. I take a deep breath. "I'm the lucky one." I hug him back.

"You guys want something to drink?" his father asks, noticing our empty glasses.

"That'd be great," Jason says.

The second his dad's out of earshot, I start in. "*The Da Vinci Code?*"

"It was either that or *Tuesdays with Morrie*! They're the last two books I read!"

"You might as well have told them I discovered *Harry Potter*."

"Too unrealistic," he says dismissively.

"And *The Da Vinci Code* isn't? I haven't even read it yet," I grumble.

"Ooh, you should. It's a great book."

"That's beside the point! What if they ask—"

Jason shushes me as his mother returns. She seems to have rounded up half the wedding party. "This," she announces, gesturing toward me, "is the girl who wrote *The Da Vinci Code*."

"You're a millionaire!" someone exclaims.

"I didn't write it. I just sold it," I say meekly.

"Do you have any other notable clients?" someone—the best man, I think—asks.

"She's handling a celebrity novel right now," Jason pipes up. "It's very exciting. You wanna tell them about it, honey?" He squeezes my shoulders.

*No, I do not want to tell them about my "celebrity novel."*

But everyone's staring at me expectantly, so I take a deep breath and blurt out the first name that comes to mind. "John Tesh."

"*John Tesh* is writing a novel?" Jason's mother exclaims. Judging by the look on her face, I might as well have just said Bigfoot's publishing his memoirs. "What's the title?" she asks.

"*I've Got the Music in Me*," I fib.

"Is it a musical book?"

"No. It's a thriller," I start. *Think, Dani, think!*

"Like *Da Vinci*?"

"Not exactly. Tesh's work is a little . . . edgier. His narrator's a crime-fighting saxophone player who winds up investigating the murder of a . . . a homeless . . ." *Prostitute? Exotic dancer? It all sounds so clichéd.* "Drag queen," I finish.

Someone—Jason, I believe—bursts out laughing.

*Damn. I should have gone with prostitute.*

Fortunately, the bride and groom pick this moment to make their grand entrance.

I've never been so thrilled to see any two people in my entire life.

Before long, it's time to cut the cake. The attention is off me as everyone focuses on the bride and groom. I stand away from the pack, watching the festivities from the sidelines. Jason is next to his brother, beaming. Finally, at long last, he has their approval. And he's lied to get it. *Why does he have to lie to feel loved?* I think of Garrett and the wedding that never was, all the plans we had that didn't materialize. We were supposed to be married this summer. For a moment, I feel overwhelmed with emotion.

I quickly talk myself out of it.

"Potential clients," I mumble under my breath. Sure, Jason's brother and his new bride may be happy *now*—but in six months, they'll likely wind up in my office, seeking my services. All relationships end. I'm living proof of that.

We manage to make it through the rest of the reception without incident, although a few people do, incredibly, hit me up for John Tesh tickets. And the best man slips me a disk containing his unfinished screenplay, *Crapshoot*.

We've just said our good-byes and are leaving the reception area when Jason's mother, Catherine, taps me on the shoulder.

"*I've Got the Music in Me*," she says. "When's it coming out?"

And here I thought I was home free. "We don't have a firm release date yet," I lie.

"I was thinking." Catherine eyes me thoughtfully, and I'm afraid she's about to blow my cover. "It really says something about John Tesh's life experiences that he's writing about drag queens."

# 34

# She's Got Some Nerve

"He thinks I'm fat."

"No, he doesn't," I tell the overweight woman sitting across from me.

"He thinks I'm a beached whale." She takes a drink of her Frappuccino.

"Kevin would never say a thing like that," I say soothingly. I'm about to launch into my spiel: *Kevin still loves you, but he doesn't think you're right for each other. Kevin hopes you'll stay friends. Kevin wishes only the best for you.*

But instead I say, "He's an ass."

She stares at me in surprise.

"He thinks he can do better than you, thinks he can get laid by some nineteen-year-old *Playboy* Playmate of the Year. That's why he's dumping you. He wants to sleep around with younger women."

"Can he?" she asks. Renée's lower lip starts trembling. "Can he get a *Playboy* Playmate?"

I snort. "No. Not even. He's not going to find anyone better than you."

She buries her head in her hands. "Then why? Why dump me?"

"Because he's a moron." I say. "Some men always think they can get more women, always think the next big thing is right around the corner."

Renée squares her shoulders. "Screw him! I can sleep around, too!"

"Come on, Renée. Be honest. You don't want to do that."

"You're right," she sobs. "I don't. But I wish I could run into Kevin at his bar with some hot guy on my arm. That'd fix him!"

My eyes catch sight of the Red Sox pendant on her shirt.

"You don't know any single guys, do you, Dani? I don't want a boyfriend, just a guy who's willing to help me show up Kevin."

"Hmmm," I say. "As a matter of fact, I might."

I'm typing out an e-mail message to Jason Dutwiler when I hear a knock on my door. I look up to see Erin Foster-Ellis standing in the entrance to my office.

"What do you want?" I ask, quickly minimizing the screen.

"I have another job for you, Danielle. I was hoping we could get started on it today."

*Is she kidding?* "You specifically requested that I no longer handle your business."

She grins, not in a friendly way. "I've changed my mind."

"You can't keep switching between me and Trey," I say, feeling my anger swell. "You're going to have to pick a communications specialist and stick with them." *And don't pick me, or you'll be sorry.*

"I've spoken with Craig McAllister. He approved the switch." *Thanks, Craig.* "Fine. What's the job?"

Erin strolls into my office and sits down. "I need you to convince Brady that we should get back together."

I nearly fall out of my chair. "Let me get this straight," I say, folding my arms across my chest. "You want *me* to reunite you and Brady?"

She nods.

"Why?"

"That's none of your business," she begins, "but I'll tell you this much—I've realized that what Brady needs is a strong, motivated woman who will set him back on the right track. He needs someone like me in his life."

"As much as I'd love to help you," I say, mock-sweetly, "I can't." I give her a cold smile. "We don't do fix-ups, only breakups."

"Oh, you'll do it. I'm not giving you a choice in the matter."

*She's got some nerve.* I keep my tone even. "I'm not obligated to take on cases I don't want. Ask Craig; he's the boss, and he'll tell you the same thing."

Erin looks me squarely in the eyes. "Maybe you don't understand, Danielle. If you don't do this for me, I'll have you fired."

I burst out laughing. "Oh, please! Like you have that kind of power."

"I do. You're forgetting something. You lied to me—a client! And I paid you for a service that you did not deliver."

"I delivered." I stare at her defiantly. I'm not backing down.

"That's not how I see it. Look at the facts. You did not pick up all of my personal items from Brady's apartment, and you did not break things off with him in person. Those were the conditions that we agreed upon, and you violated them. And you did it all because you were hoping to land a date with Brady. You were motivated by lust, and you put the name of Your Big Break Inc. on the line. I don't think your boss will look too favorably on that."

*When she puts it that way—when she adds it all together—she makes me sound horrible.*

"You're oversimplifying," I argue. "When I explain everything to Craig, he'll understand." Even to my own ears, this sounds weak. *There's a good chance I will get fired!*

"*Will* he? Because you don't look so sure."

I'm not. "Things with Brady were complicated." I struggle to explain. "I did the best I could under difficult circumstances. If you hadn't decided to ditch him two weeks after his father died, it might have been different."

"That's not your call. Your company has a rule about being an *impartial adviser*. And there's another policy about not getting personally involved. You broke both of those. I have half a mind to report you to the Better Business Bureau for false advertising."

She's got me. I take a deep breath and let it out slowly. There's nothing I can say, no point I can argue. Craig's a stickler for our five rules, and I'm in total violation of all of them.

"All right. I'll do it." I hope my voice doesn't sound as shaky as it feels.

"I suspected you would."

I feel sick. *How can this be happening?* Brady has completely avoided me since our disastrous dinner two weeks ago. Now I've got to approach him and convince him to get back together with Erin? I've got to bite my tongue, suppress my feelings once again. I've got to pretend I don't care about him.

"Here's what you're going to do," Erin says. "The easiest way for Brady to forgive me is if he thinks our breakup was all one giant misunderstanding."

"Brady's not an idiot. He'll never believe that."

"He will when you confess that you orchestrated the whole thing. You'll tell him you wrote him that breakup letter without my knowledge."

*She's insane.* "There's no way Brady will buy a stupid story like that."

"You're also going to tell Brady that you saw him at a poetry reading, and you thought he was cute, and you moved in for the kill, using your work skills to your own pathetic advantage."

I shake my head. "I don't think I can—"

"You can. Just think about how much you've got on the line. That will motivate you." She's got me trapped. I can't see a way out of this except to do what she wants.

"Now, for the time frame." Erin reaches into her Prada satchel purse and produces two tickets. "There's a new play opening in a couple of weeks called *Mélange*. I promised a friend I'd be there; I'd like for Brady to go, too." She sets one of the tickets down on the corner of my desk. "Make sure that he gets this."

"I'll give it to him. I can't guarantee he'll show up."

"It's nearly three weeks until the play. That's more than enough time for you to spin a story and convince him to come back to me." She rises to leave. "I'd better find Brady beside me on opening night or I'm going straight to Craig McAllister. Got it?"

"Yes," I mumble. I pick up the ticket and shove it into my purse.

"Danielle," Erin adds as she walks toward the door. "Even

though he's only a schoolteacher now"—she slings her Prada purse over one shoulder—"he's still way out of your league."

I want to hit her back with some clever line, some well-timed insult.

But I say nothing.

She gives me a wave as she walks out the door.

If I follow Erin's demands and tell Brady this ludicrous story, how do I know she won't go to Craig *anyway*? She's made her contempt for me clear. Why not use this opportunity to zing me not once but twice? And even if Erin does keep her end of the bargain, what's to stop her from blackmailing me again in the future?

There's really only one way to play this.

For once in my life, I'm going to be honest.

I'm going to go to Craig and tell him everything; I'm going to take responsibility for my actions. He might fire me. But that's a chance I'll have to take. And after I've confessed to Craig, I'll call Brady. I'll tell him that Erin wants to get back together. I'll offer up the play ticket and let him decide whether or not he wants to be with her. I've been meddling for long enough. It's time to butt out and let people make their own decisions.


Craig takes the news surprisingly well.

He sits across from me for twenty minutes, hands folded in his lap, listening intently while I spill the whole story. I leave nothing out: I start with the poetry workshop and move on to the seventy-five-dollar discount I gave Erin. I tell him about my e-mails to Brady, about our coffee date, about the picnic in the public gardens and the romantic dinner at his house. I tell him how I sent the anonymous letter and how I advised Brady to return Erin's personal items via FedEx. Red-faced, I explain how Erin found me and Brady together, and how now she's black-mailing me in an effort to reunite with him.

The only thing I skip over is the part about me being in my bra when Erin showed up at Brady's apartment. Some things are just too personal.

Craig nods and smiles as I go along. He's calm, attentive, interested in my plight.

When I finally finish talking, he sighs deeply and looks at me for a long time. "I've been warning you to stop ignoring our five rules, particularly the cardinal rule: Do *not* get personally involved," he begins. "And it seems you've given me promise after empty promise. You've sworn up and down that you weren't letting personal feelings get in the way of common business sense. I'm a reasonable man, I'm a patient man, but you leave me no choice. Effective immediately, Amanda will be taking over your clients."

I don't say anything. My eyes blink rapidly, trying to ward off tears. I've never been fired from a job before. I don't know what comes next. *Do I pack up my office, or does Craig have someone do that for me? Does he call security to escort me out of the building? Will I get my last paycheck? Will he write me a good letter of reference? Will I get to keep my health benefits?*

Craig keeps talking, but I don't hear any of it. I should be paying attention; he's probably answering some of my questions. I zone back in.

". . . I hope you're willing to learn Flash."

For the life of me, I can't figure out how that sentence fits into this conversation.

"I'm sorry, Craig," I apologize. "I missed what you were saying."

"Which part?"

*All of it.* "About the Flash . . . why are you asking if I want to learn it?"

"So we can move you over to maintaining our website."

*What?* "You want me to run our website?"

"Truthfully, it's something I've been thinking about for a while. You have terrific written communication skills, Dani. That flier copy you wrote? It was excellent. And your Dear John letters are the best on staff. But you're too much of a people person. You can't separate business from personal."

I stare down at my hands, afraid to look at him.

"So, therefore, if you're interested, I'd like you to take on the technical, behind-the-scenes duties: website design, copywriting. You'll also be in charge of queries that come in via our website. With all of the publicity we've been receiving lately, we've started getting a number of out-of-town clients. Most of them want us to break up with their partners via a letter. It's a quick twenty-five bucks. You'll draft the letters."

I nod.

"After some time, we can reevaluate where things stand and see if you're ready to begin working directly with clients again. How does that sound?"

My relief is palpable. "It sounds very fair. Thanks, Craig."

"I'll need you and Amanda to cross-train each other," he exclaims. "She's ready to branch off on her own. But I want you to assist her with taking over the clients. And she'll instruct you on the technical aspects of Web design."

"Amanda has time for all this?" I ask. "Isn't she busy with school?"

"She'll be graduating in a month."

"Thanks." I shake Craig's hand. "You're an incredible man. Most bosses probably would have fired me."

"True dat," he says, giving me a high-five. "But I'm not most bosses."

I grin.

"Everyone deserves a second chance," Craig says.


When I get home from work that night, I call my father.

"Dani, hi!" He sounds surprised to hear from me. It's been a while. Even though my mother and I have made a comfortable peace, my father and I haven't spoken much since the Fourth of July.

"I just called to ask if you know anything about repairing ceiling fans," I say, rushing on before he can bring up marrying Gretchen or divorcing Mom or anything else unpleasant.

"I could probably figure it out. Why?"

"My stupid ceiling fan's not working, and I don't want to call a repair guy for something so tiny. But, you know, I could use the fresh air flow. . . ."

"You shouldn't have to go without a fan," he says. "I'll stop by tomorrow."

# 35

**STAGE FIVE OF BREAKUP HELL:**
*Letting Go*
At long last, the dumpee accepts the inevitable: It's over. Deep
down, though, some part of them will always be connected to
the person who broke their heart.

It's about ten o'clock the following night when Dad gets here. He
brings Chinese take-out, but neither of us feels like eating. We
leave the unopened cartons on my kitchen counter and go into
the bedroom. He tinkers with the ceiling fan, tightening a few
screws, and suddenly it works again. It takes him all of ten
minutes.

It's weird having him in my apartment. Even though Cambridge is only a short drive from Boston, my parents rarely come
to visit me. "I was wondering if we could talk for a minute,"
Dad says. He sets down the screwdriver on the floor.

"We could do that." I plop on the bed and stare out the window, avoiding his gaze.

"So, great news about Sean!" Dad says enthusiastically.

My brother has decided to follow Sophie's lead and go back
to school. He's going to study forensic psychiatry. All that *CSI*
watching finally paid off.

"He said it was all your influence. Yours, and his new girl-friend, Sophie's. Thanks for helping him with that."

"I didn't help him with anything," I say. "Sean makes his own decisions."

"But you encouraged him," Dad counters. "That means some-thing. You two have gotten so close over these last few months. It's been wonderful to watch."

I don't say anything.

"Now that you know everything . . . I was wondering what you think of me?" Dad asks, leaning back against the wall. "I want you to be honest."

*Honest.* Something I haven't always been good at. "Okay."

He clears his throat. "Tell me what you felt when you first learned about Gretchen."

I draw in a deep breath and let it out. "I was mad," I admit. "I hated you."

"I can understand that." Dad comes over and sits down next to me on the bed. He pats my hand. "I never meant for you to find out the way you did," he says. "It must have been awful."

"It was. I went a little crazy for a while there."

"You were having a normal response."

"I'm not sure normal's the right word." I pull the photo al-bum of our trip to France off the shelf and pass it to him. "See for yourself."

Dad takes it and begins flipping through it, surveying my handiwork. Page after page of sliced-and-diced photos appear before him. "Did you cut me out of *all* of them?" He shakes his head, looking sad. "You put a lot of work into this."

"You were in so many pictures. . . ." My voice trails off.

"You know why that is, don't you?" He sets the album down on the bed.

"You're a camera hog."

Dad chuckles. "Your mother hates having her picture taken."

In my zest to massacre his image, I'd forgotten how camera-shy Mom is.

"These were all taken with *your* camera," he continues, tapping the album. "I've got a photo album back at the house with nothing but pictures of you."

Suddenly, I feel truly, desperately sad. I hang my head in my hands.

Dad puts an arm around my shoulder. "I did a lot of things I'm not proud of," he says. "I—*we*—should have been honest with you from the start. Your mom and I rationalized, told ourselves we were protecting you and Sean. But, really, we were lying."

"I've been lying to you, too, for almost a year."

"Yes, that." He squeezes my shoulders. "Why didn't you just tell us the truth about your job in the first place? We wouldn't have cared."

It's a difficult question to answer. I shrug. "I was embarrassed." I look at my hands, pick at my cuticles.

"You shouldn't have been."

"I know. It's not just that." *How do I say this?* "I think after Garrett left me, I sort of closed a part of myself off. I felt so inadequate, like such a failure."

"Dani, you were never a failure! What Garrett did to you . . ." He looks angry for a second, then reels it back in. "He was a horrible human being, and he had no right to hurt you the way he did. But you have to remember: The way someone treats you says more about that person than it does about you. Only a complete and utter bastard would behave that way."

I smile weakly. "I know. But I felt so low. And I was worried about disappointing you." I shrug. "So I lied."

"Dani, you've never disappointed us. *Never*," Dad says emphatically. "The concept of Your Big Break Inc. is kind of unusual, but it's not shameful."

I fiddle with my watch, gathering up my nerve. "Dad, can I ask you something?"

"Sure."

"Are you going to marry her?"

"Gretchen? Your mother and I aren't even legally separated yet."

"But have you talked about it?"

"We have." Dad takes a deep breath. "That's the direction I'm moving in, yes."

I thought hearing that news would make me feel worse, but it somehow makes things better. At least there are no more surprises now. I can *let go*. Move on.

We sit there in silence for a long time. But it's not awkward—it's comfortable.

"This is better," Dad finally says, "having everything out in the open."

"Yeah, it is," I agree.

Dad nods. "And the truth shall set you free."

But I haven't told the whole truth.

There's still one person who I need to talk to.


Later that night, I phone Brady's apartment and leave him what must be the hundredth message. But, unlike before, I keep this one impersonal.

"Hi Brady, it's Danielle. I wanted to inform you that your ex-girlfriend, Erin Foster-Ellis, would like to get back together with you. She's invited you to a new play called *Mélange*. I can mail the ticket to you if you want. Let me know either way."

He doesn't call back.

With Amanda's diligent instruction, I'm getting a handle on this website design thing. I've also thrown myself into updating Your Big Break Inc.'s filing system, getting everything logged in to the computer. Our client flow has become overwhelming. Our administrative assistant, Beverly, has been struggling to keep up.

I'm working late when Craig comes in. "I've got a message for you, Big D," he says, popping his head into my office.

I'm sitting on the floor, going through our filing cabinet. "Can you leave it on my desk?" I ask, trying to balance the growing mountain of paperwork on my lap.

"You need to take care of this right away."

I sigh. I pile the papers onto the floor and stand up. "All right, who's it from?" I can't imagine what could be so urgent, considering I'm no longer seeing any clients.

"Nuh-uh, I promised I'd keep this on the down-low."

"Excuse me?" I smooth the wrinkles out of my skirt.

"Just go."

"Go where?" I ask.

Craig chuckles. "Sorry. I'm getting ahead of myself. You've got a six-o'clock appointment at two hundred Boylston Street."

"Two hundred Boylston? Isn't that the—"

"The Four Seasons."

"What am I supposed to do at the Four Seasons?" I ask.

"You'll be having dinner at the hotel's restaurant, Aujour-d'hui."

I stare at him, utterly confused.

"You've got a reservation, so you'd better hurry."

I don't budge an inch. There's only one Your Big Break Inc. client who would arrange something so extravagant as dinner at a pricey French restaurant.

Evan Hirschbaum.

# 36

# Personally Involved

It's strange; I've walked past the Four Seasons dozens of times, but I've never once ventured inside. The lobby is grand, as fancy and lavish as you might expect: chandeliers and marble floors, waitstaff decked out in flawlessly pressed suits. I take a deep breath and try to keep my composure. It's easy to get intimidated in a place like this.

"Excuse me?" I ask the hostess. "I'm Dani Myers. I'm here to meet—"

She nods. "This way, please."

I follow the hostess through a sea of elegantly outfitted diners. As we make our way to the corner of the restaurant, I catch sight of Brady, sitting at a table by himself. I stop in my tracks, nearly toppling over a waiter who is carrying a tray of desserts.

*What is Brady doing here?* My heart starts racing. He's wearing a jacket and tie and looks, unmistakably, like a high-priced attorney. *Is Erin on her way to meet him? Are they already back together?*

I regain control of my legs and continue walking forward, looking for Evan.

The hostess stops at Brady's table.

"I hope you didn't mind coming here," Brady says, smiling. "I thought the Four Seasons, the scene of the infamous Magnus run-in, was fitting." He makes a sweeping gesture toward the window. "Plus, we've got this beautiful view of the Public Garden."

Stunned, I sit down.

Brady orders us champagne cocktails. He's acting friendly. It's as though our falling out never happened. Our champagne cocktails arrive.

"I haven't gone overboard, have I?" Brady asks, looking concerned. "I feel so bad about everything—the unreturned messages, the trip out of town. I wanted to make it up to you."

I take a sip of champagne. "So you really did go out of town?" I ask.

He nods. "I thought everything was settled with my father's will, but a few complications arose. I had to fly back to Scottsdale to take care of them." He lowers his gaze. "I *was* avoiding you, though." A waiter comes over and sets down a lobster appetizer. "Erin made up a ridiculous lie. She said you'd been conspiring to break us up all along." He sips his champagne.

I start to reply, but he stops me.

"She really thought I would believe her no matter what she said, and that I'd wind up hating you. She wanted to embarrass you. She didn't count on me learning the truth."

"The truth?"

"I learned the truth, learned that you weren't messing with me or playing a joke."

I think for a minute. "How did you find out?"

"Craig McAllister told me."

I blink in surprise. "*Craig* told you?"

Brady nods. "I called your office yesterday, but you were gone to lunch. I'd just gotten back from Scottsdale. Craig answered and we got to talking. He explained what happened with Erin; she really did hire you guys to break up with me."

"I'm sorry, Brady."

"Don't be." He shakes his head. "You were just doing your job. You could have told me the truth in the first place. I never would have faulted you for it."

I look down at my hands. "I'm sorry that I lied to you. I guess I was . . . I just felt like the situation was spiraling out of control and, rather than be adult about it, I let myself get in deeper. The truth is, I was afraid."

"It's okay." He leans over and squeezes my hand. "People do strange things when they're afraid." He grins. "I loved the Breakup Recovery Kit you sent me."

"You did?"

"It really meant a lot to me. At the time, I couldn't figure out who sent it. But after I spoke with Craig, I looked at Your Big Break Inc.'s website and I knew."

"I'm so glad." I take a deep swig of champagne. "There's something that seems weird to me. And don't take this the wrong way, but why did Erin suddenly want to get back together with you? It was like her feelings changed overnight."

Brady shifts uncomfortably in his seat. "She found out about the inheritance."

I stare at him. "The inheritance?"

"When my father died, I inherited money. That's the real reason I've been out in Arizona so much recently."

*The real reason? So he's lied a bit, too!*

"It's not a fortune. But enough to let me live very comfortably. It gave me the confidence, and the ability, to leave my law firm and become a teacher."

"I guess you won't be wanting this." I reach into my purse and pull out the ticket to *Mélange*.

"God, no." Brady smiles. "I just want you, Dani. The truth is, I got scared, too. Everything happened so fast. And I fell so hard . . . I tried to take things slow, but it was impossible." He squeezes my hand. "I haven't felt this way in as long as I can remember. I don't want it to go away."

"Me neither."

"Then we won't let it." Brady leans forward and kisses me softly on the lips. I hesitate for a nanosecond as a thought runs through my head. Rule #5: Do *not* get personally involved. This is the cardinal rule and must be followed above all others!

*To hell with it. Rules were made to be broken.*

I kiss him back.

# Epilogue

"I have to admit I'm shocked," Evan Hirschbaum says as we sit down to the long-awaited lunch at The Ritz-Carlton Hotel two weeks later. "I can't believe you've resigned."

"Yep. My last day is Friday."

"What are you going to be doing?" Evan asks, taking a sip of mineral water.

"I'm starting a business."

He raises an eyebrow. "What kind of business?"

"Something that's always been a passion of mine." I pause for effect. "Matchmaking."

I've had some success at it already. Sophie and Sean are a hot item, and Jason and Renée are well on their way, too. I've even been tinkering with the idea of setting up my mother and Craig McAllister. I'm not sure if I'm ready to go there yet, but we'll see.

Evan looks impressed. "From breaking people up to putting

them together. Sounds like you've got your work cut out for you."

"I do," I agree. "But I'm up for the challenge."

"I'll bet you are," Evan says, raising his water glass in a toast. "To your new career."

We clink glasses.

"I tell you what. To help you kick things off, I'll be your first client."

I eye him with surprise. "You have more women than you can handle."

"You can *never* have too many women, Dani." Evan winks at me. "You know what kinds of women I like. Let's see who you can pair me up with."

"You really want to do this?"

He nods. "The sooner, the better!"

I smile, and pull the *Mélange* play ticket out of my purse. "I've got the *perfect* girl for you."